FINDING JUPITER

FINDING JUPITER

Kelis Rowe

CROWN
NEW YORK

Text copyright © 2022 by Raquel Enes Dennie
Jacket art copyright © 2022 by Delmaine Donson
Interior illustrations copyright © 2022 by Bex Glendining

All rights reserved. Published in the United States by
Crown Books for Young Readers, an imprint of
Random House Children's Books,
a division of Penguin Random House LLC, New York.

Crown and the colophon are registered trademarks of
Penguin Random House LLC.

Visit us on the Web! GetUnderlined.com

Educators and librarians, for a variety of teaching tools, visit us at
RHTeachersLibrarians.com

Library of Congress Cataloging-in-Publication Data is available upon request.
ISBN 978-0-593-42925-9 (hardcover) — ISBN 978-0-593-42926-6 (lib. bdg.) —
ISBN 978-0-593-42927-3 (ebook)

The text of this book is set in 11.5-point Adobe Caslon Pro.
Interior design by Andrea Lau

Printed in the United States of America
10 9 8 7 6 5 4 3 2 1
First Edition

To my mom and my son, Zack.
Momma, you always made me believe I could be anything.
I believed that you believed it. Which made me want to
be something amazing. Zack, thank you for gently
asking how my writing was going in the days, weeks,
and sometimes months that you saw me not-writing.
I hope I make you proud.

I suppose you've got to make your house into a pigsty in order to have any friends—in the modern world."

Angry as I was, as we all were, I was tempted to laugh whenever he opened his mouth. The transition from libertine to prig was so complete.

"I've got something to tell *you*, old sport—" began Gatsby. But Daisy guessed at his intention.

"Please don't!" she interrupted helplessly. "Please let's all go home. Why don't we all go home?"

"That's a good idea." I got up. "Come on, Tom. Nobody wants a drink."

"I want to know what Mr. Gatsby has to tell me."

"Your wife doesn't love you," said Gatsby. "She's never loved you. She loves me."

"You must be crazy!" exclaimed Tom automatically.

Gatsby sprang to his feet, vivid with excitement.

"She never loved you, do you hear?" he cried. "She only married you because I was poor and she was tired of waiting for me. It was a terrible mistake, but in her heart she never loved any one except me!"

At this point Jordan and I tried to go, but Tom and Gatsby insisted with competitive firmness that we remain—as though neither of them had anything to conceal and it would be a privilege to partake vicariously of their emotions.

"Sit down, Daisy," Tom's voice groped unsuccessfully for the paternal note. "What's been going on? I want to hear all about it."

"I told you what's been going on," said Gatsby. "Going on for five years—and you didn't know?"

Tom turned to Daisy sharply.

"You've been seeing this fellow for five years?"

"Not seeing," said Gatsby. "No, we couldn't meet.

I was complete
to know your love, automatically.
Do you hear?
I was tired of waiting for a loved one.
I tried to conceal emotions,
unsuccessfully,
for the paternal.
I didn't know we couldn't meet.

ONE

Ray

22 DAYS

I'm finding poetry in the pages of *The Great Gatsby* this summer. My copy from middle school has started to fall apart, so I've ripped out my favorite set of pages and have glued some of the finished pieces into my journal. Gatsby's life was utterly unfair, and it came to an end because of circumstances that were far out of his control. I can relate. For my found poetry, I'm drawn to the parts of stories where the writing is on the wall and there's nothing anyone can do about it. Gatsby's goose is cooked. He'll never get what he wants most.

What do I want? Just once I'd like today to be about the day I was born, not the day my father died.

Sitting in the tree house he built for me, I push away thoughts of him dying while I was entering the world. I unravel my turquoise earbuds, start my James Taylor Essentials playlist, and try to focus.

A calm washes over me as I study the page that I've taped to a piece of lined paper. On this page, Tom Buchanan is closing in on Gatsby's lie, quizzing him about his days at Oxford as Daisy interjects about a mint julep. Shit's about to hit the fan.

Mr. Nobody.

I write it in pencil on the side of the page. I go back to the top of the page and scan, waiting to find words about Mr. Nobody. I list them as I go.

smiling, snapped, politely, content, desperately, nowhere, alone . . .

I read the list over and over again, until some words fall away and others seem to float above the page. With each pass, more words join in, calling out to me as the poem makes itself known. Then, finally, the found poetry has found me.

Smiling faintly,
I'll wait desperately to please Mr. Nobody.
Me, with him,
Standing alone.

I draw cloudy circles around the words that call to me, in order as they appear on the page. An image of a girl standing alone comes to me and I begin to sketch. When I'm done, I'll use black ink pens, oil crayons, and a Sharpie to finish it, but that will have to wait. It's almost time for me to pick up my roommate, Bri, from the airport. In three years of boarding school, this will be her first time coming here. I'm excited to see her, but nervous, too. My neighborhood is worlds away from her fancy Maryland digs.

I'm almost finished packing my things away when I hear Momma's voice.

I pretend not to hear her. I know she's standing at the foot of the tree-house ladder, but I wait for her to call twice before I shuffle to the entrance and look down. I keep my headphones on, on purpose.

She smiles at the sight of me, which has the annoying effect of making me smile back. She taps her ear. I take the hint but make a show of stopping my playlist and tugging at the cords, popping one of the earbuds out of my ear.

"Happy birthday, baby." She holds up my favorite tumbler, purple with pink stars, filled with fresh lemonade.

"Thanks, Momma. One second." I toss my pencil pouch into my backpack and climb down the ladder. She kisses my cheek as I take the cup.

"I can't wait to see what you're working on. I've always been amazed at how you turn those words into art," she says.

I take a sip of lemonade and avoid making eye contact with her.

"You excited about Bri coming today?"

"Yes," I mumble as I remove the other earbud and wrap the cord around my cell phone.

"What time you planning to head to the airport?"

I shrug and check the time on my phone before shoving it into the back pocket of my jean shorts.

"You call yourself trying to give me the silent treatment or something with all these short nonanswers?" There's a smile in her voice.

"Maybe." I take another indignant sip of lemonade.

Momma chuckles and pinches my cheek with the backs of her fingers.

"Ray, you are something else—a ray of sunshine this morning," she teases. "Come on." She bumps her arm to mine. "Come help your old momma pick some lavender. You still have a little time before you have to go?"

I follow her through the opening of the garden. The air is thick with the scent of rosemary, lavender, and lemon blossoms. We make quick work of cutting lavender stems and laying them in a basket. My mom ties the cut end of three sprigs together with a small piece of silver ribbon, for my father's headstone.

"Can I go now?" I ask, with a hint of exasperation.

"Ray, I haven't asked you to visit your dad's grave since you turned twelve." I can tell she's about to go into one of her long monologues, but I refuse to feel guilty for not mourning a person I never knew.

"This is your last summer in high school. You might not even be here next summer. I wish you'd go to the cemetery before you head back to Rhode Island. Those visits used to mean so much to you."

"The first few years you took me there, I thought I'd get to meet him, maybe get to know him."

I was clueless. He was a nurse. He liked Bob Marley and Caribbean food. That's all I know about him. She'd told me he'd become a star in the sky the night I was born, and so we'd stargaze and pretend to talk to him. Then on my birthday we'd make this big picnic to go visit Daddy. When I was really little, I thought he'd come out of his grave once a year like Santa coming down from the North Pole. I felt ridiculous when I realized the truth.

"Momma, you knew him. I never will. I don't see why I should go."

My mom doesn't look up from her hands, and I feel like shit. "If you hurry, maybe Bri won't have to wait for you too long outside baggage claim," she says.

"You sure you don't want me to drop you off on the way?" I offer as an olive branch.

"No, baby, I'm good. It's on the bus route to work. I'll be fine. You go on and get Bri. Y'all have fun skating tonight."

I want to explain to her that I don't think she's weird for returning to his grave every year. I get it—her life changed more than anyone's that night. She became a widow and a mother in a single moment. I want to tell her how much it sucks that my birthday can never just be about me. I walk away and look back as she absentmindedly wraps silver ribbon around more lavender. I've said enough. Instead of telling her that she's already made one of those, I head inside the house.

"Best birthday ever," I say *after* I slide the patio door closed.

━━━

Briana is all gloss and polish against the dingy backdrop of the Memphis International Airport—like a colorful image cut from a fashion magazine, fixed onto newspaper, and then shellacked. It's only been two months since we left school, but it seems longer. She notices me waving and, just like that, she's three-dimensional again, waving excitedly and picking up her carry-on. I don't even make it around to open the trunk before her arms are around me.

"Hey, girl, hey!" Her mass of curly hair presses into me. Briana usually smells like something sweet or edible or both. Today it's wildflowers. "Scent is tied to memories," she said on move-in day freshman year, while unloading her arsenal of perfumes onto her hutch. "I want to be unforgettable."

Bri is taller than most girls, but still not as tall as me. Her hair is a glorious mass of tumbling coils down her back, and I've never seen a more radiant smile outside of a Disney animated prince. And she laughs like a charming hyena. She's unforgettable the moment you meet her. Why she thinks she needs the help of a fragrance is beyond me.

She squeezes me and I squeeze her before shoving her suitcase in the trunk. She's already in the car by the time I'm behind the wheel.

"Nice ride! A red Jeep Cherokee—so retro! I'm excited to be here and see what these Memphis streets talkin' about! Happy. Birthday. Queen!" She does a little dance.

I smile and shake. "Okay, so, tell me about your fancy summer camp. The girls, the horses, the *boys*?"

Bri *collects* stories about boys. And I could really use the distraction. Anything to get my mind off how my mom looked before I left the house. Anything to get my mind off that stupid graveyard.

Bri only knows that my father died when I was little. That's enough. It's easier to keep things light. I don't want her to know *everything* about me. My sob story would draw her in.

And I don't do *in* with other people.

I'm totally fine with just being Ray Jr., the tall girl from Memphis with the braids that stay poppin'.

"Camp was camp. I met a super dope girl who came all the way from Ireland, and bump my camp boys, Ray—where the Memphis boys at? What are the plans for the birthday turnup?"

"We're going skating. Wherever the boys are, I'm sure you'll find them." I laugh and she shoves my shoulder playfully. "When we get to the house, we'll have just enough time for you to figure out your costume change before we dip. They close at eleven, and I need to catch as much wind as possible tonight."

Bri fans herself with a piece of junk mail from the armrest.

"Sorry my mom's AC is out. I meant to warn you about Memphis summers. It's always hell degrees outside."

"It's fine. Glad I didn't straighten my hair. This Memphis humidity is not playing." She rolls the window down farther. "But, uh, boys. Who's your summer boo?"

"I'm not hooking up with anybody this summer."

"No summer love this year? That's new, do tell."

"Summer *fling*," I correct her. "Love is for the birds. Keep that drama away from me. There's way more honesty in cutting to the chase."

"Why you always frontin', Ray? I see you watching *The Notebook* repeatedly. You love romance, admit it."

"Correction. I'm *entertained* by romance."

"Whatever. Romance is everything."

"Romance is a waste of time." I see Bri's head whip in my direction out of the side of my eyes.

"Girl, you trippin'."

"I'm just a girl with satisfied needs and peace that comes with not caring if he's gonna call the next day or ever."

Bri shakes her head. I shrug.

"Moving on. I live in Whitehaven, near Graceland. We'll go past where Elvis lived. It's kind of a tourist requirement." I exit the highway and hang a left. Small shopping centers, houses that've been converted into businesses, and old apartment complexes line either side of the street. I glance at Bri to get a read on her first impression.

"*Whitehaven?*" She says the name of my neighborhood like it leaves a bad aftertaste.

"Yes, Whitehaven . . . and it meant exactly what you think, back when the neighborhood was settled. Welcome to the Dirty South," I say, gesturing at the clusters of local businesses and ancient apartment complexes that line the road. The scent of fried chicken fills the air as we approach KFC. "Ironically, Whitehaven is a very Black neighborhood now. White flight was real. We call it Blackhaven, unofficially."

Bri's eyebrows are still raised in shock.

"Graceland is coming up on your left. All the souvenir shops, his private jet, and his famous Cadillac will be on the right." Bri stops her fanning, sits up in her seat, and cranes her neck.

"Okay, so these are the first white people I've seen since the airport."

"Those are tourists."

My eyes fall on the ever-present flower shrine near the front gates of Graceland, and my mind goes back to the lavender Momma will leave on my father's headstone today. Why'd she have to suggest I go to that grave after all these years? What is even the point?

"Well, that was underwhelming," Bri says, distracting me from my thoughts. I nod.

My stomach sinks. What is she going to think of my tiny house? Bri's family is loaded. The first time I went to her house, I was shocked by the size of the windows and the amount of food they had stored away. There are only three of them, and their pantry is an actual room with cabinets and a sink. It's like a corner store in the kitchen. Sometimes I wonder if we would be friends if we hadn't been the only two Black girls in our freshman class.

There's something about being captive at boarding school in middle-of-nowhere Rhode Island that forces a bond between girls who feel like home. I'd be lying if I said I wasn't extremely nervous about her being in my little house with its small windows and normal amounts of food. We enter the cove and roll to a stop in my driveway.

"Home sweet home," she sings.

I gnaw my lip and watch Bri scan the area. There used to be a housing project walking distance from here. It was nicknamed P. Valley because it was a hot spot for the world's oldest profession. But it was closed down years ago, so I feel like my neighborhood is coming up.

I still my fidgety hands and remind myself that a real friend wouldn't trip because of where I live. "Welcome to my humble abode," I say in my best English butler impression. "What it lacks in size and youth, it charms with snacks, hot water, and a plethora of fragrant handmade soaps and essential oils, courtesy of the lady of the house."

I bow my head and she throws hers back, cackling. Fortunately, she doesn't seem uptight about my place. Bri starts to say something but then whips around mid-sentence. I turn and see Cash, my forever next-door neighbor. Cash and I became easy friends the day I started walking home from school—when my mom started working at the hospital. We were nine years old. One day he shoved a frog in my face. I laughed and asked if I could hold it. He seemed impressed that I didn't scream and run away and told me he liked my *Star Wars* shirt. We've been like cousins ever since.

Flashing her toothiest smile, she waves as he walks past my driveway. "You didn't mention that the boy next door was *fine* with a capital *I*, honey."

"I sure didn't," I say, nudging her toward the house. "You know how long it takes you to get ready to go anywhere?"

Cash tilts his chin in a *what's up*.

"Hey, Cash. Bye, Cash. We'll see you tonight at Crystal Palace."

Bri's gonna be disappointed when I break it to her that Cash is practically married. Thankfully, tonight of all nights I plan to be too lost in the music to care.

It was a good call to shoo Cash away at the door. It took Bri a record low number of three outfit changes before she decided on the first one. We hit up the Wendy's drive-through and ate in the car in the Crystal Palace parking lot, which was already packed when we arrived.

As soon as we step through the doors, the scent of buttery popcorn welcomes us. I've been away far too long. Looking up at the giant, sparkling disco ball hanging from the center of the ceiling and hearing the music blaring, I instantly regret the lost time. Neon strobe lights create colorful patterns on the rink's glossy wood floor—practically calling my name.

I wait in line with Bri to pick up her rental skates. I don't recognize the rap song that's playing, but it's bass-heavy and I can't help but bounce to the beat.

"I see you, Ray, turn up!" Bri says, dancing with me.

I watch a little girl whose mother is squatting to tie the strings on her skates. Her smile widens when I smile back at her. They remind me of Momma and me. We spent so many nights here. She taught me to skate, but once I got to middle school I'd come here with Cash and his girlfriend, Mel, instead.

"I think it's so cool that you actually own a pair of roller skates," Bri says, rental skates now in hand. "You must be really good."

She's talking to me as she scans the room. Wearing mint-green skinny jeans and a snug powder-blue T-shirt with a rainbow across the chest, Bri may not have skated in a while, but she looks the part.

"I'm pretty good," I say, holding up my well-worn bright

turquoise skates with magenta laces and matching wheels. "You see how close this place is to my house? We used to walk up here all the time. It didn't make sense to keep renting skates."

Bri nods, eyes still roaming.

Every time we go anywhere together, she surveys the area to identify cute single guys to potentially talk to—and cute girls who could potentially be her competition. It's a sport for her. She rarely even dates any of the boys. She just collects them, her small army of admirers.

She's tried to get me in on it, but much to Bri's disappointment, I mostly just focus on volleyball, classes, and art in my spare time. Cory, Bri's neighbor, is the only boy in my life, but we just hook up whenever I go home to Bri's over breaks. He isn't needy or aggressive, and he never really tries to get inside my head. All I know about him is that his parents always travel for work, he plays basketball, and he can really work his way around a girl's body. I might be a loner, but I'm also a girl with needs. Cory always obliges, and, most importantly, afterward he leaves me alone.

Bri and I find a spot and put our skates on. Just as we're done, I spot Cash and Mel, holding hands, walking away from the lockers. Those two are the only reason I have faith that love might actually be worth it. They've been together, drama-free, since elementary school. Cash sees us, too. The glow from the lights makes their dark skin look like deep brown pearls as they move toward us. He towers above just about everyone in the place, including me, and I'm six feet tall.

"Hey, Mel," I say, bending down to hug her, then reaching up to hug Cash.

"Happy birthday, Ray. Loving those ombré braids, girl," Mel says.

"My birthday braids?" I toss my ombré hair forward over my shoulder and dramatically stroke the length of it to my waist. They're black at the roots and fade into pastel pink, pale turquoise, and silvery blue on the ends. "Thank you. They come out before I head back to school."

"This is my roommate, Bri. Bri, this is my neighbor Cash, and his girlfriend, Mel."

"Yeah. Happy birthday. It's been a while since we were all here," Cash says to me. "This was the spot."

"Remember they used to give out those free passes at school some Fridays?" Mel says, and we nod.

"We all went to elementary school together." I answer the question on Bri's face.

"Wait. So *all* you guys own skates?" Bri studies Mel's pink bedazzled skates with neon laces. "I'm jealous. I haven't skated in forever. I hope I remember how." She laughs; then her gaze fixes somewhere across the room.

It's some lanky dude with broad shoulders. She's found her boy for the night. Good luck to 'em. Cash and Mel boo'd up and Bri trying to be. I'm just here to skate.

"Ray, do you mind putting my shoes in the locker with yours? I'm gonna go ahead and get some practice rounds in before trying to keep up with you pros. Thanks." Without looking back at us, she's off.

Mel and Cash exchange amused looks. I shrug.

"Babe, let's go tell the DJ we have a birthday girl in the building," Mel says, and drags Cash away.

I'm relieved to find myself alone for a moment. I skate-walk across the carpeted floor toward the lockers. Bri is struggle-skating solo, but looking like she's having a great time. Her long coily hair is catching all kinds of wind as she goes. She turns heads without making an effort.

I hang back on the sidelines, watching all the action in the rink. The skate crews are here in numbers, easily spotted by their matching shirts or head-to-toe outfits. Little kids and families take it easy in the center island. Lots of solo skaters, young and old, are lost in their own worlds, gliding around the rink. I'm about to get out there and into my own world too when I see Cash and Mel skate-walking toward me, smiling like they have a juicy secret.

"What's with the faces?"

"Listen," Mel says.

"What am I listening for? I—"

She shushes me. "Eighth grade, first weekend of summer. You, me, Cash."

I recognize the rhythmic music from the intro to "Crank That" by Soulja Boy. The room is bouncing to the beat. They want to do one of our old skating routines.

"It's been so long. Do y'all still remember the steps?" I'm already being pulled onto the floor by Mel, so there's my answer. Cash is skating ahead of us. When we're all finally skating in the same direction, I catch up to Mel, who is skating in step directly behind Cash, who is a mountain on skates. The music transports me right back.

I begin side to side, in step to the beat, as Soulja Boy finishes the rap intro. We make our way around the rink a couple of times in line, taking the curves with our footwork in sync, warming up for the dance. I can feel the music in my bones, my body gliding to the beat. Cash smiles back at Mel and me as we round the curve, and then the bass drops. It's about to go down.

TWO

Orion

"Crystal Palace tonight, right?" Mo asks, eyes closed, arm hanging out of the passenger-side window of my car.

Skating could be a welcome distraction today, but after early morning swim practice followed by five hours busing tables and walking past barbecue pits and steaming dishwashers, I feel like I've been cooked myself. The last thing I want to do is go skating to sweat some more. It's a hundred and one degrees and Mo insists on riding with his window down, so I don't bother turning on the AC. The air coming through the windows is warm and humid and offers no relief from the heat. This is us every week, working the same shifts at Deja Vu BBQ all summer.

"I don't know about skating. I'll probably just kick back at home," I say.

"No!" Mo holds his head, frustrated. "Man, nah! We just graduated from high school; I'm not letting you hang at home with your two cats. We used to skate damn near every weekend—it's been months! Nah, you coming to Crystal Palace tonight. And we getting you a woman."

I laugh. "Mo, you know about me and girls." I get so nervous,

I can't keep up with them. Either I don't know what to say, or I say too much and come off thirsty. When it comes to girlfriends, I'm 0 for 2 awkward, failed attempts. I'm doomed for a life in the friend zone.

Mo shakes his head. "Boy, you a waste of money and good looks. We going tonight. Period."

"I don't know. Maybe. I'll text you. You bringing one of your girlfriends?" I ask, knowing the answer.

"Orion"—Mo pretends to be shocked—"am I bringing one of my girlfriends." It's a statement more than a question. "No, I will not be bringing any of my *friend girls* to Crystal Palace tonight. I'll be looking for me a new friend."

I nod. "So, you not worried about running into Karona or Sherona, what's her name?"

"Naw, man. Ka-*ri*-na is cool. She knows what the situation is. We just kick it, that's it." He adjusts the seat back to the upright position. Sometimes I wish I had it like Mo. I wouldn't collect girls, though. I just wish I had enough game to keep one amazing girl interested.

I make another left turn onto his street, which is lined with shotgun houses and duplexes. Orange Mound is one of a handful of places over here that has resisted gentrification. My dad says the City Beautiful program is supposed to be giving grants to homeowners to fix up their houses. Seems like it hasn't made it to this side of the Mound yet.

We pass my old house on the corner, three houses down from Mo's. The white wood siding is still split and chipped in places. The same four-foot-tall chain-link fence wraps around the entire perimeter of the yard, which is full of overgrown grass and weeds, but there's a new gate—slightly taller than the fence, and sturdy. I can't help but remember the day almost ten years ago when that fence, which was supposed to keep our family safe, didn't. The city bus came out of nowhere. My little sister, Nora, had just turned three. One moment, we were a whole, happy family. The next, we were a ship taking on just enough water to tilt but not sink.

A group of boys plays basketball, shirts and skins, using a bottomed-out milk crate that has been nailed to the light post for a hoop. Some girls play hopscotch in a space between two parallel-parked cars that look like they might be there for an extended stay—one is on blocks. I don't know when I stopped missing this place.

I pull over at the curb in front of Mo's house.

"All right, mane. Thanks for the ride. How much I owe you?" He knows I'm going to reject his gas money. Mo always says a person shouldn't go to sleep owing anybody but Uncle Sam. He sounds like my dad. I think they could both learn to accept acts of kindness from people sometimes. Everything shouldn't be about keeping tabs and tallies, especially between best friends.

"Moses. Boy, if you don't go on somewhere . . ."

He hops out. "Tonight," he says, then spins and disappears into his house.

I pull a U-turn and head toward home. Not looking at the old house when I pass this time. A sharp pain and salty taste in my mouth—I've bitten down on the inside of my cheek too hard again. Bad habit. When things get loud and hectic around me, like lunch rush at work, I grind my teeth or bite down on my cheek to give my mind something to focus on.

Soon after Mo disappears into his house, I turn onto my street. It's amazing how a seven-minute drive can seem a world away.

My dad grew up in Orange Mound. After the accident, we moved just far enough that we wouldn't have to pass our old street every day, but close enough that I could stay at the same public schools with Mo.

The street I live on now is lined with old oak trees and sidewalks in front of large, two-story, old-fashioned houses, with wraparound front porches and manicured lawns. There are no milk-crate basketball hoops, no children playing on the streets, no four-foot chain-link fences, and no other Black people. It wasn't until I was a lot older that I realized that even in a city like Memphis, where the majority of folks are Black, there are some places where Black people are scarce. Central Gardens is one of them. The neighbors are cool, though. Could be worse.

I pull into our empty driveway, grateful to have the house to myself. Inside, I quickly clean out the litter boxes before stripping down, leaving my shades on, dumping my dirty clothes into the hamper, and streaking upstairs. I step over Lotus, my white cat, who is chilling on his usual spot on the stairs, and make a beeline to my shower to wash away a shift's worth of barbecue smoke.

I lay my sunglasses on the desk by my bedroom door and notice the pain in my jaw. I must have been clenching my teeth most of the way home. Sunlight filters through a small frosted window in my bathroom. I rarely turn the light on in here. I keep my room as dark as possible to kind of recover from the day. When I was little, at school I'd constantly spin, or make myself louder than the noise around me, or bite on anything that would fit into my mouth because the fluorescent lights and regular classroom sounds were overwhelming. Now I just bite down on my cheek or listen to music through my headphones when I can. In the shower, I concentrate on my breathing and clear my mind. I try to be present, but my thoughts jump between Nora and the way my dad will, no doubt, be moping around the house tonight the way he always does this time every year. I can't be here. I text Mo as soon as I step out of my bathroom.

> **Me:** Ok I'm in. Pick you up at 8.

> **Mo:** My man. Bump that. I'm borrowing a shirt and getting a plate. Be there at 7.

The last thing I want to do is go to Crystal Palace and get wingmanned by Mo.

Mo has eight of my shirts neatly spread out on my bed.

"Boy. Pick a shirt and let's go," I say, pretending to be more impatient than I am.

"You can't rush this process, mane. It's gonna be girls at the Crystal Palace tonight, waiting to be chose, and I'm planning to leave with as many numbers as possible." He holds a lavender polo shirt up to his chest and looks in the mirror. He shakes his head and hangs it back in my closet.

Waiting to be *chose*? What if they're just at the Crystal Palace waiting to skate?

"They're all polo shirts," I say. "Plus, girls don't care about what shirt you wear. Just pick a color and come on."

"First of all, don't talk about girls as if you know anything about them, my guy. Second of all, unlike you, I'm not walking around here looking like Michael B. Jordan or some shit. I have to actually care what my clothes look like." He pops the collar on his shirt. "But you right. It don't matter what I wear. I got the gift of gab. If you can make a girl laugh, you in there." He's joking, but he's telling the truth.

"And unless you plan on skating solo during couples tonight, I suggest you rethink that school uniform you wearing." Mo picks up a shirt with wide green and white horizontal stripes and layers it on top of the plain white T-shirt he wore over here. "We have a winner."

My dark Levi's, navy T-shirt, and white sneakers immediately feel more uptight than they did a moment ago. Maybe Mo has a point. But I'm not trying to impress any girls tonight. That's a lost cause. I grab a navy sweater as we leave my room.

Finally. My mom is in the kitchen, scooping lemonade mix into a pitcher, when Mo and I reach downstairs. "Y'all want something to eat before you go? Your dad worked his magic with food again. He put his foot in this spaghetti."

When we've finished scarfing down fried whiting, spaghetti, and cornbread, we pile our dishes in the sink.

In the car, Mo's busy brushing his waves and looking out the windows like he's afraid he's going to miss something. I wish he wouldn't do that, because it makes him look like he's up to something. We're two Black guys in an old sports car with tinted windows: the police-suspect trifecta. My dad told me to follow traffic laws and to keep a low profile, and Mo jerking his head around like a pigeon is not helping.

"Bruh, I'm glad you changed your mind about coming," Mo says.

"Yeah, I don't know. I was talking to my dad earlier and he was being all . . . my dad. I don't know. I just wanted to be out." I didn't know he wouldn't even be there. I coulda saved myself a night of discomfort and stayed home.

"Nah, I meant, with today being . . . I mean, Nora . . . the accident . . ." Mo laughs.

Some people laugh in sensitive moments, a way to cut the tension. Mo's like that. But I like to just sit with it sometimes. Let the heavy settle into me. Bear it. Loss is suffocating, but I just breathe through it. Mo laughs again. I force a smile, to let him know I get it—I'm good.

"Aight, enough of this soap-opera shit—let me turn up this Usher. We need some testosterone in this car." He turns the radio up loud and "Yeah!" blasts. Mo's dancing way too hard as we reach the Crystal Palace. Police cars are already preemptively lined up on the curb. The parking lot is packed, but I manage to find a spot.

Mo's hand is warm on my wrist, stopping me before I can get out. "Hey, for real, though. What I was saying earlier? You good?"

"I'm good."

He smiles at that. "Then let's get in here and find wifey." He grabs the door handle. "Shit, we might even find yo' sensitive ass one."

This dude got jokes.

———

This girl keeps skating past, watching me. It got awkward around the fifth or sixth time around, so I moved from the edge of the rink and found a seat off to the side. When I'm at school or work, I'm in a constant battle to block out the light and quiet the noise to stay focused. When I'm here, I like to let all the noise and lights and music and everything wash over me. Here and underwater are the two places I can just exist as I am—be part of the world around me instead of coping with it for a change. This girl who is now skating toward me is kinda messing up my Zen.

"Hi there." She sits right next to me. Not close enough where we seem like we're together, but close enough to make it odd to not answer her.

"Hey." We watch skaters pass by without saying anything else for a while.

"Soooo . . . are you here with somebody?" she asks, turning her whole body toward me, which tells me this is happening.

"Yeah, my best friend, Mo, is around here somewhere." I go back to watching the skaters. In my peripheral, I can see her still pretending not to watch me. Where is Mo? He would love this girl. She's just his type. She's kinda tall and light-skinned with long curly hair. She's also the type of interested that he would vibe with. Something tells me she didn't just come to skate tonight.

"Mo . . . nique?"

Clever. "Moses."

We share a smile.

"You? Here with somebody?" I ask, to be polite.

She nods. "I came with my roommate, Ray."

"Ray . . . mond?" I ask, mimicking her. She laughs full-out this time. Hard. I don't think what I said was that funny, but I know what this is. Girls always giggle when they first start talking to me, until they become bored. Truth is, I'm impressed with how well I'm handling this so far. I wonder if the key to not being nervous with a girl is to not really be interested in her.

"Oh my god," she says, gawking at some skaters. "That's my roommate." She rushes to the barrier wall so fast, I hop up and do the same almost involuntarily.

I've seen skaters do routines countless times, but this crew is different. There's a guy in front, who is linebacker huge, and a girl behind him, and behind *her* a tall girl who is . . . a vision.

I'm still processing the size of this superhero trio on skates when the chorus to "Crank That" starts. They all jump, spin around, and skate backward at the same time. When the same line repeats in the chorus, the Hulk and the girl in the middle slow down.

But Superwoman—the goddess with the cotton-candy braids—moonwalks past them. She reaches the front position just as the next verse is about to begin; then they all jump, spin around, and skate forward again.

Ray's friend is losing it beside me, which is getting me extra hype too. The whole place is going off for the superheroes. I spot Mo on the side rail halfway around the rink. He points toward the middle of the rink, and I nod, letting him know I saw it too. I glance back and find Superwoman dipping and skating as the song goes on.

She's all I see.

Her wavy braids dangle down her back as she twists and turns, art on skates. She's wearing a long, loose black shirt and leggings, I think. I'm not sure about her clothes—the multicolored disco lights obscure them every few seconds—but I'm sure about her smile. She smiles again, and this weird thing happens in my stomach.

I feel Ray's roommate looking at me again.

"She's pretty amazing, isn't she?"

I stumble for words. *Did I say any of that aloud?* "H-huh?"

"Ray. She's amazing, right?"

"O-oh, y-yeah, they're all really good. Which one is Ray?" *Please let it be Superwoman.*

"The tall one."

There is a god. Before I can ask a very important follow-up question, Mo walks up and forces his way in between Ray's friend and me.

"That's right, beautiful. Orion is the tall one. I'm the one you were looking for." Mo holds his hand out to shake hers.

Ray's roommate tilts her head and gives Mo a smile that lets me know I might be off her hook.

"Moses, but you can call me Mo." He takes her hand and kisses the back of it instead of shaking it.

"Briana, but you can call me Bri," she says. "I feel like I'm supposed to say 'charmed, I'm sure' or something. Did you really just kiss the back of my hand?" She giggles.

"Yeah, because I'm a gentleman and I can tell you a lady." Mo winks. This guy is shameless, and, fortunately, it's working. Maybe I do want to be wingmanned tonight.

The song ends and everyone is clapping and whooping. I scan the rink for Ray. Hulk is hugging her and swinging her around in a circle. Is she with him? I'm gutted.

They all leave the floor and sit at a table on the opposite side from where we are. Everything in me wants to rush over there. To do what, though? To say what? This is dumb. What am I even thinking?

"Come on, let me introduce you to Ray," Bri says, grabbing my elbow and pulling me toward the table where Ray and the others are sitting. They're all still breathing heavily and hyping up the routine they just finished. Hulk sees us first. I give him a nod and we size each other up. *Did he see me watching her?*

"Ray, you were holding out," Bri says. "I had no idea you had it like that, girl. All of you. You guys were so great." They hug, and the light catches Ray's eyes just right. All of a sudden, I notice how loud it is in here. I feel my blood pulsing through my fingertips. I trip over my skates and catch myself on their table. *Excellent.*

"You guys, this is Orion and Mo." Bri blushes at the mention of Mo. "And this is my girl, Ray, and her friends Cash and Mel." They sitting mighty close. But I thought . . . Could Hulk have both girls? Nah.

I wave, but words stick in my throat. Ray seems annoyed. I

try not to stare at her, but I'm too close and she's too pretty and I'm not in control of my eyes anymore. When I finally do blink, I notice Cash watching me, stone-faced. I clear my throat.

Bri raises her eyebrows at me, nodding toward Ray. The second Ray's deep cinnamon eyes lock with mine, I forget to breathe.

"*And* today is Ray's birthday, so we're celebrating."

"Really?" I ask, way too loud, and way higher-pitched than anyone my age should say anything. Ever. Mo looks disappointed. I can see he's done the math and already coupled me with Ray in his head. She's the key to him getting to spend more time with Bri. "I mean, yay. I mean, yeah. Happy birthday, Ray." *Why am I like this?* "Y-y'all were really good out there. Obviously been skating for a while."

"Yeah," Mel says, "countless weekends since we were little kids, but none of us can touch Ray. She's queen."

"Aw, thanks, Mel," Ray says. Her voice is as unreal as the rest of her—soft, but deep and strong. "We learned that routine in middle school. I can't believe we still remember the steps." She smiles a little and I'm breathless again. It must be written all over my face, because she looks away. *Get it together, Orion. Say something worth saying.*

"Briana . . . Bri . . . she said you were roommates. What college?"

Ray snorts, then gives me a closemouthed smile.

"Aight, we getting back out there," Cash says loudly, leaving with Mel. Mo's already headed after them with Bri, stranding me and Ray.

I'm covered in cold sweat.

"High school. We go to a boarding school in Rhode Island." She couldn't appear less interested to be talking to me. The DJ announces that the next song goes out to all July birthdays, then plays the Stevie Wonder "Happy Birthday" song.

"This is me," she says. "I'm gonna go skate."

She can't get away from me fast enough. But then she turns back.

"Can you skate?" I know this question is based on my less-than-graceful entry earlier.

I exhale, which turns into an embarrassing cough-chuckle. "Y-yeah, I can skate. Not as good as you, though," I say, in a voice that sounds way more like myself. She flashes me a skeptical smirk as she checks out my black skates. A wave of boldness ripples through me. *What would Mo do?*

"Come on. Let's get out there." To my surprise she nods and skates past me. Her face is sunshine and I'm a leaf turning toward it.

Her smile deepens. What does it mean? I know the friend-zone smile. But the way she's looking at me but trying not to . . . something's different. What, I don't know, but I like it. I like it a lot.

She steps over the edge of the rink and loses her footing. I catch her by the hand and help her steady herself. We are toe to toe, face to face. She bites her bottom lip. I want . . . I don't know what I want, but it's urgent and it's her. She glances at our hands, still touching. I look at them too. I didn't even realize I was still holding on to her hand.

"You okay?" I ask. "I—I'm sorry if I . . . I just didn't want you to fall . . . so I—" *Shut up.* I snap my mouth shut and she does

30

that smile-look-away thing again. I adjust my grip on her hand so it's deliberate.

"Is this okay?" I ask, feeling bolder than I have ever felt in my life.

She hesitates for one second, then simply nods. I step onto the rink, pulling her along with me, and, to my great relief, she comes.

The chorus to the birthday song begins and her eyes light up, igniting something inside me that has lived in the dark a long time. She breaks our grip, spinning around to skate backward in front of me. I follow, as best I can.

I'm mimicking her steps, trying to look cool. She dances and sings along, twirling around one moment, then skating backward the next, then forward, facing me most of the time.

She only meets my eyes occasionally. But I don't care. I don't take my eyes off her.

For a second it's like I exist purely to be here, skating around in circles, following her, locked in her orbit. Orion is a bunch of stars somewhere in the galaxy, but Ray . . . she's the sun.

THREE

Ray

Orion holds my hand and something inside me shifts. It's weird. It's like he's here, in my world, and not just for a fleeting moment. It's like he's a fixture, whether I want him here or not. And, strangely, I don't *not* want him here.

Orion's eyes write an entire love song. Is it even possible to see someone else's love at first sight?

This boy's gonna want to love me. I can tell.

My heart breaks for him, because I'm not a girl to love.

FOUR

Orion

We skate the rest of the night. Ray can outskate me, and she gets lost in the music. She leaves me a few times to skate on my own when I can't keep up, but she always finds me again. Most importantly, she finds me when it's time to skate doubles.

Cash and Mel left a while ago. They caught up to us and said goodbyes, and Cash shot me a look that low-key felt like a warning. Now Ray and I are putting our shoes on as Mo and Bri come back from returning skates.

"We should keep the party going," Mo says. "Me and O were thinking about going down to Beale Street after this."

We were?

"Right, O?"

"Huh? I mean, yeah." It's late, and I have practice in the morning, but if it gets me any more time with Ray, I'm all for it.

Silence.

"We not smoking or drinking or nothing." Mo pleads our case. "Just chilling. You know, drawing the night out a little bit before we have to go home." Still no answer. "I know y'all don't know us, but we good guys. We could show you our IDs. Orion's dad owns Anchor Trucking. I know y'all seen those trucks with the giant anchor on the sides. We cool."

I study my feet. What kind of wingman am I? *Say something.* "Yeah, just hanging out. Talking. And who can you trust more than a guy whose dad owns a trucking company?" I wait for a laugh. Only a hint of a chuckle comes from Ray, and that's plenty.

Mo shakes his head, so I stop talking.

"Ray, I know you not trying to go home this early on your birthday, and this place will be closing in a few. We're in." Bri loops her arm around Mo's, answering for the two of them. I try to read Ray's expression but she's poker-faced.

———

The girls followed us down to Beale and we found parking near each other.

"I don't usually do things like this," I say as I wait with Ray to cross the street.

Mo and Bri decided to hang back. I look behind us, and they are sitting on the hood of my car. The light begins flashing for us to cross. We pass the roadblocks, set up to keep folks from driving down Beale Street after hours, and join the bustling crowd. Colorful fluorescent lights advertising restaurants and bars line both sides of the street. In the distance, a street drummer is banging out a mean beat—the live music from different venues mingles and gives Beale Street a life all its own.

"You don't usually do things like what?"

"Talk to girls." As soon as I say it, I cringe. She looks over at me and laughs. I am mortified. But something about her makes me want to explain myself rather than die.

"For real," I say.

When she notices that I'm not laughing, she squints at me. "What?"

"Yeah, I don't usually talk to girls that I'm attracted to." I want to be more like Mo right now, and say something that will make her laugh, but all I can seem to do is just be honest with her. She nods and watches her feet as we walk on. Our arms knock together every few steps, but neither of us moves to create more space between us. It's nice.

"So what about girls you're not attracted to?"

"Apparently I ask them to introduce me to their beautiful roommates." I shrug.

She flashes a huge smile at me, and I'm high-fiving myself in my head.

"So, I'm beautiful?" She squints her eyes at me like she's actually curious about my answer. Her playfulness sends a jolt of excitement through me. Who even am I right now? My heart is beating a mile a minute. Honesty has gotten me this far. I hope I can keep this up.

"You're the most beautiful girl I've ever seen." She slows her pace and looks at me like I just said the most ridiculous, funny thing. I'm starting to understand Mo a little more now. Any time she reacts to me, it's like I've won a prize.

"Seriously? You're so dramatic. The most beautiful girl you've *ever* seen?" she says. "Well, I am cute, so I'll allow it."

She speeds up, so I speed up.

"It's true." I take a deep breath. "It's weird because I usually don't know what to say. I still don't know what to say, but I don't care if I say the wrong thing. I just want to be here talking to you."

"You know you don't have to say anything, right? We can just walk and not say anything. It's totally fine to hang with somebody and just be, you know?"

"Okay," I say.

A slight breeze blows one of her braids into her face. She tucks it behind her ear and looks away from me.

"So, boarding school, huh?" It's the best I could come up with.

"What? You really can't just walk silently? It's a beautiful night—look around." She spreads her arms wide. As if on cue, a group of loud teens blows past us, wildly running the entire length of Beale. We laugh at their perfect timing. The last one to pass us is dressed head to toe in white—tank top, shorts, Jordans.

"Obviously, walking quietly and looking around has its merits, but I don't want to waste any time not looking at you. So, if I have to talk to you in order to look at you, we talking." That smile. Internal high five.

"Yes, boarding school," she says.

"Why?"

"Why not?"

"Right." We are quiet for a moment.

"What school do you go to?"

"There's only one high school in the city that counts. Thee High School," I say, as if her question is absurd. She rolls her eyes and pretends to be exhausted.

"What is it with you Central kids? Just say Central and keep it moving."

She hugs herself as a cool breeze comes through. Without thinking, I take my cardigan off and hover it over her shoulders so she can put it on. She slides her arms into my sweater and pulls it close to herself. Knowing my body heat is making her body warm makes my heart race a little. I slide my hands into my pockets as far as they will go.

"Thanks. It's windy out here." Her eyes search the sky like she's trying to think of something; then she smiles at the memory.

"I saw a flyer on the wall of my guidance counselor's office."

What were we talking about? I clamp my mouth shut. As long as she's talking to me, I'm good.

"This group of girls, all huddled together wearing identical white polo shirts and green-and-yellow plaid pleated skirts, caught my attention. The buildings across the massive lawn behind them looked like Hogwarts. There was one Black girl in the picture. She had extension braids and wore braces and she looked so happy." She opens her eyes wide whenever she reaches her point at the end of her sentences, which are slow and deliberate. Any time she pauses, she does this thing where she blinks a little longer than a blink requires.

"This is really happening," I hear myself whisper. Did I just say that out loud? "I mean, um . . . I don't . . ."

"Are you even listening to me?" She smiles.

That smile. All I can do is laugh because I'm caught. "Nah, I mean, I'm listening to you. You're just so expressive when you talk. Your . . ." I know what I want to say, but it's not coming out right.

"What did I just say?" She stops walking and crosses her arms, amused, but also a little heated.

I tell her what she said—everything, almost word for word. Her face changes from skeptical amusement to something more serious that's hard to read.

"Impressive," she says flatly, with a nod. She starts to walk again, leaving me behind. I jog a couple of steps to catch up with her. "I heard what you said, by the way."

"Huh?" I pretend to not know what she's referring to.

"Just now. You whispered, but I heard it. 'This is really happening.'" She almost smiles. "I've always been kind of a loner at school. I mean, people knew me, as much as you'd know any super-tall girl you went to school with, but I never really had friends."

"You didn't have friends? You seem so cool."

She shrugs. "I kept myself busy enough with art, poetry, school projects, and stuff. Cassius was my only real friend in elementary. He hung out with Mel and me, until I got tired of being the third wheel and took myself out of the equation."

"Cash's real name is Cassius?"

"Yes. Like Cassius Clay? You know, Muhammad Ali? He was named after him."

"So y'all have been friends forever. I could tell . . . I mean, he seemed kind of protective, like . . . I don't know. He kinda stared me down." Ray looks at me like she's trying to predict where I'm going with this. I think I better get off Cassius. "But you have friends now? I mean, Briana, obviously. Is it like you thought it would be? Do you smile in the class pictures now?"

"Bri is my friend. I can't say I'd call anyone else there a friend. We are kind of all captive, away at school, and have to make the most of it. If Bri and I weren't roommates, who knows? I still smile the same way in class pictures."

I don't think I've ever met a girl this open. I didn't expect a deeply personal conversation like this. I wonder how often she shares stuff with people she's just met. It's not like she's frontin' or anything.

"Interesting. Bri is your roommate and only friend at boarding school. Cassius was your elementary friend and he's your neighbor. I'm good at the friend thing. But I don't live anywhere near you—I think I'm gonna have to move."

She rolls her eyes, laughing, and my world explodes like fireworks on a perfectly clear summer night.

"I graduated in May. I start at Howard in the fall," I say.

"Howard? I was just there last summer for a leadership program. It was refreshing to spend an entire week immersed in Blackness. It's on my list too."

I'm not sure what facial expression I'm making. All I'm thinking about is her being at Howard while I'm at Howard and how suddenly my life is just too good to be true.

"I swim team. I swim. I mean, I'm gonna be swimming for Howard. Scholarship," I manage to say. *Get it together, Orion.*

"Okay. Translation—I'm attending Howard on partial academic and athletic scholarships this fall."

"Ooooh, he skates. He swims. What other hidden talents does he have?" Her eyes smile. I try to commit every inch of her face to memory. I think she likes me. As if she's read my mind, and isn't really into me, her smile fades.

"Um. What other schools are on your list?"

"Can we talk about something else?"

"Right. Yeah. I don't want to hear about any other schools anyway. I just want to think about you going to Howard, so . . ." I trail off, expecting her to laugh at the suggestion in my voice, but she's still serious. The magic is gone. The group of boys from earlier take turns flipping like fearless gymnasts down the stretch of Beale Street they have cleared, like a runway. The one in white is about to go next.

She shakes her head. "You don't even know me and you're already making future plans? I could be a stalker and you've told me where I can find you for the next four years. You might be in danger, my friend."

"If I'm lucky," I say, serious as a heart attack. She chuckles and doesn't look away this time. She stares right back at me.

"I want to. T-to know you." *Come on, O, don't get nervous now that you got her full attention.* I clear my throat. "You said I don't even know you. Well, I *want* to know you. I leave for school in four weeks. That's plenty of time to get to know someone. When do you go back?"

"Seriously?" she asks the sky. "Why?"

I hope I'm not coming off as too needy, but she is here, now, and we both have school in different states in the fall. I don't want to be in this city knowing she is also in this city and not be with her. Damn Mo or whoever for thinking I'm a softy. I'll be whatever if she'll just look at me again.

"Yeah, I mean, I want to know when you leave, so—" I start to explain, but she cuts me off.

"No. Why do you want to know me?"

I don't know how to answer, so I don't say anything. For a moment, the only sounds are the dissonant symphony of music from all the bars and the voices of people talking, laughing, and possibly fighting all around us.

"I'm just a girl who skated with you, for a night. Are you sure you want to be asking me how long we have left? You could meet another 'beautiful girl you'd never talk to,'" she says, making air quotes, "the next time you go out. Then what?"

Silence hangs between us and I let it, choosing my next words carefully.

"I've already met the only beautiful girl I want to talk to this summer. If I'm not talking to you, I will *want* to be talking to you."

She sighs.

"We skated awhile and now we're conversating on Beale," I answer. "Is it crazy that I don't want this to end here?" She's not amused by my use of the word *conversating*. I want her to smile again.

I look up. The sky is a thick blanket of deep blue, hazy with a sheet of clouds, interrupted only by the glowing crescent moon. There are no stars to wish on, so I send a silent plea up to the man in the moon. We are almost to the end of this side of Beale and will have to turn and go back soon. I glance over my shoulder and watch the lights from the buildings dance off puddles along the cobblestones and wait for something, anything, to come to mind to say next.

"You asked me why I want to know you. The true answer is I can't explain why. When I saw you, I just . . . I don't know. And talking to you, you say these things that make me . . . want to keep listening, I guess." We watch each other silently. I can't read her face; she seems more curious about what I said than anything. "Want to take a selfie? We can get Beale Street in the background."

She nods and leans into me like we've done this a thousand times before as I hold my cell phone up. I'm afraid to touch her, so my arm reaches around her shoulder and hovers. She smells like flowers, and it takes everything in me not to press my nose against her neck.

"So, when can I see you again? Can we talk? How will I know? Do you know the way to San Jose? Don't make me keep quoting R and B songs; I can go . . . all night long. See?" I try my best to look silly, making my eyebrows dance. She laughs.

"Is 'Do You Know the Way to San Jose' even an R and B song, though?"

"I don't know. It's Dionne Warwick, so even if it's not R and B, she's Black, so it stays," I insist. I nod and turn for us to walk back the way we came.

We walk quietly for a little bit. I catch her watching me a couple of times.

"Okay, Orion," she says finally.

I close my eyes for a second. Her voice saying my name, it's sweet. I exhale.

"For a guy who isn't used to talking to girls, you sure know how to string some words together." She laughs and shakes her head. I can't tell if that's a good thing or a bad thing, but I am afraid I wouldn't like the answer if I asked.

"Cool. Okay, so getting to know you. Ray. Is that short for something? Your name?"

"It's just Ray." Her answer is short and clipped, so I move on.

"Favorite color?"

"Purple."

"Favorite food?"

"Curried chicken with pigeon peas and rice."

"Okay, technically that's more than one food; also it's really specific."

"That's really the answer," she says. Something in her voice makes it seem like she's not done talking, so I wait. She watches me closely, as if she's trying to decide whether she wants to speak.

"My dad—" She pauses and looks like she's searching my eyes for something. "It was—I mean, it's his favorite, so my mom cooks it all the time. Since forever." I nod before she looks away.

Unsure why her mood seems to have shifted, I just say, "Cool."

I want to ask her a million questions until the sun hangs as high as the moon is right now. But I don't want to weird her out any more. I can't tell if she's over me talking about keeping in touch.

The closer we get to the crosswalk, the closer this night is to ending. I have to see Ray again. Tomorrow. How?

We cross the street and she picks up the pace. We make it across to our parked cars in silence. Mo and Bri are sitting on the curb.

Bri says, "Did y'all see the boy dressed like he was headed to a white party?" We nod and tell them how we got to see him flipping close-up.

Mo winks at me. I don't know how to read it, but he's up to something.

"Bri and me was talking. She's only in town for the weekend. Y'all look like you vibing or whatever. We should hang out again."

Ray is shooting wide-eyed darts at Bri, who has a cheesy grin plastered on her face. Mo is nodding, and I get it. I'm getting wingmanned. I'm so hype right now. I want to do parkour all over this parking lot.

"Pool. I mean cool. You can come to my pool," I manage to say. "My house has a pool. Come tomorrow night. Night swimming. Us and maybe a few other people?"

Ray starts, "I don't think—"

"We'll be there!" Briana shouts, looping her arm around Ray's.

Ray unloops her arm. "Thanks for the invite, but it depends on how things go tomorrow. I'll let you know. If you want, give me your number and maybe I'll call you if we can make it."

Bri reaches into Ray's back pocket and hands me her phone.

"Dang, Bri. I was gonna give him my phone, relax," she says, and playfully rolls her eyes. Then she turns to me and says, "Just

44

add your number to my contacts. Give me your phone. I'll put my number in."

I do and hand the phone back to Ray. Bri hugs Mo goodbye. I blink and Ray's already in her ride, starting the engine and, just like that, she is gone. But she gave me her number. That's something. I hope like hell that Mo's plan works.

"As if it mattered to you," she said.

"Of course it matters. I'm going to take better care of you from now on."

"You don't understand," said Gatsby, with a touch of panic. "You're not going to take care of her any more."

"I'm not?" Tom opened his eyes wide and laughed. He could afford to control himself now. "Why's that?"

"Daisy's leaving you."

"Nonsense."

"I am, though," she said with a visible effort.

"She's not leaving me!" Tom's words suddenly leaned down over Gatsby. "Certainly not for a common swindler who'd have to steal the ring he put on her finger."

"I won't stand this!" cried Daisy. "Oh, please let's get out."

"Who are you, anyhow?" broke out Tom. "You're one of that bunch that hangs around with Meyer Wolfsheim —that much I happen to know. I've made a little investigation into your affairs—and I'll carry it further to-morrow."

"You can suit yourself about that, old sport," said Gatsby steadily.

"I found out what your 'drug-stores' were." He turned to us and spoke rapidly. "He and this Wolfsheim bought up a lot of side-street drug-stores here and in Chicago and sold grain alcohol over the counter. That's one of his little stunts. I picked him for a bootlegger the first time I saw him, and I wasn't far wrong."

"What about it?" said Gatsby politely. "I guess your friend Walter Chase wasn't too proud to come in on it."

"And you left him in the lurch, didn't you? You let him go to jail for a month over in New Jersey. God! You ought to hear Walter on the subject of *you*."

who are you

FIVE

Ray

21 DAYS

Bob Marley's voice gently tugs me awake before the smell of bacon and a freshly baked chocolate cake work a smile across my face. Momma bakes the same cake for my birthday every single year. It's a two-layer buttermilk chocolate cake with lavender buttercream icing. The icing is tinted light purple, it tastes like heaven and love, and we eat it every day until it's gone.

Just like that, Orion's lovesick face appears in my mind's eye and gives me butterflies. This is exactly what I tried to avoid. I gave him my mom's landline because I didn't want him texting me. Looking at my cell phone now, I kinda regret it. I blame Bri. Thanks to her need to be entertained by boys, this one is taking up space in my mind. I was good after we finished skating. Then we just had to end up on Beale, and he just had to be fine, and he just had to give me his sweater, and I just had to wear it home. Maybe he won't miss it.

Bri's and Momma's muffled laughter snaps me back to

reality and carries me to the kitchen. I start down the hall and notice two file boxes spilling out in the middle of the spare catchall room we call the Hoarding Room. I close the door. We always take care to keep the door to that room closed when we have houseguests. Momma's slipping.

"There's our girl," my mom says, embracing me. I rest my cheek on her shoulder because that extra inch of height she has above me is just enough to make me feel dainty and because her hugs are my life support.

"Hey, Momma," I mumble, sounding sleepier than I really am. "Good morning, Bri. I hope you slept okay."

"Morning." Bri speaks around a mouthful of melon. "Don't worry, you didn't snore or anything. I smelled coffee and couldn't resist."

I pour myself a cup of coffee and am pleased to see it is steaming. Momma lays crispy bacon strips onto a plate lined with paper towels. I notice two chocolate cake layers cooling on the countertop.

"The cakes look so good. Thanks, Momma. Bri, wait until you taste this."

"Yeah, your mom told me about the icing. I've never had lavender icing before. Yummy." Bri walks over to the patio door.

"Bri, did Ray show you the tree house?" my mom asks.

"Not yet. I'm jealous. She has her own little Terabithia back there. I'm gonna go get a closer look at that garden."

Bri steps out of the sliding door. Our garden is full of medicinal wildflowers and herbs, meticulously planted in rows around a small clearing of paver stones in the grass, accented by a dwarf lemon tree planted in a whiskey barrel. The lavender plants that line the interior perimeter are the main attraction, especially in the summer.

Mom excuses herself to get ready. As always, she pauses ever so slightly at the cake-cutting photo from her wedding, then disappears down the hall.

"Happy birthday, Ray," Bri sings. She's holding a small flat box wrapped in paper covered in handwritten script. It looks like an old, elegant letter from a time when people wrote with feathers dipped into pots of ink. Twine crisscrosses the package and is tied in a simple bow on the top.

I take the box from her and open it. The journal is bound in soft, tawny leather. The back cover wraps halfway around the front and is self-secured by two leather strings. I loosen the ties and reveal thick, flower-pressed pages with deckled edges.

"I saw it and instantly thought of how all your journals are the same black leather with that elastic strap. This one will stand out. Maybe you can use it for extra special stuff."

Sometimes Bri's gifts are upgrades on things that I already have. They're actually kind of backhand diss gifts, but I know they come from a good-hearted place. Like when she got me turquoise earbuds to replace the black ones I'd used since forever with my cell. "There. Now it matches your phone case," she'd said when I'd tried them out.

"It's so pretty and extremely thoughtful—thanks, friend." I give her a hug.

After Bri and I have filled up on waffles and bacon and cleaned the dishes, my mom emerges from the hallway, showered, dressed, and ready to meet up with her friends.

"I forgot to ask, did you girls have fun last night?"

"We did. Cash, Mel, and me pulled out an old routine from middle school."

"Ms. Rosalyn, you should have seen them. I had no idea Ray was an actual queen on skates. She was amazing—rendered me totally invisible to a boy I had my sights on. All he could see was Ray."

My mom raises her eyebrows, amused. "Oh, really? A boy, huh? Y'all got in pretty late." Mom takes a dramatic sip of coffee. I love it when my mom is playful like this.

"We went down to Beale Street with him and his friend after Crystal Palace closed," I say.

My mom raises her eyebrows again, less amused.

"To walk," I add. "I wanted Bri to see Beale Street."

"So while Orion was getting to know Ray, I was third-wheeling it with his friend Mo."

Uh, I was definitely the third wheel, not Bri. It was their idea to take a walk in the first place. I keep my mouth shut and let Bri think she was doing me a favor.

"Orion?" Momma's smile cracks just a little.

"Yeah, what is it?"

"Huh? Oh. No, honey. I just wasn't sure if I heard it clearly. Orion and Mo?" She pinches off a piece of a leftover waffle.

Bri and I nod.

"What do you know about him?"

I can't hold back the goofy smile I flash at Bri, and we both burst out laughing. I used to mock her cheesy grin and chirpy voice whenever she'd talk about a new boy. I get it now.

Momma looks confused.

"His name is Orion. He's taller than me, but only by an inch or two. He swims. He graduated this spring. He's going to swim for Howard in the fall. His dad owns a trucking company. Anchor Trucking. He likes me. I'm not sure if I want him to. The end."

My mom studies my face. "Anchor Trucking. You're not sure if you want him to like you?"

"Yeah. I'm not sure if I want to be bothered."

"Baby, you don't have to be anywhere or with anyone you don't want to be. You can't control how he feels about you, but you can choose whether to invite him around or not."

"I know, Momma. It's me you're talking to, The Ice Queen. I mean, I know, but then again I don't. He's different in a way that I think probably matters. Like, I can tell he thinks I'm cute, but he never made me feel gross. It was nice. Does that make sense?"

Bri looks like she's just seen a basket full of puppies and is about to cry.

My mom nods. "Yes. That makes sense. It's called a first impression, and it sounds like he made a mighty strong one on you."

Momma seems maybe worried or something.

"You can relax, Momma—I probably won't even see him again. It was just nice . . . the way he made me feel, that's all. I'm not running away and eloping or anything," I say, attempting to lighten the mood.

"He invited us over for a pool party tonight, actually." Bri grins.

"You're going to his house?"

"No. I don't know. Maybe."

Momma's face relaxes into the soft, sad smile that I'm used to.

I've seen that smile hundreds of times—she'll notice me watching her, perk up, and insist she's okay. It happens less often since she finally donated my father's old books and T-shirts, but it's ever present around the Day.

"Y'all sure you want to be going to the house of some boys you just met?" She squints at me.

"I don't want to go to his house anyway. Bri's the one who wants to go. But I thought I'd take her around to see Memphis since it's her only full day here."

"You shouldn't do anything you feel pressured to do. I want to be sure you girls are being smart. Will his parents be there?"

"I didn't ask. I don't even want to go, really."

"There's no reason we can't do both. He said night swimming, remember? You can take me around Memphis during the day and we can hang with them after," Bri reminds me. "They seem like really solid guys, Ms. Roz. Mo said they don't smoke or drink or anything. And there'll be other kids there too. I can't think of a better way to spend my last night in Memphis."

Momma's jaw clenches.

"Mom, you don't have to worry, seriously. I'm not even all that into him—he's just really nice. If we go, I'll be sure to leave the address and phone number so you'll know exactly where we are."

A car horn makes us all jump.

"I don't . . . maybe y'all shouldn't . . ." Momma looks aimlessly around the room, as if the words she's searching for can be found someplace in the house. "If you end up going, just . . . be safe, okay? I trust you girls. My ride is here."

"Okay," I say as Momma rushes past us. My answer meets a closing door.

"Sounds to me like we're going to a pool party tonight," Bri says. "I'll text Mo."

SIX

Orion

The solar-powered yard lights flicker on just as the sun dips behind the trees. Applause erupts when I turn the pool lights on and the pool glows neon blue. From the patio, I take a bow, turn the speaker volume up, and kick back on a lounger, trying not to freak out.

Almost everybody we invited to night swimming is here. Ahmir and Niko, two of my swim teammates, take turns seeing who can hold an underwater handstand the longest. Ray and Bri are nowhere in sight. I gave them a later time so they could walk in on a popping party. Pressure's on to show Ray it might be fun to hang with me again after tonight.

"Mo. On a scale of one to not interested, this girl is a solid two. There's no more wingmanning after tonight. It's time for me to fly on my own. How?"

"I can't really tell you what to do. I just be trying to kick it. You on some falling-in-love stuff, and that's out of my arena."

"Seriously? You got me this far and you're just leaving me out here? What kind of wingman are you?"

Mo shakes his head. "Pitiful. Okay. Man, look at you . . . look at your house. Profile. Post up. Stunt on her. Keep her smiling. When the time seems right, after y'all been vibing for a minute, ask her what she likes to do when she comes home in the summers. Whatever she says, say y'all should do it together. The rest will happen naturally. Simple."

Simple. Almost too simple.

Mo's phone buzzes. She is here.

"I'll go get them. You be doing something Denzel-like when we get back here. Stunt."

I'm frozen in place when Mo leaves. *Stunt?* What does that even mean? *Breathe.* Okay. I throw two towels over one arm and grip two water bottles in my other hand to greet them. No. That's too much like a butler. I toss everything and stretch out on the lounger. I don't know what to do with my hands, so I fold them across my stomach. No. It's a party. I don't want to look like the chaperone. One of the girls screams, drawing my attention to the pool. The pool.

I dive into the middle of the pool and swim to the shallow end where everybody is. I prop my elbows up on the edge and join in laughing at the chicken fight. Instantly, I'm a little self-conscious posted up next to Niko, who only has to show up for girls to get weird and giggly. He's light-skinned with a floppy, curly fade. He's also a show-off, and even better with girls than Mo. And Ahmir is ripped. All of a sudden, I'm questioning my decision to invite half of my relay team from swim. I shake my head to clear it and try to relax into a chill party vibe.

"Yoooo, who is White Dress?" Niko asks, pressing his elbow into my arm, almost pushing me over.

I look up as Mo enters the backyard with Bri and Ray.

"White Dress is don't you worry about who she is," I say, shrugging Niko off me.

"*You* worried?" Niko asks me, amused. I ignore him.

"Look who I found," Mo announces as they approach the pool. Showtime.

I wait until she sees me and tip my head back like *wassup*. Then I push off from the wall, streamline underwater, and break the surface like a shark. I only have room to swim a couple of strokes before I get to the steps, but that's all I need.

I climb out of the pool and walk, a little slower than usual, over to greet them. I don't get a towel on purpose. I glance at Mo, who is giving me a low-key thumbs-up. I catch Ray checking me out and my stomach flutters a little bit. My abs tighten reflexively. Ray's braids are pulled up into a ponytail. She must have had a neck and ears and smooth skin yesterday, too, but it's like I'm seeing her for the first time all over again. A soft grin creeps across her face, and I clear my throat to mask a chuckle.

"Nice shorts," Ray says.

I look down, confused because I'm wearing basic navy trunks. Then it hits me—she's complimenting how I look in these. *It's working. Be cool.*

"Thank you." I tuck my bottom lip between my teeth and rub my palms together like I've seen Mo do countless times when talking to girls. She squints.

"Um. Glad y'all could make it." Ray is looking out at the pool. "So, Bri, how you like Memphis? Mo said y'all did a grand tour."

"Yes, I got to see that pyramid up close. I'd never have guessed the place was that huge—the postcards don't do it justice. We didn't go inside, though. I have zero interest in hunting and fishing. I wanted to ride that elevator to the top of the pyramid, but the line was too long. Maybe next time. The Civil Rights Museum was surreal. My family travels a lot—all over the world—so I've seen a ton of historic places, but to see where MLK got shot . . . to see where the civil rights movement was gutted . . . and how they kept going . . . how we kept going . . ." Bri shakes her head.

"Yeah," I say, "it really is a powerful thing to see up close. I'm glad you got to go." We're all quiet for a moment. Mo catches my eye and nods toward the far end of the pool.

"Come on, let me show y'all where you can put your stuff down."

They follow me to the covered section of the patio.

Bri drops her bag and quickly removes her cover-up.

"Later," she says over her shoulder as she and Mo rush to join the others in the pool. Ray and I share a little laugh at our obviously preplanned abandonment.

"Bri really likes your friend." Ray slips off her sandals.

"Every girl that Mo wants to like Mo likes Mo."

Awkward silence.

Ray reaches to untie the straps on her long white dress, and the flowy material seems to float to the ground in slow motion. Instinctively, I turn my back.

"You do realize I'm wearing a swimsuit underneath my dress, right?"

I can tell she's smiling.

"I know . . . sorry. I don't know why I did that. I see girls undress all the time . . . at swim . . . warm-ups." *Stop talking*. I turn back around.

Her gold-foil swimsuit makes her deep brown skin look like it's lit from the inside . . . like it's some kind of precious metal too. She watches me so intentionally as she twists her ponytail up into a bun and tucks the colorful ends in. My stomach goes weird. I force myself to check over her shoulder toward the pool as if I give any bit of a damn about what's happening over there. I look back at her and it's clear she knows the effect she has on me. *Say something smooth. Be cool.* What would Mo say right now? My mind is blank. Mercifully, she steps backward, turns, and takes a running leap into the middle of the pool.

Almost an hour into it and things are going as planned. The more time passes, the less anxious I am about Ray becoming bored of me like other girls have. We all have cannonball and belly-flop contests. I dominate the races. Ray smiles wide at me every time I win. When I beat Niko, I trash-talk him, like always. When I beat Ahmir, I tell him his dreadlocks are slowing him down. My jokes are a hit. I'm glad Ray gets to see me with my friends. I feel looser around them. Mo said to keep her smiling. I think it's working. I even get her to take a selfie with me—her face pressed right against mine.

Ahmir wants to race again. We freestyle down to the deep end of the pool, flip turn, and sprint back. I touch the wall for the win. Everyone is cheering and some rap song is blaring from the backyard speaker system and Ray is lost in conversation, leaning against the side of the pool, shoulder to shoulder with Niko. I don't even have to guess that he's flirting, because of that dumb smirk planted on his face.

I swim toward them and hope I'm in earshot of whatever Niko's saying before they notice me.

"*Me gusto* your face, girl. You fine as—"

"Me *do something painful* to your face if you don't back up off my girl," I say, sending a wave to splash in Niko's face. Everybody bursts into a chorus of ooooohs. Niko winces but laughs, and I force a laugh to soften the blow.

Everyone is still splashing and whooping when it hits me that I just called Ray my girl. Her eyes are burning holes into mine. She's smiling so wide that I notice a soft dimple on her other cheek.

"Your *girl*?" Ray says. She laughs and floats past me on her back, swimming toward the other side of the pool.

"You coming?" she calls out as she turns and swims away. Everybody hypes me up as I catch up with her.

We face each other, treading water, exchanging silly smiles for a few seconds.

"'*Me gusto* your face'?" Ray says mockingly. "Niko is something. He was really trying to spit game in Spanglish."

"Yeah, Niko's fluent in Spanish—had a Spanish-speaking nanny for that sole purpose—but he's Black and Serbian. He's fluent in that, too."

"Okay. Multilingual? Nice," Ray says. A tiny bolt of jealousy runs through me. "Does he always do that? Try to steal your *girls*?" Her smile is so sweet. I'm embarrassed that she thinks he plays me like that all the time, but not enough to be defensive about it.

"I'm not worried about Niko. We been swimming together since we were like eight years old. He's like my brother. Plus, I actually never had a *girl.*"

Ray raises her eyebrows.

"Nah, I mean . . . I've had girls, but not anyone serious or . . . not anyone to be around for long . . . to bring around." Not smooth.

"How long can you hold your breath?" she asks, mercifully changing the subject.

"Just over two minutes," I say. "Two minutes and nineteen seconds, to be exact."

"Really? What are you, part dolphin?"

"Part shark. I practice a lot." I shift to the right and she mirrors me, so we're moving in a slow circle, facing each other. "How long can you hold yours?"

"I don't know. I've never counted. Want to count for me?" She stops circling and treads in place.

"Yeah."

"Okay. On three," she says. "One, two . . ." On three, we both sink below the surface. I would hold my breath down here forever if I could look at her just like this. The pool lights play with the water against her iridescent swimsuit and dark skin, giving off sparkles of light as she steadies herself in the water, slowly moving her arms and incredibly long legs for control. She smiles at me and tiny bubbles escape her mouth. Jeez. She returns to the surface. I follow her.

She is gasping for air. "How long did I hold it?"

I burst out laughing.

"What?"

"I forgot to count."

One of her pink braids has come loose and is plastered across her forehead. Without thinking, I swipe it aside and tuck it behind her ear. Some pop dance anthem is blazing through the speakers, but it might as well be a symphony of violins. Her mouth slowly curves into a grin and her eyes go soft. In the movies, this is probably where I'd ask to kiss her. I wish I were as bold as the guys in the movies.

"Pizza." I regret it immediately, but there's no way to backtrack. I announce that I'm ordering some to the group before leaving the pool.

"Aye, thanks, O. I only had cereal today. I'm hungry as hell!" Niko calls back.

I order the pizzas and run into Ray as I reach the door.

"Hey, where's your restroom?"

I show her to the powder room.

"Don't go back out yet, okay? Wait for me. I'll be quick." She goes into the bathroom and closes the door behind her.

I walk over to the sliding doors that lead to the backyard. The cannonball battles have ended and almost everyone is just chilling around the pool. Mo is stretched out on one of the double loungers next to Bri. He says something that must have been a punchline because everybody within earshot bursts out laughing. I hear the bathroom door open behind me.

"Thanks for waiting. Do you want to show me your room? We getting to *know* each other, right?" The way she says *know* sends my pulse racing. I think she means it in the biblical sense, where "to know you" means "to bone you." Half of me hopes this is just all in my head, because the only person I've ever *known* is myself, but that half of me is at war with the half that wants to know Ray in every sense of the word.

"Sure. Glad I made my bed today . . . um . . . I mean glad I cleaned my room . . . not . . ." *Hush.* I can't look at her, so I just go. She follows me up the stairs.

"Watch out for Lotus. He lives on this step." I reach down and scratch Lotus's forehead with one finger before stepping over him.

"I've never seen a cat with one green eye and one blue eye before." She follows me into my room, and Jinx walks in right past her and jumps onto the middle of my bed.

"Another one? Where did he come from?"

"This is Jinx"—I pet Jinx's head—"and *she* shows up just like magic, don't you, girl?" I stop petting Jinx when I realize I have just baby-talked my cat in front of Ray. I want to vaporize.

"One white cat, one black cat . . . are there any more?"

"No, just Lotus and Jinx. I got them two years after the . . . I got them after we moved here."

Now that a girl is in here, it occurs to me how juvenile this place is, with the blue walls and airplane posters all over. Why do I still have Hot Wheels displayed in my room? *Facepalm.* At least it's clean. We are alone. I just have to find the perfect time to ask what she likes to do.

Ray runs her fingers along the spines of the books stacked on my desk. She checks out my swim Wall of Fame—mounted shelves holding plaques and framed action shots, rows of medals and ribbons hanging from hooks, and tons of square selfies from meets tacked to the wall.

"Junior Olympics? I'm gonna take a shot in the dark here and assume you swim a little bit."

I muster as much cool as I can. *Stunt.*

"Yeah, I swim a little bit."

Ray smirks and smiles, admiring everything. Suddenly I feel less insecure about my Hot Wheels.

"Now all the selfies you ask for make sense."

"Yeah. My dad used to always take pictures of us—the family—all the time. He'd snap shots at the most random moments. When I was little, he was really into photography and developing film and all that. I guess it rubbed off on me." Ray nods. Her face goes serious, almost kind of sad, before she turns back to surveying my room.

"Do you play these?" Now she's touching one of the three acoustic guitars that hang from mounted hooks on the wall. I like how she keeps touching my things. I wish I could say yes and then play an Ed Sheeran song for her, but I'm too damn shy.

"Yeah. I only know a few songs from taking lessons off and on over the years. At first I took group lessons, but I couldn't focus—the music from the other guitars."

Then swim started to take up more of my time, and I dropped it. Swim is life. Sometimes, I still learn to play songs on guitar from YouTube.

"Do you sing, too?"

In the shower, in here with my cats, but in front of humans—no.

"I don't sing the songs, just mostly play the instrumental." I try to sound nonchalant. Our eyes meet and her eyelids go heavy. She reaches out and gently tugs at the leg of my trunks, so quickly that I wonder if it even happened. I look down at her hand and keep looking at that same spot on my trunks a few seconds after she let go. When I look back at her, she bites her bottom lip.

"Play something for me," she says, and sits on the edge of my bed like it's nothing. Mo's plan is working too well.

I pick my favorite guitar. My heart is beating out of my chest. Mo said to stunt on her. I'm shirtless, holding a guitar. I think this qualifies as a stunt. The guitar is already tuned, but I pretend to tune it anyway. I never play or sing in front of my parents with my eyes open. As a kid I'd close them because I believed it made me invisible. I summon some courage, take a deep breath, look Ray right in the eyes, and strum the intro, picking strings one by one. I'm glad it's a short intro, because watching her watch me is making me cringe on the inside. I clear my throat and stop playing.

"You recognize it?"

"Bob Marley. 'Redemption Song.' *Legend* is one of my favorite albums." Her smile is so wide that her eyes nearly close. Something flutters inside my chest. "Yeah, my mom has played that album in our house my entire life. There's usually a record spinning when she's home, but this one has always been in heavy rotation."

"We have something in common," I say. Her smile starts to fade. I clear my throat.

"I have to close my eyes to play the rest . . . so I can concentrate."

The last thing I see before I close my eyes is her smile diminishing.

"That's it," I say, and shrug, when I'm done.

"Nice. Bravo." Ray exaggerates a slow clap. That hungry look is back on her face.

I hang up my guitar to take a few deep breaths and scream silently. Now is the perfect time to ask what she likes to do.

"What's that?" she says, making me jump when she touches the scar on the center of my lower back. She might as well be touching everything on me from my waist down. I step just out of her reach and reflexively touch it myself as I turn to face her.

"Spinal surgery baby . . . as a baby . . . I was born with a tethered spinal cord."

Ray looks embarrassed.

"Damn. I shouldn't have asked. . . . I didn't mean to . . ."

"Nah, it's cool. There's a funny story, actually. My parents told me that I had been born with a shark fin, and they had it removed because I swam too fast. I was four, so I believed them."

"Aw!" Ray looks like she's just seen one of those viral wedding proposals on Instagram.

She stands up and her towel slips. She catches it and tucks it at her waist before sitting farther back on the bed. She says something about the shark fin being the cutest thing. My ears are ringing now because Jinx walks across the bed and nuzzles Ray's hand until she pets her. Ray does it like she has done it a thousand times—like it's the most natural thing for her to be in my room, on my bed, petting my cat. My cat, whom I envy right now.

"Why don't you come join Jinx and me over here?" She looks me up and down, dead serious.

"Huh? On the bed?"

"Yeah. On the bed." She continues to pet Jinx and leans down on her elbow, stretching out on her side, and I can't deal.

I clear my throat and look over at my door, either to identify any possible escape routes or to decide if I should close it. I look back at Ray, who's still watching me like I'm dessert.

"Pizza." *Again, Orion, really?*

Ray looks confused. I'm in panic mode. I'm not ready to be on the bed with her yet, but she's clearly ready. Mo would call this a win, but I want more of . . . I don't know . . . *her* . . . before on-the-bed stuff. If I tell her I'm not ready for all that, will she wait around for me to be ready?

"Pizza," I say again like a caveman, and point toward the window behind her. I walk around the bed and look down at the backyard. *Pizza.*

Ray followed me when I walked to the window, because the front of her body is now pressed against my side. She's looking down at the backyard now too. Pizza boxes and party guests dot the sitting areas around the pool.

"Yeah. Um. Maybe we should get some pizza before it's all gone." I clear my throat, trying to sound cool. "I should have been carbo-loading today. For practice. We have a pretty intense practice in the morning. Swim."

"Or we could do some pretty intense practicing in here," she says, and rubs her cheek against my shoulder.

I don't know what to say, but I know that I'm not ready to do this yet. I'm dumbfounded. Speechless.

Ray huffs out a chuckle and rolls her eyes. It's a punch in my gut.

"Let's just go eat," she says.

"Um . . ." Defeated and tongue-tied, I run out of the room, leaving her there. I want to stop myself with every step I take toward the door, but I'm spiraling. I pause at the bottom of the stairs to get my head right. I'm too embarrassed to look back at Ray and too crushed to face Mo. I'm actually holding back tears. I hate this.

Mo climbs out of the pool when he sees me approaching the door. We reach the table stacked with pizzas at the same time.

"Boy. Let me handle these pizzas so you can get upstairs and handle yo' business." He nods toward the house with a dumb look on his face. I shake my head.

"There's no business being handled in there, Mo. She is in my room, and I don't know . . . ," I say. Mo swats my hand away from the pizza boxes and shoves me toward the house.

"In your room? Get in there. Get it. Go. Bye." He jams a pizza box into my hand, then guides me to the door. How does Mo not understand that I don't want to *get it* yet? I mean, I want to get it . . . I'd love to get it, at some point, eventually. Truth is, I've never wanted to get it more, but right now, just watching Ray and coming up with ways to make her laugh is everything.

I can't do this Mo's way. Honesty won me some points early

on. I have to go with that. I open the box of pizza and take a giant stress bite out of the first slice I grab. I'm just going to go upstairs and remind her that I'm the nervous type, and that I like her, and ask her, hoping against hope, to let me see her again.

She looked at Tom, alarmed now, but he insisted with magnanimous scorn.

"Go on. He won't annoy you. I think he realizes that his presumptuous little flirtation is over."

They were gone, without a word, snapped out, made accidental, isolated, like ghosts, even from our pity.

After a moment Tom got up and began wrapping the unopened bottle of whiskey in the towel.

"Want any of this stuff? Jordan? . . . Nick?"

I didn't answer.

"Nick?" He asked again.

"What?"

"Want any?"

"No . . . I just remembered that today's my birthday."

I was thirty. Before me stretched the portentous, menacing road of a new decade.

It was seven o'clock when we got into the coupé with him and started for Long Island. Tom talked incessantly, exulting and laughing, but his voice was as remote from Jordan and me as the foreign clamor on the sidewalk or the tumult of the elevated overhead. Human sympathy has its limits, and we were content to let all their tragic arguments fade with the city lights behind. Thirty—the promise of a decade of loneliness, a thinning list of single men to know, a thinning briefcase of enthusiasm, thinning hair. But there was Jordan beside me, who, unlike Daisy, was too wise ever to carry well-forgotten dreams from age to age. As we passed over the dark bridge her wan face fell lazily against my coat's shoulder and the formidable stroke of thirty died away with the reassuring pressure of her hand.

She insisted.
He won't.
He realizes
his little flirtation is over.
gone
without a word.
a pity.
tragic.

SEVEN

Ray

Orion literally ran away from me. I collapse onto his bed, baffled. Why even bother with this guy?

Jinx is stretched out on the bed beside me, where Orion should be. I get up from the bed to take another look around his room.

Above Orion's dresser, the whole wall is full of posters of aerodynamic cars and all kinds of airplanes. The ceiling fan in his room even has an aviator feel to it, like propellers on an old World War II aircraft. Maybe he wants to be a pilot or design planes. There's an impressive shrine to his swim life, which explains his amazing shoulders. I recognize Ahmir and Niko in some of the group photos and selfies. There's one with his parents—everyone in this family is hot. One section of the wall in the far corner of his room is half covered with a wall-mounted case of tiny compartments, and every one holds a tiny toy car. He probably still has every Hot Wheels he ever got. Adorable. Seems like a guy his age would have taken all this stuff down by now. Orion is a puzzle.

He was so nervous about me being in his room. And he's

honest about his feelings, which makes me feel simultaneously sorry for him and kind of like I can trust him with my life, which is unsettling. I basically offered myself to him on a platter, and he ran. Here is this super-fine guy who seems clueless about how fine he is, alone in his room with me . . . *me* . . . no parents in sight, and he actually ran away. He jumped every time I touched him.

He said he wanted to get to know me . . . we should be making out by now. I've always been chased, never the other way around.

Outside his window is a sweeping view of his backyard and the pool. Below, it looks like Mo is coming inside—no doubt to find out if his friend scored.

"So, Jinx. Ready to go downstairs? Your daddy not trying to get anything going up in here." Jinx blinks at me, as confused as I am. What kind of boy turns this down?

I take my time going down the stairs, being nosy. His house only has two stories, but there is a door next to the landing where the stairway zigzags down. My curiosity gets the best of me. Part of me hopes this immaculate Midtown mansion has a hoarding room. I turn the knob to see if the door opens. It does.

The room appears to be an office. A stream of light comes in from the stairwell. I make out dark wood floor-to-ceiling bookshelves, a leather couch, and a bank of windows that must overlook the backyard. There have to be hundreds of books in here. A massive desk sits against the wall just left of the door. The office is neat, but there are stacks of papers and books cluttering the desktop and the floor surrounding it.

An envelope that kinda looks like Crestfield mail catches

my interest. I know I shouldn't, but I can't help stepping inside to get a closer look.

Jinx springs out of the room. I stumble back with a yelp. Where'd she come from? Jinx is judging me for being a nosy houseguest, I bet.

I hear the patio door close, and though everything in me wants to peek back at the letters on the desk, I don't. Instead I pull the door closed and follow Jinx down the rest of the stairs to the kitchen.

Orion is there, chowing on a slice of pizza. His gold chain, stuck to his skin, glints as he swallows, cheeks still full of pizza. He likes me—he just doesn't know what to do with me. It's written all over his face. I bet he'd be the perfect boyfriend for the right girl.

"Um . . . I guess . . . I get nervous. You make me nervous. But it's only because I like you. Can I call you? After today? I want to see you again."

This boy . . .

"Maybe," I say, with a smile that I hope he can see through. Because it's really hard to say no to a boy who is so hopeful, especially when an incredibly annoying small part of me wishes I could relax into this and see where it goes.

EIGHT

Orion

20 DAYS

I've been lying here watching my ceiling fan spin since before
the sunlight started to stream into my bedroom. Jinx has been
scratching my door for about as long. I must have slept, but
I feel like all I've done is toss and turn and look at our selfies
since Ray left last night. I posted our photo from Beale Street
on IG. Everyone in the comments is asking who she is. We're
both smiling and the lights in the background are blurred. It's
taking everything in me not to make it my cell background. I
want to see her again. I need to see her again. She gave me my
sweater back before she left last night. I'm so dumb—the first
thing I did when I got to my room was hold it to my nose. It
mostly just smells like me, but there's a hint of her flower smell
near the collar. I slept with it near my pillow.

How am I supposed to spend the rest of the summer knowing she's here and knowing I'm not hanging with her? I grab
my phone.

Me: Ray. I need her in my life man. What to do?

Mo: Boy, u have her number. U know where she works. Bri told me, remember?

Me: But I can't just show up at her job, can I?

She doesn't even know I know where she works.

She said MAYBE I could call her.

But what if she was just being nice?

Dad bursts open my door and Jinx pounces onto my chest. I scream. He's still in his pajama pants and isn't wearing his glasses, so he must have jumped out of bed in a hurry to get in here. From the look on his face, he's annoyed about it.

"You see the time? Get up, boy. You tryin' to be late for practice?"

"Um . . . no, sir . . . I was just about to get—"

"Aye, who is this girl on your IG?" He flashes his phone screen.

"Huh? Ray. I met her at Crystal Palace. Why?"

"Why? Boy, nationals is around the corner. Now is the time to be laser focused on training, eating, and sleeping. The last thing you need to be doing is chasing a girl around." He pauses like he expects me to say something. "Aye, don't worry 'bout it. Just be downstairs in fifteen—I'll drive you," he says, closing the door. He is gone as quickly as he appeared. I shove Jinx off my chest with an apology and search my sheets for my phone, which went flying when my dad busted in. There's another text.

> **Mo:** If you don't get off my phone and go plead your case to that woman . . .

He's right. I get all tongue-tied around her, but I can't not see her. Maybe I could text her the selfie . . . to remember me by. We look good together. Nah, that's corny. I should just call her and tell her I want to see her again. But then what would I say after that? Plus, what if I call her and she doesn't answer or doesn't call back? Then any attempt to contact her after that will just be weird.

If I ask myself too many more questions, I'm gonna talk myself out of it.

I throw my covers off and wipe the crust from my eyes.

I have to see her in person. But first I need to get to practice.

━━━

I always come to practice a half hour early. I like having the pool to myself to warm up before things get loud. I wore my swim shorts here. My fade is on full Afro today, so I grab a swim cap from my bag, throw my shirt in, slide a pair of mirrored swim goggles over my cap, and stop at the mirror. I've been working hard on dry-land workouts lately, and definitely look as strong as I feel.

I slip my feet into my pool slides. As soon as I exit the locker room, the familiar scent of chlorine calms me. Between thinking about Ray and my dad sulking on the bleachers missing Nora, I can't get to my Zen, at the bottom of the pool, fast enough.

I walk to the deep end, press my goggles firmly against my eyes, and dive in. The water is a cool shock to my system. In the muted silence, I feel like I'm flying. I freestyle a few laps and keep getting flashes of Nora's smiling face.

I can't focus on my laps, so I get out of the pool, stretch, and get ready for some deep dives. Feet together, I take several deep breaths in, filling my lungs before stepping off the edge. I start my watch, press my hands against my thighs, and let my body weight carry me twelve feet down to the bottom.

This is my favorite part.

When I'm alone down here, the sounds of the world shut off. There's just my heartbeat, the light reflecting off the water, and my tightening lungs. All I focus on down here is staying alive. There's no room to think about anything else.

I stand on the bottom, suspended, watching the lights play before closing my eyes and focusing my mind on surviving. My lungs start to burn and I wait as long as I can before I open my eyes. I've been clearing the surface at two minutes nineteen seconds for the past couple of weeks, but I want to try to inch past that today. I close my eyes again until my chest feels like it's closing in on itself, and push off the bottom of the pool. I stop my watch just as I break the surface.

"Your mother hates that shit." My dad stands right beside the pool. "How much did you add this time?"

I check my watch. "Two seconds." I pull my goggles onto my forehead and wipe the water from my eyes.

He watches my face like he's trying to figure something out. "That's a lot of Mississippis."

When I was a kid, he and my mom would find me completely submerged in the bathtub. The first time, my mom hauled me out of the tub, and I was yelling "nine Mississippis" over and over again, excited. I don't remember a lot of things from when I was four years old, but I remember seeing my mom cry for the first time. My dad was there too, but he's not the crying type.

My dad comes closer to the edge of the pool and smiles. It reminds me of how he'd look at me after he'd let me beat him in a swimming race when I was little. Even when he's saying he's proud of me or he loves me or whatever, there's a *but* lingering behind his words.

He shut down after Nora died. I noticed it right away, and I think that's why I've always just tried to be the best kid I can be for my dad.

I look up at him now, and just like that, he blinks his smile away as if something reminded him that his heart was showing.

He clears his throat. "All right. Well, you better finish up. We didn't come early for you to be late. Team huddle in ten."

There's an awkward silence between us before my dad goes back to the bleachers. I wish that I could press rewind—that my dad was like before, that Nora was here, that I'd been smoother with Ray. I pull my goggles down over my eyes and sink back into the pool.

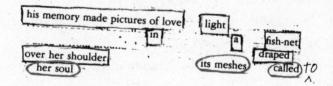

his memory made pictures of love | light

in | a | fish-net

over her shoulder | draped

her soul | its meshes | called to

his memory made pictures of love
light in a fish-net
draped
over her shoulder
its meshes
called to her soul

NINE

Ray

Bri was still asleep when I snuck up here to the tree house. There was just a hint of light outside, but it's brightening now, and the birds are waking up too. I slept in spurts last night. Couldn't stop thinking about Orion—so sweet and innocent. Obviously a hopeless romantic. He wears his heart on his sleeve. I wish I could forget about him and leave him to find a girl who can cherish that and let herself turn to jelly and believe, stupidly, that their love will last forever. I'm not trying to end up like Momma, weighed down by memories, longing for a love she can hold on to about as much as she can hold sunlight in a fishnet. Stuck in a revolving door of memories and never stepping out of it. No thanks.

The first poems I came across in my journal today were from *Their Eyes Were Watching God*, where Janie's life is about to be shattered. There are only five lines on the last one, so I challenge myself to find a truth. Almost instantly, I watch the words snake around the page, revealing a poem about a woman grasping hopelessly at memories of a love she can never really hold, and never will again.

As an experiment, I pull out my book and find the place where the sun rises for Janie, as if for the first time. She has met Tea Cake and they've entered a flirtation. They are approaching the sweet spot of their courtship—the push and pull, the dance. Again, I find a poem quickly. . . .

With, a, compliment
With a smile
He, played, her.
This time, she offered him nothing.

Determined to find an upbeat piece, I search for the sweet part, the pull, but the only poem that wants to speak today is the push. Rather than my usual black and shades of gray for the art, I depict the first hint of dawn in deep shades of blue. As soon as I finish, I pack up my things and head into the kitchen. The last thing I want is Bri asking to come into my tree house.

━━━

I turn the kettle on, grind coffee beans, and pour them into the French press. Not long after the kettle whistles, Momma emerges from the hallway. I'm already holding out a steaming cup of coffee for her, which she gratefully takes in both hands as she disappears into the back garden for her Sunday meditation.

I wander down the hall past framed collages of me hugged up with Momma through the years.

The door to the spare room, where all our discarded-yet-not-trash stuff ends up, is cracked. Unusual. Bri is humming in the shower, but I still cut a glance around to be sure I'm alone and slip inside the Hoarding Room. My footsteps are soft, because I'm officially in sneak mode. The boxes that caught my eye the other day are stacked in the corner. I slip the door closed, holding my breath, and it shuts with the tiniest click. I hurry over to the boxes, my curiosity burning in me like an appetite.

I go straight for the top of the stack and remove the lid, revealing a photo album of pictures of my parents from back in the day. I've seen these before. Each photo must have a story behind it, but Momma rarely tells them, even when I ask. Aside from the wedding photos, the only one I know about is when they graduated from nursing school, and that's because they're in their caps holding their degrees. I always thought talking about the dearly departed was how people got over the loss, but for Momma, that seems too hard to do. I set the album aside and notice three identical leather-bound journals that I've never seen before. I sneak a closer look.

I grab one and tug at a paper tucked into the back cover; it's a photo of my father leaning against a black Camry. He can't be much older than I am now. It's like looking into a mirror. We have the same square shoulders, high cheekbones, deep brown skin, and legs that account for most of our height. Momma often says he left so much of himself behind in me. Why has she kept this photo hidden away?

I open the journal to the first page, expecting to see an entry, but it's just full of sketches of a full moon and stars on a shaded night sky. Elongated mermaid tails that curve into figure eights are peppered among scribbled fragments of sentences. I've seen old sketches of my mom's before. I know I got my talent from her, but it's like she stopped after I was born . . . after my father died.

Moon, Jupiter, help him, angel

Words and phrases related to the crash, some in smooth calm strokes and others written erratically, are scattered across the pages. They remind me of my poetry, except the same words and phrases are repeated and not arranged in any way that makes sense. My head is swimming.

I turn the page and press the open journal flat. Sketches of lavender form a vignette around the edges. My father's name—my name—is written over and over on the tiny leaves of the plant. There's a full page of a person with a mass of dreadlocks. The face and one loc are left white. My dad never had locs but both my parents loved Bob Marley. Why didn't Momma finish the drawing? I flip through blank pages and find an entry, but it's not dated.

The reaper, the angel, saw Ray take his last breath. I wasn't seeing things. I hadn't been alone. I could only accept and forgive when I met him today. So much time has passed. So much loss.

I turn the page, and the rest of this journal is empty.

Forgive? Who was there?

I grab another journal, and it is completely empty but for one word on the first page.

Honeysuckle

Bri knocks on the door as she opens it. I drop the journal and loose pages fall out.

"Bri!" I yelp, and collect the papers from the floor around me.

"Oh shit, sorry! I didn't mean to scare you. What are you up to in here?"

I quickly slide the journals back into the box and replace the lid. "Nothing. Just being nosy." I rush Bri out of the room and close the door.

"Dude, what the hell? Did I just walk in on something?"

"No, no . . . it's just that . . . you saw that room. It's a disaster. We don't have a lot of space, so everything just gets tossed in there. I heard you in the shower. I thought I had time to . . . but I didn't hear the water go off. . . . Anyway, you never saw that room, okay?" I realize Bri is wrapped in a bath towel.

"I conditioned my hair," she says, and gestures toward her dripping-wet head.

"Oh my god, okay, right. Towels. You need a towel for your hair." I hurry and grab a clean one. I give it to Bri, who's in my room now, with apologies before closing the door to give her privacy.

Back against the door, I'm frozen. The journal pages play

on repeat through my head. *Honeysuckle.* I noticed it on my father's headstone back when I used to visit with Momma. I loved the nectar. That stuff grows wild everywhere in Memphis. A whole journal for just that one word? Maybe she attempted to write again after the flowers started showing up on his grave. Maybe that was when she stopped drawing altogether.

When I pass the closed door of the Hoarding Room, I get a sinking feeling in my stomach. I don't like snooping through my mom's things, but I have to know if there's anything—about the accident or about my dad, their life together—in those other journals.

———

Bri and I are about ten minutes into the drive to the airport. National chain restaurants and drugstores give way to larger expanses of shipping yards and nondescript business parks. "Hit the Quan" by iLoveMemphis blasts from the radio, and we do the car-seat version of the dance. Bri stops abruptly and reads her phone.

"Mo sent me a meme. He also said Orion is driving himself crazy trying to figure out how to see you again."

I guess I wasn't cold enough when we left. I didn't even say "nice to see you." I just said "thanks" and "bye" and thought he'd take the hint. Ugh, why did I give him my number?

"So you gonna make him your summer boo or nah?"

"Why would I do that? He's not even my type."

"You mean the type who looks like a Calvin Klein under-wear model and gets those little cartoon hearts in his eyes as soon as you walk into a room?"

"Exactly. That's why he got my home number and not my cell. I don't plan to be in touch with him. I peeped his lovesick-ness a mile away. I'm not the girlfriend type, and he's definitely the type to write love letters. Orion deserves a girl who wants all that stuff."

"Whatever, Ray. I've seen you with guys before. For all the hearts I see in Orion's eyes, there's something different about you, too, when you're next to him. I saw y'all holding hands when you were about to skate to the birthday song. And at the house, when it was Mo's turn to belly flop in the pool, I saw who you were watching, girl. I know you. . . ."

No, you don't. No one does.

Not even me, these days.

She's picking at layers of something I'm not ready to see. What do I even say? With silence to fill, she just keeps filling it.

"Admit it: you're already gone for him. I see you," Bri says, pointing two fingers at her own eyes and then at me. "I'm speaking facts."

I try to think of a rebuttal, but all I can do is squint and shake my head.

"Whatever, Bri."

"Mm-hmm. Just saying, he's a nice guy. Who knows what could happen?"

I know what happens when people fall in love. It might not always be accidents, pain, and death, but it does end eventually, and all you're left with is an endless cloud of memories tucked away. No thanks.

"Okay, fine, but so what if I happen to find him attractive? And, yes, he seems to be a genuinely nice person. Any other guy would have totally hooked up with me by now. He didn't even try. He's too innocent."

"And these are reasons you're *not* trying to go with him? Real talk—if he calls you, pick up the phone. Have a fling. It's summertime. If you not feeling it, bounce. But Ray . . . if you feeling it . . ." She starts doing body rolls in her seat. "Feeeeel it." We laugh.

Me feeling things is what scares me.

To my great relief, the tall grayish building that is the Memphis International Airport comes into view.

"Yes, Mother," I say.

Once Bri has her luggage, we give each other a squeeze.

"Now go on. You gonna make me late for work," I say.

What I don't say to Bri, as she walks through the sliding doors of the airport, is that I'm not calling him. But if he reaches out . . . I'll give him a shot.

The shift manager, Amy, agreed to put me on dishes *and* said I could listen to my music while I work today. On a regular day, I'd be happy to make flavored espresso drinks and reheat sugar-crusted breakfast pastries for the customers at Rituals Coffee Bar and Unique Gifts. But today I can't be bothered to keep track of orders or to engage in small talk with people while they wait to pay. Momma was in the shower when I got back home. I was gonna ask her to drop me at my bus stop on her way to work, but I was already cutting it close.

As soon as I'm seated on the bus, I type and backspace until I settle on a text to Momma.

> **Me:** Coffee talk? The accident.

Work is coming at a steady clip, and James Taylor is singing through my earbuds about going to Carolina. I've been rinsing and loading and unloading and stacking pretty much nonstop since my shift began. It's a pleasant break from dealing with customers, and a great distraction from the accident and my mom's journals. Plus, I can't stop thinking about Orion.

I prefer my life the way it was back when I wouldn't be wondering what it would be like to kiss him—back when I wouldn't be thinking about his smile or the faint scar on his forehead or the way that he seems to look *into* me.

I slide the last dish into the washer and dry my hands. It's break time. In the bathroom, I splash my face with cold water, hoping that'll knock some sense back into me. I make myself an iced coffee and grab a raisin bagel. It's a small lunch. Apparently, thoughts of Orion and my appetite cannot coexist. I pay for my food, then turn around to find a seat.

And freeze.

The boy in my head is standing near the entrance of the gift shop.

I watch Orion take a deep breath and say something to

himself. He's blocked by a curtain of jewel-toned beads that separates the shop from the cafe, but I can still see him clearly. James Taylor belts in my ear: "How sweet it is to be loved by you!" For a split second, I fight the urge to squeal with excitement. The next second, I curse myself for wanting to squeal at all. Then I curse James Taylor for being so optimistic about love. I stop the music, rip out my earbuds, and shove them into the big pocket of my apron along with my phone. I take a few deep breaths. *Calm down, Ray.*

Orion drifts over to a display of refrigerator magnets. I put my food down on the nearest empty table and place a napkin over my cup. Smoothing my edges and making sure my headband is tight, I am suddenly aware that Orion hasn't seen me with my natural hair. Bri helped me take my braids out last night after we got home. I'm annoyed with myself for even caring what he thinks, but I smooth my hair again and walk across the cafe, through the beaded curtain, and into the gift shop.

He looks like a Gap ad in dark jeans and a plain white tee. He doesn't turn around, and I'm close enough to see that he is looking at a magnet depicting Godzilla's body with a tawny cat head, stomping through a burning city with the word *Cat-astrophe* branded across the top in blood.

"Cat lover?"

Orion drops the magnet he was holding and fumbles his way to return it to the display.

"Nice," I say, hoping the light teasing masks my excitement.

"Sorry, hey." He faces me, smoothing his hands on the pockets of his jeans.

I smile bigger than I intend to. He chuckles nervously.

"Hey. How are . . . why are you here?" Part of me wonders if I conjured him up and willed him here with my thoughts.

"Me? Oh. I was just passing by. You work here?"

I try to read his face, and can't decide whether or not he's joking.

"Maybe I heard this is the best place in town to buy cat magnets." His face cracks and he flashes that smile of his, and I go into a mess of nervous giggles. *Get it together, girl.*

"Ha-ha," I say, dripping with sarcasm. "Seriously, how did you know where to find me?"

He looks down at his feet and grins to himself before facing me again.

"I, uh . . . Mo. Bri told him that you didn't have to work until after she left. Mo asked where you worked. Here I am."

"Mm-hmm."

"I . . . um . . . you know . . . I just wanted to see you. . . ."

His honesty never fails to make me uneasy.

"Oh?"

"Yeah. I'm just glad you were here the first time I showed up, because I was gonna keep coming back every two hours until closing time." He shrugs and slides his hands into his pockets.

"Hmm." I'm skeptical. But then I start smiling. I have to remember to ice him out. This is usually easier.

"You changed your hair," he says, checking out my messy Afro. "You look pretty."

"Thanks. Bri helped me take my braids out last night."

Orion seems distracted.

"I can't believe you have been working so close to my hood all summer and I haven't seen you. Do you work here every summer? I'm actually frustrated thinking about all the days we were walking around not knowing each other."

"Seriously, Orion?"

He places his hand over his heart and flashes an ecstatic smile.

"Say that again," he pleads like his life depends on it.

"Say what again?"

"My name. I like how you say it."

I pretend to be over it. "Orion . . ." His smile is the definition of glee.

"Are you busy? Like, can we hang a bit?"

"I have about ten minutes left on my break." My cheeks hurt from blushing. I cheese like the Cheshire cat as he follows me back through the beaded curtain to my table. How am I this goofy for this boy? I fix my face before we sit down.

"I'm really glad you came to my pool," he says.

"It was fun. Your cats are so cute." I sip my iced coffee and tear off a piece of the bagel, offering him some. He shakes his head.

"No work for you today? At the BBQ place? I have my ways of gathering intel as well." The brightest smile takes over his face again, and suddenly it's hot in here.

"Nope. I had swim practice this morning—lifeguard duty tomorrow. I won't be back busing tables until Friday." He leans forward on the table, crossing his arms and holding his elbows. He smells like Irish Spring and mouthwash. His textured Afro is glistening. I imagine him in his bathroom at home, preening just to come see me.

"Did you drive today?" he asks.

"No, I rode the bus. Why?"

"I wish you didn't have to ride the bus," he says.

"How am I supposed to get where I want to go?" I got teased for riding the city bus in middle school. I attempt to sound more intrigued than triggered. "I drive my mom's car sometimes when she's not using it. What do you care about me riding the bus? It has nothing to do with you." So much for not sounding defensive.

"I guess it doesn't have anything to do with me, other than I want you to be safe. Don't a lot of sketchy people ride the bus? Someone could follow you or hurt you or something. And don't you trust your own driving more than some random bus driver, who—"

"Who is a professional, certified to drive a city bus? Also, the last time I checked, *I'm* not sketchy and have been riding the bus since I was thirteen. I'm good. Just because you know I exist now, I don't all of a sudden need extra protection."

The second I stop talking, I regret everything I just said. I want to turn back time and not be so defensive. I want to be soft like he deserves. He has been nothing but sweet and thoughtful and he's crushing on me and I suck.

Orion's arms tense up and he looks pensive and a little . . . amused? I can't tell if my tone bothered him as much as it bothers me.

"Sorry?"

I look away without answering him. I should be the one apologizing, but the words just won't come. I feel like an idiot.

"I—I just wanted to offer you a ride, Ray. I'm sorry that what I said offended you. That was not my intent. I know you ride the bus like a pro. It's just . . . sometimes with bus drivers, you just never know." He slicks a hand over his head and sighs.

"Look," he goes on. "I—I've never been around someone that makes me feel like you do. I—I'm never comfortable around girls, but with you it's . . . you're different. Like, I feel like I could just say whatever and you wouldn't make me feel weird for it. You don't expect me to be . . . I don't know, a certain type of way. I think you're amazing. We'll both be leaving for school . . . um, when do you go back?"

"Mid-August," I say, feeling horrible that he's spilling feelings after I just snapped on him.

"See? I leave around the same time and I want to spend as much of whatever free time we have left hanging with you. But if you want me to leave you alone . . . if you tell me to leave you alone . . . I will."

This is the same boy who literally ran from me yesterday. He's clenching his jaw. His face is begging me to say that's not what I want.

And I mean . . . it's not . . . I think.

His lips pull back into an almost-smile that makes the butterflies in my stomach go nuts. He knows I don't want him to leave me alone. I should get up from this table and go as far away from him and his stupidly beautiful face as possible. This tall, sensitive boy who wants to do nice things for me for whatever reason and sees through my frontin' and won't take my shit. It's maddening.

I exhale, and something shifts in me. "I'm sorry too. Caught a lot of flak for bus riding for years. I get defensive. . . ."

"It's cool."

Silence hangs between us and we just let it. I plop another bite of bagel into my mouth, and he happens to be reaching for a nibble at the same time. Our fingers touch and stay there longer than is needed.

"I accept your offer to take me home. Thanks."

He flashes surprised puppy-dog eyes for a split second before a relieved smile washes over his face. "Cool. What time do you get off?"

"Six."

He smiles harder. I break our gaze and notice the way his gold chain sticks to his dark brown skin and disappears under the neckline of his pristine white T-shirt, making me feel . . . deliciously frustrated. And we haven't even kissed yet.

"Maybe we can hang out after . . . if you're not busy."

He sits back in his chair and fidgets with his hands, ecstatic. "Yeah. Naw, I'm not busy. I'm all yours . . . I mean, I'd love to."

We laugh.

"I do need to get back to work."

We stand at the same time. I wave, turn, and walk away. I can't help but sneak a look at him. He's still standing there.

"Orion . . ."

He smiles, and I know it's because I said his name again.

"You can't wait around here until I'm off work. That would be weird."

"O-oh, right." He shrugs, embarrassed. "O-okay, I'll be out front. Right at six."

He turns to go and I miss him already. I put my earbuds in and hit play, "How Sweet It Is" blasting.

TEN

Orion

After I left Ray's job, I drove Jinx crazy pacing in my room before crashing onto my bed. I docked my phone, and until it was time to leave, I played "Find Your Love" by Drake on repeat and just stared up at the ceiling in bliss and hope and disbelief that Ray was happening to my life.

I pull up in front of the coffee shop a few minutes early. I just want to take it easy, get to know her. I cringe thinking about how I ran from her when it seemed like she wanted to hook up. I have to make up for that.

I remember what Mo said about posting up, so at six sharp I get out and lean against the passenger side. I take my shades off and leave them in the car. I cross my arms, then uncross my arms and stick my hands in my pockets. I cross my feet to look more relaxed. I wish I had put real shoes back on instead of slipping into my pool slides in a rush to get here.

Ray appears in the doorway and I jump, almost to a salute. I rub my hands against my jeans and plant my feet on the sidewalk to keep from running to her.

"Hey," I say, way too enthusiastically.

"Hey." She's chewing on her lower lip.

"Um, you sure about this? I don't want you to feel . . . I may have been kinda pushy. . . . I'm happy to walk to your bus stop and wait with you. I just . . . I mean . . . if . . ."

"I'm good, Orion. I want you to take me home." She smiles when I open the car door for her, but she seems uneasy. I hope she's really okay with this.

"You know how to get to Whitehaven down Bellevue?" she asks as I fasten my seat belt. That's the long way, but I nod. "Okay. Turn right onto Brooks Road when we get to it and I'll give you directions from there."

A few minutes into the ride, we haven't said very much to each other. I steal glances at her at the stop signs and she's watching the world through the window. She's still killing her bottom lip. I haven't seen her nervous since we met.

We ride through the heart of the Cooper-Young District, passing the shops and restaurants that college students and Midtown locals seem to like. I hang a right onto East Parkway after we pass the thrift store with its elaborately styled, headless mannequin displayed outside.

"Is it me, or does that thing always have sequins somewhere on it, no matter what day of the year?" Ray asks, perking up.

"Yeah. It's always something loud and wild and with a hat."

I turn on the radio and put my shades on at the next red light. Finally we look at each other and I grin involuntarily. The corners of her mouth threaten to curve up, and I'm transfixed until a car horn blares. The light has turned green.

"Nice aviators," she says. I can't tell if she's being sarcastic or is actually impressed.

"My shades? Thanks. They help me focus." I glance over at her, and she drops her eyebrows. "You know how when people put their car in reverse, they turn the radio down so they can focus?"

"Yeah. Bri's car does that automatically."

"My shades dim the light so I can focus on whatever I'm doing—class, work . . . driving." She nods, but I can tell she doesn't get it.

"I have SPD. Sensory processing disorder." Ray looks confused. "Like, say you're holding a conversation while walking in a crowded mall or studying next to a humming AC or in a classroom divided into work groups. For me, SPD means there's no filter—no such thing as white noise. Everything is on the same frequency. I have ways of dealing with it now, but as a kid, there was a limit to how much of the world I could take in before I just crashed. I'd chew on anything in sight and wild out from time to time. I got kicked out of schools. After a while my mom quit her job and homeschooled me, and I didn't go back to regular school until fifth grade."

"Wow. I've never heard of SPD. No filter. You seemed fine at Crystal Palace."

"That's different. I was just there to have a good time. Nobody was asking me to do math or remember a task list. I know it sounds weird, but music, especially loud music, relaxes me."

"That doesn't sound weird." I can feel her watching me, but I'm afraid to look at her. Why did I need to tell her about my diagnosis? That's the opposite of stunting.

"Turn left on Neely," she says, and I do.

After a couple more turns, we pull into her empty driveway.

She tells me to park under the carport since her mom's working the night shift. She's not giving me make-out vibes like she was the other day, but I'm still nervous as hell, racking my brain to come up with things to talk about. I follow her through the door, into the kitchen. Instinctively, I leave my slides by the door.

"Welcome to Casa de Ray. Can I get you some water or juice or anything?"

"No, thank you."

She nods for me to follow her into the den. "Hey, I'm going to change, okay? Make yourself at home. Feel free to file through my mom's vinyl or whatever. I'll just be a few minutes."

Through the open blinds on the patio doors, I spot the coolest tree house I've ever seen. The lone oak tree has to be at least thirty feet tall. The entire back fence is covered in vines. The whole thing looks enchanted.

"Whoa. I've never seen a tree house like this. It looks like you could live in there. Who built that?" I turn and realize that I'm alone.

Her house looks like it's stuck in the seventies. There are plants sitting and hanging everywhere, a velvet couch and wood paneling on all the walls in the den. Botanical drawings are clustered in one corner above wall-to-wall shelves. Books about gardening, cooking, natural remedies, and some fiction titles that I recognize spill over onto stacks on the floor.

I crane my neck to see what I can of the huge garden in Ray's backyard when the scent of flowers and mint announces her presence. She's mid-yawn, stretching her arms above her head.

"I feel like a human again!" She has changed into purple

leggings and a powder-blue tank top. She stands next to me and looks out at the garden too. My stomach churns. I take a deep breath and tell myself to stay cool.

"I said make yourself at home, and I see you did just that." She looks down at my feet.

"Yeah, I prefer to be barefoot whenever possible. Is that weird?"

"Hey, I'm barefoot too, so if it's weird, we weirdos." She wiggles her toes next to mine.

"You smell good." I say it without thinking. I close my eyes, wishing I could turn invisible.

"Thanks. I used soap." We laugh. She steps closer to me, and for some stupid reason, I move away. *Breathe.* How am I going to kiss her if I can't even stand next to her . . . alone . . . in private?

"You sure have a lot of library books," I say, taking her attention off me.

"We're kind of obsessed with using the library," she says, moving closer to me again. This time I don't move away. "My mom refuses to buy any book unless it's a reference book of some kind, and she'll only buy that one new if she can't find a used copy. She reads a lot. Me too, but I usually spend a lot of my downtime in my tree house writing, painting, or drawing . . ."

"It's so cool you have your own tree house. What's the story with—"

"O-or in the garden," she cuts in. "Mostly it's my mom's space, but we spend a lot of time out there . . . pulling weeds, or picking lemons and herbs for whatever." She goes on talking a lot about garden stuff. I'm only half listening to her because she just cut me off.

"Can I see it? The garden. Can we go out?"

"Sure," she says, sounding more upbeat than she looks. I follow her outside.

Three large raised garden beds line the house. Some herbs and flowers are also planted directly into the ground around the sides of each box. There's a lemon tree too. I didn't know lemon trees had flowers. Ray continues naming plants, and hasn't looked directly at me once. If she were a bird, she'd fly away.

We step into the shade of the lemon tree, standing so close our fingers brush. I take a chance and loop my pinky around hers, and to my relief she doesn't pull away. She stops talking and we stay like this just long enough for things to feel awkward. Finally, her eyes find their way to mine and I exhale.

"Hi," I say.

"Hi. S-sorry, I'm a little nervous."

"I didn't know you got nervous."

She laughs.

I swing our hands gently, hoping it relaxes her. "Thank you for letting me bring you home today. I feel like I won something."

At that she cracks up, and now I really have won a prize.

"Well. You're welcome?" She giggles.

"This spot is really cool," I say, looking around the garden. "I can see why you love it out here."

"Yeah. This is more my mom's spot. She spends her Sunday mornings out here meditating. It's like her church. She says there's no place she'd go on Sundays to be closer to God than outdoors between the ground and sky, and if you close your eyes and breathe deeply enough, for long enough, your soul remembers it's part of the universe."

"Damn. That's deep. Do you meditate too?"

"Nah," she says, and her eyes dart toward the tree house.

I look over there too and she removes her finger from around mine. She's watching her hands and wringing them. There's something about the tree house.

I sit on the ground with my back against the lemon-tree barrel and she joins me. After a while she reaches her hand out and I take it.

"Come on," she says, and helps me stand up. When I'm on my feet, we are standing so close that I can smell her lip balm— something fruity. I realize that I'm staring at her mouth when her playful smirk turns into a full-on smile. Our eyes meet and she shakes her head at me a little.

"You're here to get to know me, right?"

"Yeah." My heart is racing.

"Follow me."

The tree house is cradled between three wide boughs of the tree. It sits about ten feet above the ground and has a wrap-around porch. Several massive wood beams and smaller metal rods act as signposts and support beams. A BEWARE OF DOG sign dangles, barely holding on.

"You had a dog?"

"No, but I thought it seemed like the kind of sign that should guard a tree house."

"Man. A garden, a tree house, and a phantom dog—your childhood must have been a regular fairy tale." I stand aside so she can be first up the ladder.

"Yeah, the one where the father dies at the beginning," she says. She freezes on the second step. Her back is to me, but I can tell by the way she holds her head down that she didn't mean to blurt that.

"Hey, I know. . . . Um . . . Mo told me. . . ." Her grip on the ladder tightens, and I wish I could undo the past few seconds. Things were just starting to go well. "That night on Beale Street, he asked about your folks, and Bri told him that your dad . . . I'm sorry if . . ."

"It's fine. It's not a secret or anything. But all fairy tales start like that, right? The orphaned child survives the adventure, saves the world, and lives happyishly ever after." She looks back at me and shrugs, hard. "Anyway, since we came out here with no shoes on, like Flintstones, be careful with your feet on the steps."

I try hard as hell to not look at her body as I follow her up the ladder. I'm not successful. Her hips shift left to right in front of me, and her shirt ripples in the wind.

Once we are both up there, I walk the full length of the porch, which wraps around three sides of the tree house. I feel like a little kid again.

"Can I see inside?"

She gnaws her lip. "Yeah."

We're both at least six feet tall, and we actually fit in here. The ceiling is probably about a foot overhead. The room is pretty bare except for paintings hanging from a clothesline.

Built-in shelves line two of the walls, empty except for a vase of dried flowers and a few mason jars of pens, pencils, and paintbrushes near a desk. I open and close a screen door that leads to an empty screened-in room. A light breeze whips through. I want to ask again who built this, but I'm not going to push it. My gut tells me she's avoiding the subject.

"This place is unreal," I say.

"Yeah, it's my spot." Ray nudges a wooden stool farther beneath the desk with her knee and neatens an already-neat stack of papers.

"So you're an artist."

"Nah. I just like creating beautiful things." She opens the two windows and props open the two doors, then turns on the fan, which is plugged into an actual working electrical outlet.

"So . . . an artist, then," I try to say with a straight face. She laughs. "You gonna be an art major?"

"Okay, I am an artist, but math and science are my jam, so I'll major in something in one or both of those departments for sure. Art is just what I do for fun. It's kind of like my form of meditation."

"You're like da Vinci . . . Leonardo da Vinci—an artist and a scientist. An engineer," I say. Her eyes blink into an easy smile. She seems impressed by what I said, so I keep talking. "Engineering . . . electrical. That's what I'm thinking of majoring in. But that kind of thing is all I'm good at. You? Your art is amazing. I hear they have a nice art department at Howard. I'm just saying."

Part of her desk is full of loose pages from books. Some of them have been turned into paintings with words floating around them, and some appear to be sketches in progress. They are mostly in shades from black to gray.

"I like these. But isn't it bad karma or something to destroy a book?"

Ray shrugs. "I only use pages from books that are taken out of circulation from the library. I like to think of what I do as giving books a second life. These pages will actually be glued to larger sheets of paper, bound, and made into a new book. A book of fiction dies and becomes an illustrated book of poetry. Reincarnation."

I hold up a particularly layered piece that looks like words from several pages put together. "What do you call this? It looks like graffiti. Collage?"

"Yeah, that one is a collage. Found poetry. That one's a little unusual, since I added words to it. Usually I take a page from a book, pick words that make up a poem, and cover the remaining words to make art."

"Cool." I pick up a pencil drawing of a girl with her back turned, standing alone on a pathway underneath an arch. Before I can read the poem, Ray snatches it away.

"No." She doesn't look or sound angry—anxious, maybe. "Sorry. I'm not finished with that one yet. I didn't mean to yell, just . . . sorry."

"Nah, I'm sorry. I should have asked before touching your stuff." She opens a notebook and slips the page into it, then slides it underneath a stack of finished pieces. "What book are these from?"

"*Gatsby.*"

"That story was messed up."

"Yeah. Happy endings are for fairy tales. All Gatsby did was love a girl. He lived and died for a love that he would never have. There is no redemptive quality of love whatsoever in that book. Love brings out the worst in everyone. Everyone."

"Damn."

"What? I'm just saying. I guess it reminds me that things don't usually work out, and that's just life, and that's okay because that's what's real."

That's dark. I point to a set of pages arranged in a grid on the corner of the desk.

"*The Bluest Eye. Their Eyes Were Watching God.* I guess you're working on these ones next? Do you only read sad-as-hell books?"

She doesn't answer. When I look over at her, her eyes dart away from me and she's biting her lip. Again.

"There it is. You know, Orion, it seems like whenever I answer one of your twenty questions, you have something to say—about everything out of my mouth. First I have to hear about how I'm too fragile to ride the bus, and apparently I should just shit on a whole lifetime of excelling in math and science to major in arts and crafts, and now I'm a glutton for punishment who only reads depressing books? You said you wanted to get to know me—like, damn, am I wasting your time?" She walks out of the tree house, clearly upset.

Shit. I follow her out and she is sitting on the porch floor with her back against the wall. Tears sting my eyes. *Do not cry.* I want to tell her that she's wrong. What I've been saying and what she's hearing are two totally different things. But whether I agree with her is irrelevant. She's upset, and it's my fault.

"Ray. Ray, I'm sorry." Fighting back tears, I clear my throat and take deep breaths as I wait for her to say something.

She doesn't say anything. I sit down next to her, as close as I can get. If she recoils when I touch her, I'm going to die. My arm is pressed right against hers. She doesn't look at me, but she doesn't move away. I raise my knees and rest my head in my hands, take a deep breath, and speak as gently as I can.

"I don't know why I keep saying the wrong things. I don't mean to come across as critical. You're so amazing. I ask questions because I'm interested. *You're* interesting. I just want to . . . I shouldn't have made assumptions about your books. I shouldn't have questioned your major. I didn't mean anything by it. I just . . . I wasn't really thinking."

"You crying?" I can't tell if she's annoyed or amused. Or something else.

"N-no." I blink real fast.

She glances at me, her expression softer. Her voice is softer. "You're so in your feelings right now."

I stumble over words, trying to make an excuse or explain it away, my father's face rippling in my mind. He hates that I cry easily.

"You really do wear your heart on your sleeve, don't you?"

I shrug and nod. "I guess."

"I like that about you."

She smooths away a tear I apparently missed. "I really do," she says.

"I'm so sorry. Can we start over?"

"Can we just not talk about my art anymore, please?"

"Bet," I say.

"One day you'll have to tell me how you're so well read. I'm surprised a seventeen-year-old star athlete has read Toni and Zora."

One day . . .

"I'm almost eighteen—in September. And I would love to tell you about anything . . . *one day.*"

She fights back a smile.

The sun is lower in the sky now, and the tree is alive with what sounds like hundreds of birds singing as they settle in for the night. Ray walks around the corner of the porch and comes back with a can of mosquito repellent. She sprays her feet and arms, then sits back down next to me.

"It's almost mosquito hour." She gives the can to me, averting her eyes. I spray myself. "I'm sorry I blew up on you. I get defensive. It's not my favorite thing about myself."

"Don't worry about it. I like that you tell me exactly how you feel. I always want to know how you feel."

She looks out onto the yard.

"Do you have anywhere to be? Can you stay and watch the fireflies?"

"Fireflies? You mean lightning bugs. You haven't been gone long enough for lightning bugs to become fireflies, come on . . ."

She blinks at me, deadpan.

"My bad, you're right. I'm sorry, it's fireflies."

We laugh.

"Yes, I can stay. Even if I did have plans tonight, I would cancel them to stay here and watch the *fireflies* with you."

"Okay, Orion." She huffs.

"Okay. Say my name again."

She looks at me. I try to smile, but the feelings welling up inside me won't let a smile through. Our arms are touching and I want more.

"Orion," she says. She must be reading my thoughts because her smile quickly fades to . . . I don't know. It's like she wants to ask me something.

Suddenly, I'm burning up. Like my body just remembered it was ninety-something degrees today. Sweat beads on my forehead. I can't get enough air into my lungs. She looks through me and I don't want her to look away.

We're sitting so close that I feel her breath on my face when she speaks. I lean in.

She does too.

I inch closer, her name a whisper on my lips. "Ray, can I . . ."

Before I can ask, her mouth is on mine. At first, only our lips touch, but then she moves closer and I feel her tongue against mine. Almost reflexively, I reach up to hold her face closer and deepen the kiss.

She pulls away. "I'm, um, I'm gonna bring us some waters. Want anything to snack on? Fruit? Anything?" Before I can even answer, she's climbing down the ladder and leaping across the stone path, like a gazelle, back toward the house.

"Bananas," I shout at her back. It's like I've been yanked from a dream. One moment I'm kissing her, *really* kissing her, and the next she's giving me a thumbs-up and disappearing into her house. I'm breathless and my entire body is pulsing. *What happened?* Maybe all my questions really did push her away. Maybe

I suck at kissing. Nobody's ever complained before. Maybe I'm getting friend-zoned. Maybe I read her all wrong.

Crap. It's *pizza* all over again, except this time, she's the one running.

Did I really just ask for *bananas*?

ELEVEN

Ray

I stand in front of the mirrored wall in the kitchen nook and scold myself for being the total opposite of chill. I'm not hungry or thirsty. I had to get out of there. Why couldn't I just focus on how amazing his mouth felt, or how amazing the rest of him would feel, and just go for it? The journal Bri gave me for my birthday sits on top of a stack of cookbooks, almost taunting me. I grab a pencil and scribble the words clawing at me, determined to be free:

What if?

I shove the journal aside. This is ridiculous. I'm being ridiculous. He was kissing me, and I was feeling . . . feelings. It was too intense. So different from every other time I've kissed anyone. But something about him being that close to me, and being . . . him . . . It was too much.

I wash a bunch of grapes and seal them in a bowl. How could he even want to kiss me after I unleashed on him like that? Twice in one day. This would be easier if he had just wanted to hook up. *That* I'm good at. Orion is working his way under my skin to the parts I don't share—the breakable parts. Giving up the breakable parts is a sure way to misery. Look what love got Momma. And people jump from relationship to relationship, looking for what?

I crack an ice cube tray and fill two water bottles from the tap. I peel a few bananas and slice them in half before sealing them in a container. He says these big things to me that make me feel . . . an oddness. A warm oddness I've never felt before. I want more of it with every passing second that I'm in here. I don't know what to do with these feelings. I don't know what to do with him.

I sling the bag of fruit and water onto my shoulder, slide my feet into flip-flops, and grab Orion's slides before heading back to the tree house.

When I pass the mirror this time, I check myself out. My Afro is fluffy and a little longer on the top and shorter around the sides. I wish I could relax into Orion's gaze. I want to know how it feels to just enjoy him being into me and trust that maybe a love between us would be different and not end in misery. I told Bri I'd give him a shot, but at a summer fling, not at anything involving all these damn feelings.

I search my eyes for the girl who would happily do a blind-folded trust fall into love. She's nowhere to be found.

━━━

In the darkness, I can feel Orion watching me as I walk back across the yard. His frame is a statue in silhouette on the tree-house porch. I wonder if it's too late to try to shift gears with him—to just let tonight be whatever it's gonna be and end things after this. I should have gone home after skating that night. If only Orion weren't so sweet.

I plop his shoes down on the porch, and Orion takes the bag of fruit and water and then my hand, supporting me up the rest of the ladder. I don't really need his help, but I let him.

"Thanks for bringing my shoes," he says.

"You're welcome. It'll be pretty dark when you leave—probably not a great idea to walk across our wilderness barefoot then."

We sit back down on the floor with an overturned milk crate between us. I empty the bag onto the makeshift table.

"These are for you."

"*All* these?"

I want to remind him that *thank* and *you* are probably the words he was looking for, but I just nod.

"Thanks . . . for peeling them and everything." He looks at me like cutting bananas deserves sainthood, which makes me blush.

"It was nothing." I shrug.

Within seconds he fills his cheeks with fruit and shoves another piece in. He notices me watching him and stops to chew.

"Swimmer," he says, laughing. "I'm always really hungry."

He wipes his mouth clean.

"How long you been swimming?"

"Since forever. My parents found out it was a great sport for kids with SPD shortly after I was diagnosed and I been swimming ever since."

I don't know what to say next. His energy is a little off. I wonder if it's because I ran when we kissed.

"What about you? Any sports?"

"Volleyball. Not trying to play in college, but sports make the applications stand out."

"Cool, you any good?" he asks, and the smirk on his face confirms the tease I hear in his voice.

"Boy, I'm amazing. Don't play," I say, relieved that he's joking around.

"So, um, why did you stop? Did I . . . was it . . ."

His question catches me off guard.

"It was . . ." I shake my head and try to gather my thoughts. "No, you were fine. It was . . . I really liked it. I guess I just needed to put the brakes on a bit. The train was about to kinda go off the rails."

"Okay. It's just that last night, you seemed like you were cool with the train going off the rails. So when you quit like that . . . I don't know. I was worried it wasn't good or something."

"No. You were perfect." I smile at him, not really sure what to say next.

"Take a selfie with me?" Orion asks.

"Another selfie for the archives? Okay." I'm pretty sure it's just an excuse to get close to me. He pulls his phone out of his back pocket and quickly maneuvers around the crates until he's beside me. His arm is around my shoulder and I cozy in beside him, almost cheek to cheek.

He's so close.

A draft catches my toes, and goose bumps instantly cover

my body. It takes my every ounce of focus not to lean over and kiss him again.

He holds the phone up and snaps a few pics. I look up from the phone and our faces almost touch again. He's watching me instead of the phone's screen, and he doesn't look away, his gaze running across every inch of my face. I glance at his mouth and back to his eyes and hope that he takes the hint. I won't run away this time.

But he clears his throat and scoots just far enough away from me that our arms don't touch. *Wrong hint, Orion.* I can't tell whether the sinking feeling in my stomach is from rejection or the butterflies dying.

"Which one?" He holds up his phone to me. "I like this one."

"That one's nice."

"I would text it to you, but my texts don't go through to your number."

"Yeah, it's my landline—my mom's house phone."

"House phone? But I thought you gave me your cell."

"I know. I just figured we wouldn't need to be in touch after I go back. So . . ."

"Oh." He nods, deflated, and leans back against the wall.

"You know what? I'm going to turn on some music." I scurry inside and power on my boom box, just as "Another One Bites the Dust" begins. "I keep this radio tuned to the River FM. You can come look through my CDs to find something else to listen to if you want."

"CDs?"

"Yes, CDs, what about it?"

"Nothing, it's just that you don't see CDs much anymore."

"Well, you're seeing them now. Enjoy."

Orion's beside me in an instant. He clicks the CD cases as he flips through the box of about twenty that I accidentally left up here yesterday.

"Let's see . . . Billy Joel, Mariah Carey, REM, Jewel, Stevie Nicks, Beyoncé, Lauryn, Smashing Pumpkins, Beyoncé, Cranberries, James Taylor? Beyoncé *again*?" He lists the CDs mostly to himself. I step closer to him, but he moves away, fidgeting. He wants me. He wants me not. I sigh and walk out onto the porch.

Orion joins me shortly afterward. "No luck with the CDs," he says, sitting down next to me. "You love Beyoncé."

I look at him, deadpan. "And what about it?"

"Wait. Nope. I mean . . ."

"Relax. I'm working on not biting your head off for at least another twenty-four hours, but make it easy on yourself and don't diss the queen."

He drops his head with his hand over his chest, relieved.

"What's up here is just the tip of the iceberg. My full music collection is in my room, and yes, there is more Beyoncé."

The radio station switches over to my favorite love-song dedications show.

"Confession time. In middle school, I would listen to people call in and tell their love stories and make dedications with Delilah," I say.

"Confession time? Same." Orion laughs to himself, looking so bashful that if his skin weren't radiantly ebony, I swear he'd be blushing.

"You for real?"

"Yes, I swear." Orion nods matter-of-factly and shrugs.

"That's where I got into Billy Joel and Van Morrison's 'Brown Eyed Girl.' People *stay* requesting that song," I say. Our eyes meet.

"Yeah, I love that one." Orion loosens up and moves closer to me. It feels good. "I—I used to sing it . . . play it on my guitar all the time."

"Thinking about your girlfriends?" I ask.

"Girlfriends? Nah. With swim practice, meets, school, and everything . . . I mean, I've had a few unsuccessful attempts at it, but me and girls just . . ." He's fidgeting with his hands.

"I wanted to *be* Van Morrison's 'Brown Eyed Girl.' To mean that much to a person that they'd want to sing about me. To make those kinds of memories with someone, to be that in love. But I was young and ridiculous." *And afraid.*

In seventh grade, the year boys discovered I was pretty, I mastered gracefully rejecting their advances. The older I got, the more persistent they got. It was annoying. So a swift clapback or stank-eye quickly replaced my mannered rejections. I can see Orion watching my face, but I refuse to look at him right now. I don't want him to . . . I don't know . . . see too much.

Then Orion's smile fades.

"What?"

"I like you," he says.

I smile and look away from him, but the Ray in my head jumps onto his lap and devours his face.

"Do you know 'Sweet Caroline'?" I ask him instead.

Orion grins. "The Neil Diamond song? Yeah, white people

love that song. I'm one of a handful of Black guys on my swim team—trust me, I know the song."

We share a laugh.

"Yep, I know we've both participated in more group sing-alongs of 'Sweet Caroline' than we care to admit." Orion gives me a playful side-eye. "You know you get into it. Tell me I'm wrong."

"I can't even front. You, me, and everybody else—that song *goes!*"

Orion contorts his face and begins to sing the bridge to "Sweet Caroline," trying to sound as much like Neil Diamond as possible. He stretches his hand out to me: "'Hands touching hands . . . Touching me, touching you.'"

I join in and belt out, "Sweet Caroline!" He points to me and I sing the horns part of the chorus—"BUM BUM BUM"—and we both erupt into laughter.

"Come through with the vocals, though. I heard you, Orion—that little run on Caroline?"

"Nah, you were just hearing things. That's like saying it takes vocals to sing Christmas carols. Everybody can hold a note for 'Jingle Bells.'"

"Whatever. Something tells me you're the guy who sings along to 'Jingle Bells' and people turn around to see who brought the vocals, but okay."

We turn the radio up and watch the fireflies flicker in the yard below us. The sounds of the night creatures, the ice cubes knocking against the metal water containers as they melt, love song after love song playing on the radio. My fingers twitch for my journal, the chords wriggling through me, giving me words for things . . . things I didn't know I had words for. The radio switches to "Nothing Even Matters" by Lauryn Hill, and somehow we're sitting even closer.

"Do you want to look up? It's better to stretch out on the other side. There's a space in the branches—we can see the stars. Come on."

We gather a lavender-and-yellow quilt I keep in the tree house and walk around to where the porch ends. I lie down flat on my back and he steps over me and lies down too. Our arms touch.

He joins our pinkies. "You spend a lot of time doing this?"

"Not as much as I used to. My mom and I used to come out together, especially . . ."

"Especially what?"

This is where you try, Ray. Let him in.

"My mom and I used to come out here a lot. Especially around my birthday . . . to see Jupiter rise with the moon." I can't remember the last time I said my first name out loud.

"Cool. You got a telescope?"

"No, we don't have a telescope. You know you can see some planets without one."

"Right. Venus."

"Yeah, Venus. How'd you know that?"

"I don't stargaze, really, but when your name is a constellation, you look up from time to time." He grins at me, tapping his temple like that meme. "So you and your mom would look for Jupiter around your birthday?"

"Yeah. It's visible most of the year."

"Can you see it now?" he asks.

"I see Orion's belt," I say, feeling clever.

"Very funny. I know that one. It's the three stars in a row . . . there." He points, and I only pretend to see it. My stomach is in knots because, for reasons that I wish I understood, I don't want to be half of myself with Orion—this nice boy who has come out of nowhere and made me feel things. I want him to know me.

"I know how to find Orion, but I want to see Jupiter," he says. He scoots even closer to me. I roll onto my side and prop myself up on my elbow. Our faces are so close, his scent wraps around me like a blanket.

"Look," I say.

He studies the sky as if that's what I mean. When I don't say anything, he looks over at me. Instantly, I lose my courage.

"Tell me something about yourself," I say. "Something that I would be surprised to know. Something you haven't told me yet." I need him to trust me with something before I can trust him with myself.

"Oh. Okay, cool." He rolls onto his side too. "Something silly, like a cool trick I can do, or something real?"

"Something real. Something you don't really talk about much."

He rolls onto his back and blinks his eyes closed for a moment. "Okay . . ." He exhales. "I had a little sister. She died around this time almost ten years ago—same day as your birthday. I didn't say anything earlier because . . ." Orion's words hang like rain clouds in the silence between us. Heavy with meaning. He glances at me before looking back at the canopy of branches above us. "My dad would always take pictures of us. He was never without that camera. We have an entire album of her baby pictures. Nora . . . her name was Nora. My mom made albums for each of us when we were born, with all these little notes and things added in. She gave me mine as a graduation gift. Nora's book ends before she even started kindergarten."

Orion's eyes glisten with tears. "After Nora died, my mom took the last picture out of her book and framed it. She's sitting in the grass outside our old house, holding a yellow flower close to the camera lens. Any time we were in the yard, she would look for those yellow flowers—the ones that are weeds—and bring them to me. The flower is a blur and covers up part of her face. That picture used to sit on the mantel in the living room with our other family pictures. One day I came in from swimming and noticed all the family pictures we had with Nora were gone."

I want to tell him that I know what it's like. To have a family that feels like a puzzle with a missing piece. I never knew my father, but his absence is tangible. I can't imagine how different it must be to have known and loved and lost someone so dear. I don't know what to say, so I don't say anything, but I work all my fingers between Orion's.

He's quiet for a long time. "In front of our old house in Orange Mound, a bus driver ran a light. I didn't even see Nora slip through the gate. One second I was digging a hole to China—she had piled yellow dandelions up beside me and we were gonna bury them. She wanted to see if they'd all combine and grow into one giant yellow tree. She'd taken a break—was playing with a beach ball. The next moment . . . she didn't even look like she got hit. She just looked like she was sleeping. She was just three years old."

He stares upward, and a tear streams down onto his ear. I squeeze his hand, holding on tighter, words stuck in my throat. Now his issue with me riding the bus makes sense.

"My dad was away. Trucking. He stopped driving the rigs after that. With the money from the settlement with the city, we moved to Central Gardens and he started a short-haul trucking company. He doesn't drive anymore, and his company only takes short-distance hauls. He doesn't want to send drivers on the road away from their families."

Orion wipes his tears, and I realize that I'm crying too. I don't look away, or try to explain. Seeing him so vulnerable, and understanding his tears . . . something shifts deep inside me, and suddenly I want him to understand mine, too.

"That real enough for you?" he asks with a breathy chuckle. "Your turn. Tell me something I don't know about you. It doesn't have to be sad like my thing." He laughs again. I smooth the tears from my face, and with the bottom of my tank, I wipe his, too.

"Thank you for sharing that with me. I'm so sorry about your sister. It has to be a hard thing to talk about—to remember."

I lie back down next to him and he lifts his arm just enough that I can work my way under it. We lie there, pretzel-armed, fingers locked, gazing up at the sky.

"Remember when I told you curried chicken was my favorite food? And how my mom plays that Bob Marley album all the time? Those were my father's favorite things. His folks are from the Caribbean. After he died, she just hung on to everything—like cooking his favorite food, playing his favorite album, even wearing a dress that he loved. It's how she copes with his absence." She also copes by not talking about him. She left my text on read. She'll wait a few days and text me about something else and hope that I move on like I usually do. But not this time. I just told Orion basically everything I know about my father in a matter of seconds. But I understand clamming up about sensitive topics. I don't even tell people my real name.

"Aw man. Ray, I . . ."

"That's not all. My father built this tree house." I pause and breathe and acclimate myself to this new world where I reveal sacred things to a boy I've only known a few days. "You asked earlier. Momma said that when they started talking about having a child, they drove around the neighborhood, and this cove was the first place they stopped. The house wasn't much, but my father fell in love with this oak tree. She wasn't even pregnant yet, but he said this was the house he wanted, so he could build a tree house in this perfect tree for their children to grow up in. He made it big enough so that he and Momma could come inside too. But he never got to play in it, because he died the day I was born."

A throaty sound escapes Orion that sounds like tears. Orion's free fingers brush my arm. I don't look at him, because if he's crying again, I'm going to sob. The wind goes out of me. Tears blind me, but I continue.

"Sometimes when I'm up here, I imagine what it would have been like, to have memories of him, playing in here with me the way he dreamed. I don't know a whole lot about that night. He just drove off the side of the road with my mom in the passenger seat. He lived long enough to call nine-one-one, but he died before they got there. Apparently someone stopped to help. My mom gave birth to me right there in the wreckage."

I think Orion might be crying again, but I don't check to confirm because it might make me even more emotional.

"*Jupiter* was the first word she said when she woke up. She had focused on it . . . and the moon while she waited for help to arrive. S-so that's my real name: Jupiter Moon Ray Evans. If you tell people your name's Jupiter, they have questions, you know? I'm not gonna go around lying, fucking up my karma just to keep my tragedy my business. So I just go by Ray. It's easier to explain that you're named after your dead father. Fathers die all the time. Plus, it's true. And most people don't pry when you're a Junior. Fewer follow-up questions." I feel raw and exposed. My breath catches in my throat as I untangle from Orion and sit up, hugging my knees.

He sits up too. "Ray, I said yours didn't have to be sad like mine."

I can't help but laugh. Then we're both laughing and trying to stop crying as the radio competes with the chorus of cicadas.

"Jupiter." He reaches for me. Without hesitation, I close the distance between us, settling into the comfort of his one-arm embrace. I rest my head on his chest and reach my free arm around his waist and squeeze him.

"Jupiter Moon Ray Evans," he says softly. "Pleased to meet you."

Now I understand why he asks me to say his name. When someone comes into your life, knocking the earth off its axis, them speaking your name . . . it's like a spell. I feel heady, like I'm floating. A man on the radio croons, "It's for real what I feel when I'm with you," and it's messing with my emotions. I want to kiss him again.

I tilt my head up and nuzzle my nose into his cheek, kissing it softly. Everything that matters in the universe right now is on this blanket. Orion gently squeezes my arm, but he doesn't move to kiss me.

"Jupiter and Orion," he says, looking at me, "we go together." "I'm just saying what's already in the stars."

I have no idea who I am right now. I've never been this emotional in front of anyone. With anyone. Never. I smile so ridiculously wide that it hurts my face. My heart is racing. I want him to see how much I want to kiss him, how much I need to kiss him.

Then, like a twisted comedy, it happens again. Orion breaks our embrace. He reaches over and interlocks his fingers with mine. *What the hell?*

"Can I call you Jupiter now?"

I search his face for an answer to any of the questions running through my mind.

"Yes. But only when it's just us. And don't say anything to Mo, please. The way he and Bri gossip . . . Bri doesn't know all the details about my dad, and I want to be the one to tell her."

He nods firmly. "Thank you . . . for letting me see you today."

I don't know what to say. He's so open about his feelings, which makes it hard to be annoyed with him for not kissing me again, which makes me annoyed with myself for having feelings at all. We should be making out right now. I can't speak.

"I have swim practice in the morning; I really need to get home." He checks his phone. "Shit. My dad's been blowing up my phone. He's gonna kill me."

"What, you have a curfew?"

"Not really. Just . . . swim training is early. I have a big meet coming up, and he already made comments about me being out late these past couple of nights—not taking swim seriously. Anyway, walk me out?"

I follow him down the ladder back to earth.

We hug, and I breathe all of him in. He doesn't even try to kiss me goodbye. I don't get it.

I watch him get into his car and back it out of the driveway. When he's gone, I can barely see Mel sitting on Cash's lap on his porch. They wave as soon as I notice them. I throw a *what's up*, inexplicably angry at them, and close the door.

She turned to Mrs. McKee and the room rang full of her artificial laughter.

"My dear," she cried, "I'm going to give you this dress as soon as I'm through with it. I've got to get another one tomorrow. I'm going to make a list of all the things I've got to get. A massage and a wave, and a collar for the dog, and one of those cute little ash-trays where you touch a spring, and a wreath with a black silk bow for mother's grave that'll last all summer. I got to write down a list so I won't forget all the things I got to do."

It was nine o'clock—almost immediately afterward I looked at my watch and found it was ten. Mr. McKee was asleep on a chair with his fists clenched in his lap, like a photograph of a man of action. Taking out my handkerchief I wiped from his cheek the remains of the spot of dried lather that had worried me all the afternoon.

The little dog was sitting on the table looking with blind eyes through the smoke, and from time to time groaning faintly. People disappeared, reappeared, made plans to go somewhere, and then lost each other, searched for each other, found each other a few feet away. Some time toward midnight Tom Buchanan and Mrs. Wilson stood face to face, discussing in impassioned voices whether Mrs. Wilson had any right to mention Daisy's name.

"Daisy! Daisy! Daisy!" shouted Mrs. Wilson. "I'll say it whenever I want to! Daisy! Dai——"

Making a short deft movement, Tom Buchanan broke her nose with his open hand.

Then there were bloody towels upon the bathroom

Where you touch
I won't forget
Looking with blind eyes
lost

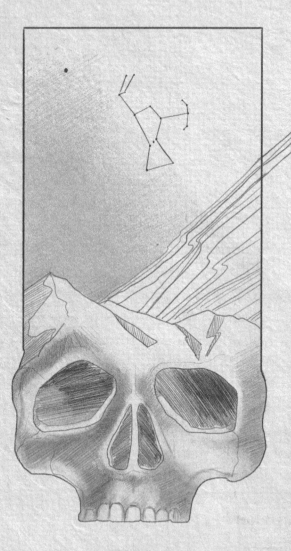

TWELVE

Orion

18 DAYS

This is my last chance to qualify for the 100 fly at the US Open, which is what I've worked for my entire swim career. Freestyle is my specialty—I qualified for that event already, and I'm swimming the last leg, freestyle, on the 4 x 100 relay team. But the butterfly stroke just looks so damn cool. I hit the qualifying time twice in practice last week, so I'm feeling really good about my chances today. In my dad's perfect world, I'd be competing in every event. No matter what happens, I've still got my ticket to the big show with my strongest stroke. Qualifying for the butterfly would just be icing on the cake.

My dad drops me and my mom off at the pool stadium entrance. A steady stream of families and swimmers wearing their team colors flows into the arena. I'm feeling fly in my white TN Southeastern Regional Championships hoodie with the word *freestyle* printed in huge block letters down the right sleeve. I wish Ray could see me swim.

It's early, but the sun is already hot—perfect weather for

an outdoor swim meet. My mom chats with some other swim moms while we wait for my dad to find parking. Team warm-ups begin in a few minutes, and waiting for him is biting into my pre-warm-up ritual. He likes to give me a pep talk before I race, so I try to wait patiently. I don't need it now as much as I did when I was a kid, but I let him keep up the tradition because I can tell it's important to him.

I put my headphones on, but before I start my race-day playlist, I go to my photos and look at my selfies with Ray.

It's been two days since I left her tree house. The way my dad came down on me when I got home the other night, I didn't want him to catch a whiff of me making plans to see Ray before this race. The only way to keep him off my back has been to stay hyperfocused on my diet and training. I've called and left voice messages. Every day. I don't even know what to say, so I just ask her to call me back. But she hasn't. Maybe what we shared in the tree house was too much. Or maybe it wasn't enough.

At my house, I ran away from kissing her. At her tree house, she kissed me and then ran away. I was so confused by that, I didn't want to make a wrong move, especially after all the talking we did. She was so vulnerable. She seemed nervous about me even being up there at first. I don't know. Why wouldn't she return my calls for two whole days after she bared her soul to me? After we kissed? When she broke and ran into the house, I thought for sure I was on a one-way ride to the friend zone. Then, after we swapped secrets, it seemed like she wanted me to kiss her again. I wanted to so bad, but I just couldn't bring myself to do it.

Whenever we do kiss again, I want it to be because we're both so turned up after spending time together that there's nothing we want to do more than just kiss on each other. But she won't even return my calls.

I can't let another day pass without talking to her. I can't give up. I'm calling her again tonight.

"Is this the reason you're all starry-eyed these days?" My mom looks over my shoulder. I swipe my photos closed and pretend to not hear her even though my headphones are still silent. I open my playlists and she taps me on my shoulder.

"Hey, Momma." I shift my headphones above my ears. "What's up?"

"That was a real question, which I know you heard."

I laugh and shake my head and hope she won't make me talk about Ray. But she plasters a funny grin on her face with her eyebrows raised, and I can't resist. I drop my head for a beat, then tell my mom what she already knows.

"Yes, ma'am. I met her at Crystal Palace. I really like her."

"I figured that much. I don't recall ever seeing you so goofy in the face." She pinches my cheek and I pretend to swat her hand away. I can't hide my cheesy.

"The Instagram pictures are just adorable. I tried to be nosy, but you haven't tagged her on anything."

I've posted a selfie of us each time we've been together. The first one was on Beale Street the night we met. It was the only one I captioned: *Me and the Birthday Girl.* The others from the pool party and her tree house simply have star emojis.

"She's not on Instagram."

"Well, are we going to get to meet this captivating young lady?"

"Are we going to get to meet who?" my dad asks cheerfully, startling us both. I slide my phone into the front pocket of my pullover.

"Orion's new young lady friend from those pictures on his Instagram," my mom answers. Her words obliterate whatever cheer my dad brought with him from the parking lot.

"Come on, honey, the boy is minutes away from his last meet of the season and you talking about some girl?" My dad calls my mom pet names like honey, sweetie, and baby whenever he's upset. She purses her lips and waves him off.

"As if anything I say could put that girl on his mind any more than she is already?" She watches my dad's face for a response. His grimace almost cracks into a smile.

"Listen." My dad checks his wristwatch, a stopwatch that he wears to meets so he can time my races. "You got fifteen minutes before warm-ups. That's fifteen minutes to get in there and get your head right. Focus on what you need to be focusing on—hitting that time on the hundred fly." He glances at my mom, then turns me around by my shoulders to face him. It's time for my pep talk. My dad grips the tops of my shoulders and looks me in the eyes.

"Who is your competition, son?" he barks.

"My fastest time," I bark back.

"What about the other swimmers?"

"I hope they ready to race."

"Who are you, son?"

133

"The Shark."

"What you come to do today?"

"Eat."

"Get in there."

"Yes, sir."

My dad gives my shoulders a final squeeze and a slap. I hug my mom and bend down for her kiss. The left cheek. Always the left. Maybe Ray will be here next time and she can kiss the right.

"Swim fast and pretty, baby," my momma says.

"Yes, ma'am."

I make it poolside with about five minutes to spare before officials open the pool for warm-ups to begin. As always, I walk to a lane that has the fewest number of people waiting to get in and stand between the blocks, with my toes on the edges of the pool. I look out at the water, take a few deep breaths, and close my eyes.

I visualize myself poised on the starting block and waiting for the signal to start. I'm off the block in an instant and gliding through the water. Perfect form. Perfect breath. Perfect speed. Flying. Tight flip turn. Repeat. I race a few times in my mind before I open my eyes. Then I focus on the lane, imagining the same perfect race with my eyes open.

There are nine events before mine, so after warm-ups I put my sneakers back on to keep my feet warm and sit on the bleachers behind my lane. I search my phone for my race-day playlist—twelve hype songs that I play on repeat. I press play, tuck my phone into the front pocket of my hoodie, and continue with my visualizations.

Today, it's hard to not look at Ray's pics on my phone. It's hard to not think about her. When I finally can't resist the urge, I whip my phone out and pull up the photo of us in her tree house. Eminem is rapping the chorus to "'Till I Collapse," and instead of thinking about how hard I'm about to race, my mind goes back to the moments before I took this picture. That kiss. Her mouth. I pinch my fingers and spread them on the image until her face fills up my entire phone screen.

The music is still going when Niko slaps my shoulder. "Hey, lover boy, heads up—*vámonos*," he says with a smirk, and gives me the thumbs-up.

It's almost time for me to line up for my race. Two more races and then it's my turn. I'm in the first heat for the 100 butterfly. I nod at my coach and then instinctively look to where my parents always sit when we race here.

My dad is standing up, with his arms crossed, looking right at me. If his eyes had lasers, my phone would have been zapped out of my hands the second I took it out of my pocket. I'm for sure going to hear about my head being in my phone instead of in the race. I kick off my shoes, drop my headphones, slip my hoodie off, and hustle to get in line. I jump and stretch and warm up while I wait, sneaking glances at my dad while I do. He hasn't moved an inch and hasn't taken his eyes off me. I've got to hit this time today. I did it twice at practice. *Please let the third time be a charm.*

I'm off the block the second the buzzer sounds.

I'm the Shark, streamlining just below the surface, fast, long, and strong. I break the surface right on my mark and I'm flying. Perfect form. Perfect breath. Perfect speed. Flying.

Tight flip turn. Repeat.

The water moves over me like a sheet. And I crush it, one stroke at a time. The wall grows clearer. Close, I'm so close. I push, visualizing the win until my fingers press the cold, hard wall.

I know I just swam the best 100 fly of my life.

My eyes shoot up to the scoreboard. EVENT 10, HEAT 1, LANE 4, PLACE 3.

A wave of emotion rushes over me and I feel the urge to cry when I see that I hit a new personal best official time for this event.

Then my blood runs ice cold when I realize that my personal best is still 1.2 seconds away from qualifying for the open.

Later, my mom tells me I did great. My dad asks me if I'm proud of what I did and congratulates me on a strong race and coming in fifth overall for the event. We don't talk about the missed qualifying time. I think my mom probably asked my dad not to bring it up, because he'd be too pissed to talk about it without getting emotional in front of everyone. I'm definitely gonna hear about this when I get home.

I eat with a few coaches and teammates afterward since it's my last meet in Memphis as a Bluff City Triton, and also because I want to buy myself some time before facing my dad.

My mom is in the kitchen washing dishes when I walk into the house. I don't see my dad downstairs.

"There he is," my mom says, offering her cheek for me to kiss. I do.

"Hey, Momma. Where's Dad?"

"He's in the study."

"How is he?"

My mom looks at me like how my dad is doing is the last thing I need to be worried about. It's just that I know he's gonna blame Ray.

"Baby, how are *you* doing?"

"I'm good, Momma. Really."

"Your father is pretty frustrated, but I talked him down," she says with a wink and a smile.

"Thanks. He was a little more intense today than usual. Did he say anything to you about me being on my phone before the race?"

"You know he did. He was pissed. But I want you to know that your father's extra edge isn't really about you and that national meet." She dries her hands off and motions for me to join her at the table. "You must have noticed, Orion, that every year, your father has a very difficult time when the . . . the day of the accident comes around. He blames himself for not being here. For some reason, he thinks that if he'd been home, he'd have been outside with you guys or we'd have all been out there together. Nora wouldn't have gone after that ball—maybe she'd have asked him to go get it."

I don't say anything because I want her to keep talking. We never talk about the accident. This is my first time hearing about how my parents deal with the loss. I had no idea my dad blamed himself. All these years.

"Nora would have turned thirteen this year. A milestone birthday. For weeks, he's talked about how he wishes he could go back in time and fix everything."

"I know. I didn't realize how much he—"

"He's pretty much been on edge—with me, at work. He hasn't volunteered with the Boys Club in months. So if he gives you a little more bite tonight, just keep in mind he's hurting."

I nod. I always knew deep down that Nora's death was present in the space between my dad and me. Now knowing that he blames himself for what happened . . . it just makes me feel sad for him.

As soon as I reach the landing on the stairs, the door to my dad's study swings open. I jump, but play it off as if I'm trying to stop my momentum. He closes the door to his study and stands there looking at me, quietly, as if he's waiting for me to say something.

"Dad, I—"

"You know, son? You practice damn near every day. You work all season to qualify for the open, and what? You'd rather look at Instagram pictures of *some girl* than keep your head where it needs to be?" He spits out the words *some girl* like they taste bad.

"Dad, I qualified in the hundred free *and* the relay. I did my best today and missed the mark, but I still get to compete. And she's not just *some girl*—"

"*That . . . girl . . .* is the reason you been coming in here late at night and showing up to practice half-asleep. You surpassed the qualifying time twice in practice. *Twice.* Then choked when it was time to make it count for something. You choose the week before the race to go chasing tail? I knew that girl was gonna be a distraction soon as I saw her on your page."

Every time he says *some girl* or *that girl,* my whole body tenses up with red-hot anger. I remind myself what my mom said about Nora. He's hurting. But if he spits that phrase again, I feel like I'm going to combust. I take a deep breath.

"Dad. It's just a race. I'm going to the open in two other events. I've had bad races before, and today I was amazing. And that girl has a *name*." My dad shifts his stance and pushes his hands into his pockets. I flinch because neither of my parents tolerates a smart mouth.

"Check your tone, boy."

"I'm sorry. But if you want to credit somebody for me swimming my best hundred ever, credit *Ray* for that." I look into my dad's eyes, and for the first time, I see sadness in them. The fight goes out of him. He just stands there blinking at me. I feel angry and embarrassed for him.

"Excuse me, Dad." I walk past him up the stairs.

But I still catch him mumbling, "I knew she was going to be a problem," before I close my bedroom door.

I pace around my room until my nerves calm down. I dock my iPhone, put my favorite Drake song on repeat, and crash backward onto my bed. I lie there with my eyes closed, my mind instantly working over what I'm supposed to say to Ray—to my Jupiter—when I call again tonight. If she answers. Then I jump to a sitting position, startling Jinx.

The other day when my dad woke me up and told me not to be late for practice, he mentioned Ray. He asked who *that girl* was on my Instagram. But it was something about the way he said it that makes my stomach lurch. It's not like he doesn't want me to date anyone—he's always riding me about not having a girl. Why is he so charged up about Ray?

I wake up two hours after I crashed on my bed, in the same

position I landed in. Drake is still singing "Find Your Love." It's dark outside. I check my phone to see if, by some miracle, Ray has called me back. She hasn't. I've called and left so many messages already, she and her mom are going to think I'm a stalker if I keep this up. Why did she give me the landline when she has a cell? I have to call her again, and this time it has to really count. It might be the last chance I have to say anything to her, and she has to know how I feel.

"What do you think, Jinx? Think fiftyleventh time's a charm?" Jinx blinks and stares me down until I build up the courage to pick up my phone. "Here goes."

"I love her and that's the beginning
and end of everything."

— F. SCOTT FITZGERALD

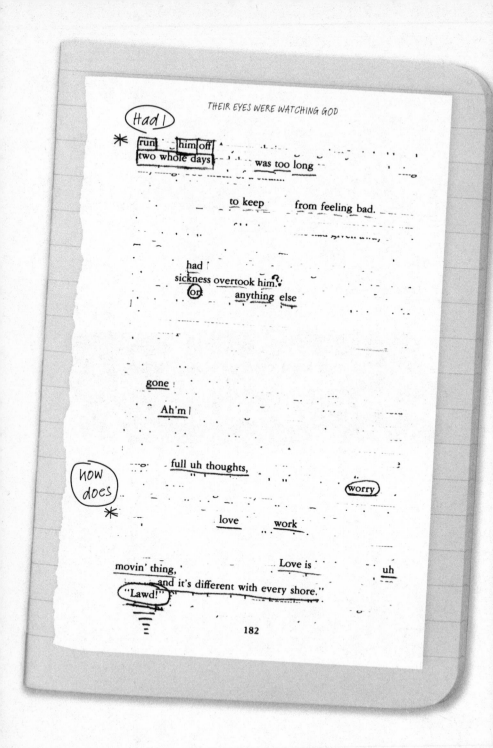

Had I

run   him off
two whole days   was too long

to keep   from feeling bad.

had
sickness overtook him?
Or   anything else

gone

Ah'm I

how does   full uh thoughts,   (worry)

love   work

movin' thing,   Love is   uh
and it's different with every shore."
"Lawd!"

182

Had I run him off?
Two whole days,
was too long to keep
from feeling bad.
Had sickness overtook him? Or something else?
Gone.
Ah'm full uh thoughts.
Worry.
How does love work?
Love is uh movin' thing and it's different at every
   shore.
Lawd!

THIRTEEN

Ray

17 DAYS

The past three days have been like some kind of twisted purgatory for me. I don't know what I did to deserve this psychological torture. My mom has been tiptoeing around my text asking to talk about the accident, and I haven't heard one word from Orion since he left without kissing me again. This is why I don't deal with people. This is why I don't deal with boys. Fucking drama.

It's like I can't even find poetry anymore without Orion showing up all over it. I close my notebook and loop my pen into the rubber strap binding it closed. I can't take it anymore. I throw off my fuzzy shag blanket and hop up from the couch when I hear Momma coming down the hall. I innocently block her path to the kitchen when she passes through in her teal scrubs smelling like fresh laundry.

"Momma?"

She sighs. "Not now, Ray. I'm about to leave for work."

"You're avoiding me."

She stops in her tracks and gives me a *the hell did you just say* look.

"I mean . . . it *feels* like you are not wanting to talk about my text."

"Ray . . ." She pinches the bridge of her nose. "We'll discuss it later. Okay? I don't know what questions you have but . . . talking about the accident is . . . just let me get in the right headspace first. What's the big rush, anyway? You never ask about it."

I always ask about him, though. *The big rush is you avoiding me. I ask less because you never seem to want to talk about him or the accident.* I don't know why she feels like she has to hide things from me. My whole life—I see the way she cloaks her sadness with smiles. The way a shadow makes its way over us around his birthday and especially around mine. I hear her crying herself to sleep, and her conversations with friends about who she's seeing and how she's "not looking for anything serious." But she's never mentioned any guys to me. She never talks at length about her life with my father all those years before me. Too many shadows and disappearing journals. Too many secrets.

"Okay. Later, then. Promise?"

She warms up at that and gives my arm a squeeze. "Thank you for understanding, baby. Later. But soon, I promise."

I grab a glass of lemonade with a sprig of basil in it and plop back on the sofa. I shove away thoughts of the note and Momma, and my mind drifts to Orion. I told him things that I haven't told anybody other than Cash and it's been three solid days and I haven't heard one peep from him. He has my number. *What the hell?* I wish I'd given him my cell phone number. I'm sure I would have broken down and at least texted him by now.

How am I already becoming this person?

Ugh. Why do people choose this? Was my story about my father too much for him? Is he over me blowing up on him? Oh god, he probably thinks that I have daddy issues and decided he doesn't want any of my drama. I hate that my stomach is in knots trying to figure out what I did wrong. I check the answering machine for the hundredth time even though the phone hasn't rung all day. No new messages.

Maybe I should just call him? The phone works both ways, after all.

No. No, he was the one who went all *your eyes* and holding my hand and showing up at my job . . . and avoiding my kisses and ghosting me. *He* should be the one to call *me*.

I fall back on the couch and throw the blanket over my head. Momma's keys jingle in her fingers. "Ray, come lock the door. I'll be back late."

I groan and shuffle over to click the lock closed, then press my back against the door. Why did I let that boy hold my hand? Why did I let his sweet laugh and eyes weave up and through me like a tapestry? Now . . . he's a part of me.

My cell phone buzzes.

Bri: He call yet?

Me: No

> **Bri:** You sure you don't want me to ask Mo what's up?

> **Me:** I'm not trying to look thirsty.

> **Bri:** But you are tho.

> **Me:** Parched as hell, but he will never know. lol

Bam! Bam! Bam!

I yelp and whip around at sudden banging on the door. Cash is there, with a self-satisfied grin, peeking through the cast-iron bars in the storm door.

"Cash, you scared the shit out of me." I open the door and glare at him. "What do you want?" His smile melts into concern.

"Damn, girl. I was just playing. My bad. You good?"

I roll my eyes at him and open the door wider, inviting him in, then walk past him and plop back down on the couch with a loud sigh.

"Wassup, Moonray? Why I feel like you was already pissed off before I pissed you off?" Cash walks into the den and sprawls out on the floor. He's so massive, he rarely sits on our vintage gold-velvet sofa anyway. The floor in front of the patio doors is his spot.

"Honestly? Everything is kinda fucked up right now. My mom is being weirder than usual about my birthday . . . you know." Tears that I didn't know I've been holding in begin to fall. "And Orion—remember that guy from Crystal Palace? He—"

"On god, if that n—" In a second Cash is up, pacing and seething. "Did he hurt you? On GOD, Ray, I'ma fuck him up." Cash stops in front of me, fists clinched at his side, watching for my answer.

"Cash, boy, calm down," I say, wiping away my tears. Cash nods, studying my face as he eases himself back onto the floor. I can't tell if he's relieved that Orion didn't hurt me, or disappointed that he doesn't get to fuck him up. "He hasn't harmed me in any way. Well, not intentionally . . . not really."

"He musta did something, you in here crying and shit. I seen his car over here the other day. He was here a long-ass time, too. He ain't been back, and here you crying. . . ."

I shake my head. "Cash, I love you for having a beat-down at the ready, but you gotta chill. It's just dumb boy stuff. I'll spare you the details, but I'll be okay." I smile at him reassuringly, until he believes me and his face cracks into a hint of a smile too.

"Aight. Good, 'cause I'm not trying to hear about all that kinky shit y'all was prob'ly in here doing anyway."

"Shut up, Big Head." I hurl a couch cushion at Cash and he flicks it away like it's a fly. "Why are you here anyway? What you want? Disturbing my peace."

"I gotta want something to come see you now? Damn. Used to roll up and just kick it. Now I need a reason? Barely seen you all summer except for your birthday." He tumbles the cushion back my way and I put it back in place.

"I know. Sorry. That's life these days. You're in football camp all day; I'm working or whatever. But I'm glad you came by, even if you on my nerves."

We spend the next hour catching up.

I walk him to the door.

"Aye, tell ole boy if he mess with you I got something for him," Cash says, holding up a fist. I slap his fist and gently shove him out the door.

"Bye, Cash."

Brrrriiiing. I hope it's Orion calling, but then remember he doesn't have my cell.

Caller ID says it's Bri, but I don't answer. I don't feel like hearing any of her optimism. I should eat something, but I have no appetite. I grab a water bottle, my earbuds, and my journal and go up to my tree house. I'm a whole person with hobbies. Why am I wasting time wishing for some stupid boy to call me anyway?

━━━━

I flesh out sketches and finish paintings on different pieces for nearly three hours. On my way out, I spot the stack of pages I selected from *Their Eyes Were Watching God.*

I hadn't planned on creating more poetry today, but the page on the top of the stack stops me in my tracks. It's the first page of chapter 11, where Janie hasn't seen Tea Cake for an entire week and has decided she doesn't even want to see him anymore . . . ever again . . . except she does. She'll go crazy if she never sees him again. This hits annoyingly close to home. Why did I have to choose a tragic love story?

I power on the radio and sit down with the page.

She was afraid

I sketch a cloud around this phrase before I scan anything else on the page. I know this will be the first line of whatever poem I find here. I read the page, underlining words as I go, and sketching clouds around the poem as it reveals itself to me.

She was afraid he might think she was interested. If she ever saw him again, she decided to treat him cold. She struggled with her secret.
She smiled. He put his guitar under his arm and she was music.

This one doesn't deserve colors nor shades of gray. Just black. It matches my mood. Blacking out an entire page with a Sharpie is satisfying. I feel more in control.

As I walk into the house, I notice the red light on the answering machine is blinking. There's a voice mail.

"H-hello? Um, this message is for Ray. It's me, Orion. We left things . . . I wasn't sure how we left things. I drove past your job a bunch of times. But with you not returning my calls, I wanted to give you space. Um . . . I didn't qualify for the hundred fly yesterday. But I'm still going to nationals week after next to compete in the hundred free and a relay with Niko and Ahmir. Anyway, maybe I can tell you about all that the next time we watch fireflies . . . one day. I miss you."

FOURTEEN

Ray

16 DAYS

The sound of something hitting my window again and again wakes me up. Gray light glows through the blinds. The sun is just beginning to rise. I lean off the side of my bed and slowly pinch the blinds open. I squint until my eyes adjust to the dim light. There's no movement in the bushes. It's about time for the tapping to come again, so I wait. I jump as bits of dirt hit the glass. Sitting up, I pull the blinds away from the window, and scream before clamping my hand over my mouth.

Orion is standing there, holding a handful of mulch in one hand and waving to me with his free hand.

"What?" I shriek-whisper, and shake my head.

I disappear from the window and race out of my room. My mom's door is shut and the house is dark, so I know she's still sleeping. I'm glad that I actually slept in cute pajamas last night and not my usual oversized tee. I stop running before I exit the hallway because I don't want him to see me being all excited when he blatantly decided to not kiss me, then didn't call for days, but said I haven't returned his calls? What calls? His voice mail was cute or whatever, but three nights and three days too late for me to be all bubbly right now. I didn't call him back on purpose. I'm glad the ball is still in his court. He's the one who ghosted. I put on my best *you interrupted my sleep* scowl and open the front door.

"What are you doing here?" I whisper, squinting more than is necessary.

Orion nervously wipes his hands on the sides of his pants.

"You totally pebbled my window," I say, fighting back a smile. "Next time, please just hold a boom box over your head and blast 'In Your Eyes' until you wake up the neighborhood. Pretty please?" I joke dryly.

"Huh?" he asks, confused.

"*Say Anything*?"

"Say what?"

"The eighties movie. Never mind. Why are you here?" I wave him in, but he shakes his head and doesn't move.

"I don't want to come in. I can't come in. I have to get to work . . . me and Mo are counting kitchen inventory before opening."

"Pause," I say, holding my hand up for dramatic effect. "You show up here at the butt crack of dawn, interrupting my sleep. . . . I need you to start over. Here's a suggestion: explain to me why you *didn't* kiss me again when we both know that was the move, and then ghosted me for three solid days." I fold my arms tight across my chest and raise my eyebrows.

"Oh . . . um . . ." Orion chuckles. "Nah, I was . . . I shouldn't have . . . Ray, you have no idea how much I wanted to kiss you—how much I *want* to kiss you—but I want it to be . . . we were both so emotional, and . . ." He puts his face in his hands, then throws his head back.

I soften my glare. He's so fine. And sweet. And he pebbled my window like a boy on TV. I wish I could throw my arms around his neck and kiss him, but he should squirm, just a little, for the agony he put me through, disappearing the way he did.

"And I called you a million times. I mean, I didn't say much on the messages, but you never called me back."

"What? Lies. We check voice mails every day and I never got any messages from you until that one last night."

"Well, I don't know. . . . I called. I'm not lying, I promise. They were short messages . . . maybe . . . I don't know, but you have to believe me."

He called me? A million times?

"When did you call?"

"I called when I thought you'd be home from work, between four and six o'clock, like three or four times a day."

I wasn't home. But Momma was.

"I called you yesterday."

"I know." Hearing that he's been calling me . . . now I feel bad for not calling him back.

"Listen. I want to take you out . . . on a date. A real date. Can I take you out? Are you busy tonight?" He shoves his hands deep into his pockets. I watch his feet step closer to me, but my mind is swimming.

He just asked me out. He didn't ghost me. He called a million times. Momma was home. Could she have deleted his messages? But why would she?

"Ray?"

"Huh? Yes . . ." I pause longer than I need to, willing myself to be here in this moment. I force myself to smile. "No, I'm . . . Okay, yes. I'm busy tonight, but not tomorrow night. I'd love to go out with you then."

Orion grabs his chest. He clears his throat and takes another step closer to me. Reflexively, I tuck my mouth into the top of my pajama shirt because I don't want him to smell my morning breath. He smiles and I smile too. He hooks his fingers into my free hand and takes another step closer, pulling me into him. My stomach lurches. I'm still standing inside my doorway, so we are almost eye to eye.

"Good." His eyes drop to my covered mouth and he bites his lip like he's about to put it down or something. "I'm looking forward to it. And when we kiss again . . . you not gone wanna run away. Watch." His mouth curves into a mischievous grin.

I'm glad my mouth is covered, because if I smile any wider, I'll look like the Joker. If I were a cartoon, my eyes would swell to ten times their normal size and hearts would fly in circles around me. My mind flashes back to his missing voice mails and I shake the thoughts away.

"So where are you taking me?"

"This open mic series that I think you'll like. I can pick you up at seven."

"Cool. Open mic . . . you bringing your guitar?"

"Nooooooo no-no-no. I told you, I only play for Jinx and Lotus." He shakes his head and chuckles. "And you, of course. I missed you."

I don't know what to say to that, so I don't say anything.

"Can I have a hug?"

"You can have a hug tomorrow night after this magical kiss I'm not gonna run away from." My cheeks ache from smiling so hard. "Give me your phone," I say, holding out my hand. "You can't have a hug, but you can have my cell phone number."

He hands over his phone, casually and without hesitation.

Before Orion gets into his car, he puts a phantom phone to his ear and points at me.

"I'll believe it when I see it," I say.

I pause at the answering machine on the way back to my room. He said the messages were super short. Maybe they just registered as hang-ups or whatever? Besides, there's no way my mom would go through all that trouble. Deleting voice mails? No way.

I can't think about this stupid old answering machine one second longer. There's too much to geek out about.

I sprint back to my room and dive onto my bed and bury my aching face in my pillow. I roll over onto my back and hug my giraffe to my chest. I text Bri.

> **Me:** He just showed up! He's taking me out!

I tap the screen to call her. I am in blissful disbelief that a boy just pebbled my window and that I'm going on a date. A real date.

FIFTEEN

Orion

15 DAYS

The sun's dipping, and I'm almost to Ray's house and kicking myself for promising her an amazing kiss. What was I thinking, putting that kind of pressure on myself? But I had to promise her that our streak of missed kisses ends tonight.

Ray's front door swings open as I approach, and a woman who looks like she could be Ray's hot older sister smiles politely back at me. "Hi there. You must be Orion." As tall as Ray and with thick dreadlocks piled on top of her head, she looks regal.

"Hi. Yes, ma'am, Ms. Evans. Nice to meet you." I step past her into the kitchen. I scan for Ray, but she's not there. I turn back around to face Ms. Evans as she closes the door behind her. She studies my face with a slight smile. I wonder what Ray has told her about me—about us.

"Marigolds," she says. It takes a moment for me to realize that she is talking about the bouquet of flowers that I brought for Ray.

"Yes! Yes, ma'am." I hold the bouquet out toward her and

she sniffs it. "And peach roses from my backyard." I almost go on talking about how my mom planted the marigolds and rose-bushes the year we first moved into our house and how she fusses over them all the time, weathering them in the winter and pruning them back and so on. Instead of saying all that, I bite both my lips to prevent myself from rambling.

"Beautiful. Marigolds and roses in your backyard?"

Just say, "Yes, ma'am." "Yes, ma'am."

She nods.

"I noticed that you garden as well," I say.

Her eyebrows rise.

"Ray showed me. I came by . . . um . . ." I clear my throat.

"I garden, yes." She leads me into the kitchen and pulls out a pitcher of water from the fridge. Thankfully, she ignores what I said about having seen the garden before.

"Would you like some water?" She doesn't wait for my answer. She just fills a little green glass and hands it to me.

"Yes, ma'am, thank you." I drain the glass in one go.

"Orion, you've made quite an impression on my Ray."

"Yes, ma'am—I mean, she's great too. She's made an impression on me, too. She's a great girl. The greatest girl." *Orion. Stop. Talking.* I try to take another sip of water from the empty glass in my hand. Her closemouthed grin widens into a smile, and she laughs a little. She pours more water for me and I thank her.

"I'll let Ray know you're here. Excuse me, dear." She disappears down the hallway.

I finish my water and pace back and forth between the kitchen and the adjacent den. Herbs wrapped with twine are hanging upside down above the windows all around the kitchen. I stop to smell one that has lavender mixed in among some leaves.

"Lavender and sage." I jump at the sound of Ray's voice and turn to see her walking toward me. You know how in movies the girl comes down the stairs in her prom dress and everything slows down and the angel music plays? That's real. Something fluttery happens in my chest, and time slows down just long enough for me to see her brown eyes sparkle when the light hits them just right. Just like the first time I saw her. Her dress is the night sky—deep blue and full of tiny gold stars. I exhale.

"Huh?" I utter the only syllable that comes to me.

"Lavender and sage," she repeats, then reaches up and touches the bundle, and she smells so good. "We harvested some from the garden to dry."

"Oh . . . hey." That's three words and three syllables so far.

"Hey," she says.

"You smell good. I brought these for you." I hold the flowers out to her. "They're from my backyard."

"Thank you, they're beautiful." She takes them and presses them to her nose. "Nice kicks."

Self-consciously, I look down at my feet. She moves closer so that our toes are just inches apart.

"Same shoes."

She inches ever closer, and our black-on-black high-top Chucks are almost toe to toe. The look in her eyes makes my insides flip, in the best way.

"I like your hair."

She smiles and swipes her finger behind her ear, but there's no hair to tuck—her hair is brushed back into a huge puff in the back. It frames her face like a halo.

"Hi," she says, our faces so close I can hear her breathing.

"Hi." I want to kiss her, like, really kiss her, but I'm hyperaware that her mom is in the house somewhere. Plus, I promised her a magical moment, and this isn't it. "Let's go."

I take the scenic route down Riverside Drive. It's a romantic stretch of road, with a nice view of the city, that runs along the banks of the Mississippi River. The iconic M-shaped Memphis-Arkansas Bridge lit with thousands of lights reflects off the water on one side, and a steep, grassy hill is topped by restaurants and condos on the other. Ray gets excited like I thought she would, peering through the window. Which is good, because I want to bring her back up here after the show.

The bridge lights hit different when you see them up close like this. I've cracked the car windows just enough so we can hear the river in the background, even over the low hum of Usher singing about making confessions.

We sit silent most of the drive, but it's not awkward; it's comfortable, like I'm more at home than I've ever been. Her hand is wrapped around mine. A couple of times she lets go to fuss with her hair puff in the mirror. I keep telling her it's perfect. She's perfect.

"If this hair would just—"

"Anything about you that feels 'out of place'—trust me, it's right where it's supposed to be."

She pokes my cheek and I pretend to try to bite her finger. She thinks I'm playing. But I'm not. "I mean it."

She closes the mirror flap in my car and rolls her eyes, but keeps holding my hand. "Thanks. I know you do."

The parking lot is full, so I drive through the adjacent neighborhood and find a spot. It's a bit of a walk, but I'm glad to get to walk with Ray, our fingers laced together. I've held her hand every single time I've been with her, as long as I've known her, including the first day we met. Even if that was by accident at first, it still counts. I wonder if she's noticed that too?

I squeeze her hand and caress the outside of her thumb with mine. I shake it to get her to look at me.

"What's going on in that beautiful mind of yours?"

"This is my first date, you know."

I'm dumbfounded. I don't want to make a big deal about her reveal, but *what?*

"Yep. First date. I mean, I've been *with* guys, but I've never been *out* with a guy before. Like, on a date."

"Oh." I search her expression because I want to know how to respond. She doesn't seem embarrassed or emotional . . . just open. "I'm glad your first date is with me. Full disclosure, this is my first time on a solo date. In school, I went to the movies a couple of times with groups and girls I was crushing on. Kid stuff."

We cross the street into the parking lot.

"Speaking of groups, Niko and Ahmir might be here tonight."

"So we're not solo, then."

"Naw, we are. Just saying, we might see some familiar faces, that's all." She squeezes my hand, and for the first time, I feel what it's like to belong to somebody and for somebody to be mine.

As I predicted, Niko and Ahmir are here with another guy from swim who we call Hollywood because he looks like Zac Efron or one of those typical white Disney stars.

"Wassup, O-Dog!" Hollywood is the only person on earth who calls me O-Dog. The only reason I let it fly is because I think it makes him feel cool.

Ray is holding back a laugh. I know she's gonna tease me about it later.

"Sup, Hollywood." I dap him up—the other guys as well.

Niko wastes no time stepping to Ray. "Hey, beautiful. You still fooling with *ese cuate* over there?" He points a thumb at me. We just laugh.

After hanging with Niko for a beat, Ray and I get drinks.

I check my phone for a text from Mo.

"Come on," I say, and lead Ray through the dense crowd toward the front of the venue.

"You think we'll find seats up there? It's pretty crowded." This is going just as I hoped it would. I want her to see me taking care of things—making this night great for her.

"It's cool—we have a seat."

"Hey, there's Mo," she says, sounding a little annoyed. She probably thinks he's the third wheel tonight.

"Hey, hey, hey! Ms. Ray." Mo bows, then leans forward and gives her the church hug, where you reach around like you about to embrace, but hands on backs are the only parts that touch.

"Hi, Mo," she says, and I could swear her mood shifts.

"You changed your hair! Nice."

"Thanks, Mo. Orion didn't tell me you would be here—you good?"

"I'm good. You know, I been texting with your girl. Bri's cool people. Technically, I'm not here. I just came early to hold these seats for y'all, as a favor to my boy over here."

"Really?" Her shoulders visibly relax, and she gives me a smile—the one with the dimples. "That's so nice."

"Yeah, Black Culture Night fills up quick, and Orion said he wanted to sit up close with you. It wasn't nothing for me to post up for y'all. Anything for love."

He makes googly eyes and we all laugh. Mo and I do a handshake and chest-bump thing, and just like that he's gone.

Ray and I sit shoulder to shoulder in our seat. The emcee has hair like Basquiat and he introduces himself as the master of ceremonies, pronouncing all the consonants and drawing out the vowels. Ray slides her fingers between mine as we wait for him to finish his opening monologue. I watch her fingers do things to my hand that feel like they should be illegal in public.

Palms of hands should be one of the bases.

The first act is a student who plays a drum that is strapped over his shoulder. At one point, a bald girl approaches the stage, matching her steps to the beat of his drumming. Her body is fluid, and whenever she stops to pulse to the rhythm, it's like she moves the air in the room and the crowd pulses too. It's hard not to imagine people outside seeing the building itself throb and sway.

"Cool, right?" I say to Ray as they bow to our applause.

She gives a standing ovation with the rest of the room. "Very!"

There's a lull before the next person takes the stage. Ray scoots closer.

"You enjoying your first date so far?" I whisper, my lips purposefully almost touching her ear.

"I am. This place is really dope."

She turns her face toward mine and I have to consciously force all my blood *back* to my brain. She reaches for her drink, mercifully creating space between us.

"They were incredible," she says.

"Yeah. I always look forward to the spoken-word artists, though. I'm blown away by how honest and open poets are willing to be sometimes."

There's a faraway look on Ray's face as the emcee asks if we're ready for the first spoken-word artist of the night. We join in the applause and turn our attention back to the stage.

SIXTEEN

Ray

A girl who looks to be about our age saunters up to the microphone. Even though she's dressed in solid black from head to toe, her bright, dewy face and bouncy hair make her look like springtime personified. By the time she reaches the microphone stand, the entire place has gone dead silent.

Orion gently squeezes my hand as he watches her the way the congregation watches a preacher—like he needs something from her. Like he expects something to feed his soul. In a way, I guess, that's why most people are drawn to one art form or another. Art is soul food.

I wish I could deny the twinge of jealousy that snakes through me.

Pretending I'm cold from the AC, I hug myself, and he instantly wraps his arm around me and rubs my arm, like I hoped he would. I feel a little silly, but this strange new feeling—wanting and receiving this kind of attention—is nice.

"Last year around the holidays I changed my name to Buttercup. I know that sounds drastic to some of y'all, but I'm an artist, and sometimes we do drastic shit." Her voice slips into an Erykah Badu impersonation when she alludes to the song "Tyrone." The audience crescendoes into laughter and applause.

"Y'all love us for it," she continues. "We love y'all, too. We need y'all to bear witness to our drastic shit. My name change was part of my resolve to resist the dark—to reject it." She takes on a more serious tone.

"If Buttercup is too strange for you, you can call me B. Bees command us to bear witness too, don't they? Bees and buttercups find their home in the sun. I wrote this a couple of weeks ago as I watched the sun rise over the river, like a bridge to heaven over troubled water. This is about love and light. It's untitled, because it is what it is."

She grips the mic with both hands and pauses for a long while, then raises her gaze to the audience.

You loved me deep.
Your hands caressed skin, flesh, sinew, bone, marrow,
    blood.
Deep.
Your mouth conjured.
Your words coaxed and conquered my soul.
Hands clenched and beckoned my spirit to rest.
An ember stoked by deep love
made promises as sure as the grave.
Eternal fire.

Her voice is loud and powerful and defiant. Snaps erupt from all over the room to let her know we feel her. She barely moves as she performs, standing firm like a warrior. Her eyes land on mine briefly before she squeezes them closed and continues. Oddly starstruck, I glance at Orion to see if he noticed, but his eyes are still on her.

> I want to go outside in the rain,
> Into night so thick that it presses against my skin,
> In shades of indigo that mask my blues until I believe
>   they've gone away.
> Dark.
> Outside in the rain at midnight
> Where, in the shadows,
> I could offer up my self to be baptized.
> Washed. Forgiven. Made clean.
> Cleansed until the blues that your love left behind
>   pool at my feet and seep back into earth.
> Deep.
> Down where dead things sustain the living.

She's still a rock, but the edge has left her voice—there's despair where anger once was. I glance over at Orion and he's watching me. He raises his eyebrows as if to ask if I'm okay, and I nod yes, less jealous now, also falling under her spell. He squeezes my arm as we turn our attention back to Buttercup.

She walks to the edge. With outstretched arms, she lowers herself to her knees and sits back on her heels.

> An ember in the ashes of our past, stoked by deep
>   love, made promises as sure as the grave.
> Eternal fire.

I want to go outside in the rain at midnight, where
    maybe I could forgive
myself.
Where, maybe, I could walk again.
In the sun.

The cafe erupts into applause. I smile in her direction—she winks at me as she begins to make her way back to her seat, clasping her hands in prayerful thanks and bowing slightly as she goes.

Clapping for her, and looking at Orion—being in this place, so alive with energy and expression—I feel open in ways I have never felt before. I could get used to this.

SEVENTEEN

Orion

"Where are we going now?" Ray asks as we shuffle through the crowd toward the exit. The open-mic part of the night is done and we're not staying for the cover band.

"Someplace where we can talk. I think you'll like it."

I lace my fingers through hers and we make our way out of the cafe.

"Aye, see you at practice. Come ready to race," Niko says when we pass him, Hollywood, and Ahmir on the way out.

I park in the neighborhood near the river, a short walk to the top of the bluff, a steep hill that overlooks Riverside Drive. Ray helps me spread out a quilt that I brought just for this. The Memphis-Arkansas Bridge is lit, and we can see part of the Pyramid from here too. It's perfect.

Other people are spread out, lounging on the hilltop. Ray sits cross-legged and looks out onto the river below us. The riverboat is lit up too and packed with people on the upper and lower decks. It looks like a postcard, inching toward the glittering bridge.

"You good?" I ask.

"Yeah." She flashes an embarrassed smile. "I loved it. I just didn't expect the open mic to get me all in my feelings."

"Right? The poem that one guy did about being a lonely child . . . and Buttercup . . ." I shake my head.

"Mm-hmm. Can we talk about why you go to that open-mic night all the time, but haven't graced the stage with one of your guitars?"

"I told you. I'm shy," I say with a shrug. "Just the thought of standing on that stage makes my anxiety hit one hundred." She looks at me like she's trying to figure me out. I just shrug again.

We stretch out on the blanket and lie side by side. Ray's body is warm next to mine and the tiny bumps on her arm give me the guts to move even closer. Her arms are behind her head, and I lie in the nook below her elbow.

"Do you remember the last time you played outside?" Ray asks, eyes on the sky. "Like, as a little kid. Like, the very last time?"

I think about Nora, and that day. That seems like the last time for me, but I played outside plenty with Mo and the other kids after that.

"No, I can't."

"Right. Cash came over the other day, and we were talking about the old days and all the ridiculous stuff we got into growing up. And I realized that one of those days was the last day we played. Everybody has one. But we have no way of knowing that that's gonna be the last day we go inside when the streetlight comes on."

"Cash was over there?" As soon as I ask it, Ray's deadpan silence makes me regret it. "Naw, I mean. That's . . . that's deep. And also true. I never considered that: the day childhood ends."

Ray shakes her head at me. "Yes, Cash was over. He lives right across the cove. Are you jealous?"

"Naw. No, I'm good," I say, my high-pitched voice giving my lie away.

"Don't worry, it's not like that with me and Cash. He's my play cousin."

Somehow that still doesn't settle with me, but I let it go.

"Have you ever seen the sky at night, away from the city?" she asks.

"Yeah," I say. "I went camping with the Boys Club when I was in elementary school—a place where you can camp in yurts and cabins. I'd never seen so many stars."

"I saw them for the first time camping with my mom. I don't remember where, but I was around six or seven. We stretched out on a blanket, just like this. I used to think we could see more stars because the people who lived there didn't have electricity, so they needed more stars for light." She laughs and keeps searching the sky for the memory. "When I got older, I couldn't shake the feeling that maybe there is more to the stars than we know. . . . I have a theory." She looks at me expectantly.

I nod my head. "Tell me."

She could be talking about types of mushrooms and I'd want to watch her face and learn about them all. I roll over onto my side and prop my head up on my arm, so I can see her better.

"It's not really a theory—it's more like a question, and I really believe in the answer that I've decided on. It's totally unscientific. Mostly."

"So . . . *a theory* . . . in theory. Got it. What's the question?" I try to keep a straight face and fail. Ray rolls her eyes.

"What if we are the *stars*?" she says, looking up. "I read that something like forty-eight hundred stars die every second. Only four humans are born per second. That's a significant difference, which makes for a weak theory, but if you take into account all the other living things with souls, everywhere in the universe, including parts we haven't explored, it starts to come a little more into focus. What if every time a star dies in the sky, life is sparked on earth? Think about it. Almost every element that makes up the human body was made in a star. Fact."

"I'm following. Nothing is just what it is with you. I think it's dope how you see below the surface of things. Of books and stars. This what I been missing out on all these summers. You been right here."

Her smile widens, and she looks back up and keeps talking. "And if we do come to life from the stars, as pure light, then the sky—outer space—must be heaven. Especially if we return there after we die, as reincarnated stars." She pauses and watches for my reaction.

"Space is heaven?"

"Think about it. The conservation of energy—it's the law of the universe. There's no creation or death of energy, only the transfer of it. When we think about the circle of life, we think in terms of earth science, the animal kingdom—living things consuming other living things, and waste, death, and decay supporting the ecology and continuing cycle of life down here. But *how* are we here? And where is our energy transferred when we die? It's all the universe, man."

"So what about hell?" I ask, drunk on her words.

"I've thought a lot about that, too. I think the evil that we do here, the part of our light that fades into darkness, that part goes into black holes, where some stars go to die, never to become stars again. Dark energy is slowly transferred into dark energy. Once something gets sucked into a black hole, that's it. It's gone forever. What if black holes are hell, eternal death, or whatever?" She looks at me with so much wonder in her eyes. I want to kiss her. I think she senses it, because she smiles a little bit. I'd do it, but I want to hear more of her theory.

"Go on," I say.

"Black holes are forming at a slower rate as time goes on, but the stars are steadily being born. The stars are going strong. Also, humans are killing each other at lower rates now than ever before, believe it or not, if you look at the entire history of human life on this planet. What if black holes are forming more slowly because evil on earth is slowly diminishing? What if one day, good wins, and there's no more need for black holes because everything on earth is starlight? Maybe that will be the heaven on earth that the holy books across religions write about. Maybe The One that everyone is waiting for is actually a metaphor for goodness inhabiting the earth . . . through the stars . . . through us?"

"That's deep as hell. Deep as a black hole," I say.

She laughs hard. "You think I'm silly."

"Never. I think you're brilliant and amazing. You're not like anybody. If you're a star, you're the brightest one."

I want to say she's the one my planet revolves around. But that's probably too much to admit on a first date. Instead I hook my fingers into hers. Her hair is like a halo around her head against the patched blanket. I move over her, letting my shadow eclipse part of her face. She grins and it's daylight again. Something happens in my chest. I bet this is what people mean when they say their heart skips a beat. Maybe this is where people got the idea that we love with our hearts. "Where did you come from?"

"The stars," she whispers, and traces her finger along my nose, stopping on my lips.

A fire burns through me. All over me. In my head, I picture myself leaning down and kissing her.

I say a silent prayer and lean in.

My phone buzzes loud in my pocket, startling the shit out of me. She laughs and moves over so I can fish it out of my jeans. I sit up.

> **Mo:** Hey Mr. Romance. U hit that yet?

"Important?"

"Not in the least."

Ray sits up and bumps my shoulder. "Anything interesting?"

I move a strand of hair from her face and trace my thumb along her jaw. "Nothing as interesting as you." She's bashful and her lips part. *Kiss her.* Just as I lean into her, a giggling group of girls plops down right next to us on their own blanket.

Ugh. Magic. I promised her magic. This is not happening.

"Let's take a selfie—we can get the bridge in the background." I hold my phone up.

We spend another half hour there, mostly just watching the sky and holding hands. I tell her about the swim meet and how excited I am about nationals. The way she smiles at me while I talk about swim makes me want to qualify for the Olympics. More people have joined us on the hill—too many. So we decide to call it a night.

When we pull up to Ray's house, neither one of us is ready for the night to be over, so we decide to go back to the tree house.

Her mom's Jeep is in the driveway. "You sure your mom won't care? It's kinda late. I do have to train in the morning. We could—"

"She's cool," Ray says. "Come on."

I follow her through the back gate to the tree house.

"No tears this time," she says as soon as we're up the ladder and on the porch. "Deal?"

"Deal."

The streetlights beyond the back fence cast a glow over the porch, which is just enough light for us to see. Ray grabs her quilt from inside and we lower it to the floor together. Our eyes meet, and we laugh because we both know why we came up here.

She starts to say something. I'll never know what it was, because before she can even say a word, I go for it. I don't want to waste any more time with words. I step forward, cup her chin, and bring her lips to mine.

She deepens the kiss, opening her mouth, and every inch of me tenses up as our tongues tease and touch. I'm not even sure that I'm breathing. Ray is my air.

She breaks the kiss, looking into my eyes. *Not pizza again!* But the next second she's on my lap, pressing me against the wall as our mouths move together again. She feels so good. I grasp on to her, pulling her closer to me. My entire existence right now is kissing her and holding her and wanting more of everything. And hoping that whatever that love song on the radio is, it stays on forever.

We stop to look at each other for a moment between kisses, coming up for air, before connecting again—our eyes and mouths and bodies saying everything either of us needs to know. We go on like this for a long time.

She positions my hand over one of her breasts and I feel electric. She says something with her lips still pressed against mine. A bolt of agony shoots through me because I feel her pulling away as she gently presses her hands against my chest, creating a little space between us, breaking the kiss.

Her face is glowing and we are both out of breath. I look into her eyes, wanting to ask why, then realize that she's waiting for me to respond to whatever she said.

"Huh?"

"Are we gonna do this?" She presses another kiss against my lips and waits for an answer.

If *this* means what I think it means, I'm not ready to do that. I want to. Eventually. I want to . . . with her . . . but not tonight.

Not like this. "Um. I want to. You have no idea how much I want to."

She looks down and back up at me with her eyebrows raised.

"Okay, maybe you have *some* idea of how much I want to, but I actually should get home. I have to train in the morning." Thankfully, she nods, understanding.

I run my hands along her thighs and hold her hips, because it feels good—her on me like this—but I know it's about to end.

"See? I told you you wouldn't want to stop," I say. She chuckles.

She responds by leaning back, pulling me down on top of her, and kissing me again until neither one of us wants to stop, but one of us has to.

She stands and helps me up from the floor. I pull her into a hug.

"Um. Orion? I thought you were in such a hurry to get out of here," she says, tapping me on my shoulder until I release her.

When we climb down the ladder out of the tree house, I kiss her one more time, just to see what it feels like again to kiss her because we both want to.

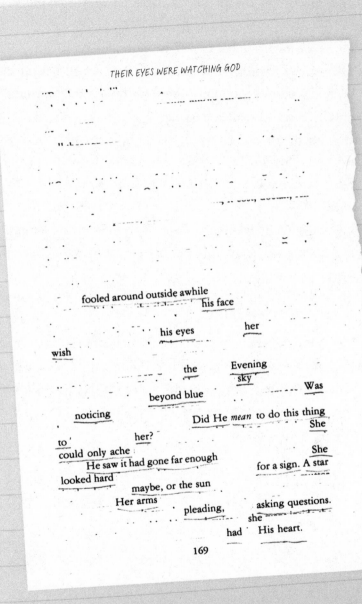

fooled around outside awhile

his face

his eyes   her

wish

the   Evening

sky

beyond blue   Was

noticing   Did He *mean* to do this thing

She

to   her?

could only ache

He saw it had gone far enough   She

looked hard   for a sign. A star

maybe, or the sun

Her arms   asking questions.

pleading,   she

had   His heart.

169

Fooled around outside awhile.
His face. His eyes. Her wish.
The evening sky, beyond blue, was noticing.
Did he mean to do this thing to her?
She could only ache. He saw it had gone far enough.
She looked hard for a sign.
A star, maybe, or the sun.
Her arms pleading, asking questions.
She had his heart.

EIGHTEEN

Ray

13 DAYS

It's been two days since my date with Orion. I've become one of those girls I used to judge so hard in my head—silly and goofy-eyed over a boy. Bri teases me about it and I'm too far gone to care.

I mentioned Orion's missed messages to Momma and she was as confused as I was about why none of his messages were recorded. When I told her I gave him my cell phone number, she seemed surprised and maybe a little annoyed that I was even still talking to him.

I move a seat cushion from beside where Momma sits on the couch and place it on the floor in between her feet, where I've been sitting for the past hour. I lean back down and return to pinching off small sections from a bundle of synthetic hair and passing them to her to add onto individual braids. I picked soft, wavy, shoulder-length black-to-lilac ombré hair this time, for a mermaid bob effect—switching it up for my senior year.

I wore my hair parted down the middle in two French braids most of my life, including my freshman year at Crestfield. There was something about suddenly being one of few Black girls in a white community that changed me in subtle ways that I didn't notice until well after I'd already changed. I don't think I would have noticed if Cash hadn't said anything.

When I came home for the summer after ninth grade, Cash pointed out that I kept running my right hand over my right ear, swiping away phantom long, loose hairs from my tight French braids. After a year surrounded by white girls constantly tossing their hair out of their faces or sweeping it over from one shoulder to the other, I realized that I had picked up that behavior—like when I got my braces off in eighth grade but kept licking my teeth and closing my lips over braces that were no longer there.

I wasted no time getting box braids installed that summer. I've taken them out and gotten them reinstalled every winter and summer break since then. My natural hair is only about eight inches long, stretched out. I keep it trimmed short because it's easier to wash and go in between styles. I love the way I feel between braid installs on school breaks, when I can finger-comb it and let it air-dry into a fuzzy Afro. I get to be one hundred percent just me under the sky for a few weeks out of the year. At school, I just don't have time to do the daily maintenance required to keep my natural hair healthy, so I keep it in fly protective styles with braids.

For me, that's a big deal.

"Well? I've been trying to let you bring it up, but you've been mighty quiet about Mr. Orion," Momma says, surprising me.

"I didn't know you were interested in hearing about him. The last time I said his name, your whole vibe changed."

She also acted like that when I brought up the accident again. But I'm not saying that yet. One thing at a time.

"The first time you said his name, you said you might never see him again." She pulls the braid tight and loops in another piece of hair, the feathery lilac ends hanging over my shoulder. "You've seen him three times since, and you've given him your cell phone number, which is a far cry from never. So what's going on with you two?"

I haven't stopped thinking about what's going on with us . . . what went on with us the night before last. My body is still buzzing from the way we touched. "Nothing out of the ordinary, Momma. He's a cute boy who likes me. We've hung out a few times. Typical."

"Do you plan to hang out some more?"

I hold up a section of hair. She takes it and starts another braid.

"Maybe."

She stops braiding my hair, and I can feel her side-eyeing me through the back of my head.

"Okay, yes. Jeez, Nosy. Yes, I plan to hang out with him again, as much as possible, actually, before I go back to school." I chuckle, but she doesn't.

"I see. Tell me about this Orion who moved your hang meter from never to as much as possible in the span of one week." She sounds chill about this compared to how she was the last time Orion came up, but she's restarted this same braid three times now. She never has to start a braid over.

"He's nice. He loves his cats. He's an amazing swimmer—he went to Junior Olympics when he was fifteen. He's going to the US Open in a little over a week. He plays guitar." I stop talking because I'm beginning to feel giddy, but I don't think Momma's trying to hear all that.

I wait for her to respond, but after a few moments of nothing, she goes on braiding quietly and the silence lingers, aside from a few deep sighs from her that I don't think I'm supposed to notice.

"Well, I don't have to ask how you feel about the boy. I can hear it all in your voice. I have to be honest, baby, I'm not thrilled that you're getting involved with some boy right before he goes off to college. It seems like a lot of buildup, just to drop off in a couple of weeks. I want to be there whether you sink or swim with this thing, but to do that, I need to know you're in the water. Promise me you'll let me know if it starts to get serious. We don't keep secrets from each other."

The one time I actually like a boy, a decent boy . . . This could be my first love—why can't she just encourage it?

"We don't keep secrets from each other?" On top of everything else she hasn't said over the years, she's hidden the journals. I went back to search them again the other day, and they were gone.

"What is this tone?"

"I'm just saying, I didn't know we were so open with everything in this house."

"Ray?" Her voice is all *I know the hell you not*, but I have to keep going.

"I saw your journal." As soon as the words escape me, I

wish I could stuff them back in, but fear and I-don't-know-what-else propel me forward. "The one you kept after I was born. That's what my text was about." I take a deep breath and brace myself for whatever she might come back with, but she just keeps braiding, which agitates me. "If we don't keep secrets, why did you never mention the journals? Who did you have to forgive?"

She reaches her hand out for another section of hair.

"Baby. Whatever you saw . . . that notebook was therapy and recovery work. It's full of made-up details to help jog my memory. Writing prompts—homework between sessions. There's nothing to . . . whatever you think you saw. There isn't anything . . ."

Whatever I think I saw? "Please don't do that, Momma. I went back for another look at the journal and it was nowhere to be found."

She stops braiding as I continue.

"Whether there's anything to what I *definitely* saw or not, you didn't answer my question. Why didn't I know that you re-membered? I've asked you for details before. You said you don't recall. The faceless angel with dreadlocks who fished you out of 'the sea of darkness' . . . the mermaid-tail sketches . . . Those might be made-up things from a writing prompt. But you clearly wrote that you met and forgave the EMT. That's a big deal. I'm just saying, it's weird to keep that from me. And you're hiding it from me still, because you moved the box when you saw that I'd disturbed it."

She starts braiding my hair again without a word. My heart

is racing—accusing my mom of things—but I can't carry these questions around inside anymore.

"Ray, one day, when you're a mother . . ." She takes a long pause. "There are things we keep from our children, not to deceive them, but to protect them."

"But I'm not a child anymore. I'm seventeen."

"I had no reason to share it with you. It's just ramblings of a grieving widow and a scared mother. I don't know who the man was. There's nothing in that journal that would have added anything good to your life." She tilts my head down for the next braid and mutters, "Especially not now."

"What does that mean?" She's so committed to keeping those journals shrouded in secrecy.

What else is she hiding?

"And you're never old enough to think it's okay to rifle through my personal things. That was a messed-up thing to do. You'd have a fit if you thought I'd been in that tree house of yours looking through your art journals."

Wow. She's trying to turn this around on me.

We sit in silence as she finishes the rest of my hair.

━━━

When she finished my braids she couldn't get out of here fast enough. She jumped right into the shower and told me not to wait up. As soon as she leaves for her night out, I go to the Hoarding Room. I'm never going to see that journal again, but there must be something else from those days that could hint at why the hell she's being so tight-lipped. I start with the box of journals, and, as expected, the used ones are missing.

Next I thumb through a box of old pictures. Every year she goes through these plastic photo albums of her and my dad, spanning their entire relationship. I stop on a picture from their nursing-school graduation. They look so happy. I've never seen my mom smile like that in my entire life. I load the books back into the box, and before I close it, I notice a loose picture sticking out from below the albums at the bottom. I tug on the corner of the photo and it slides right out.

It's a photo of me at my dad's graveside when I was five or six. I have the same one—Momma framed it and gave it to me before I left for boarding school. Except this one isn't cropped. My mom is at the top of the hill, leaning on the car, watching me. She doesn't seem to know someone is taking our picture. I flip the photo over.

Thank you for meeting with me. I hope this helps.

I don't know who took this photo; obviously my mom does. She never mentioned that the photo framed for me had been cropped. I've always assumed she took it. She's never told me otherwise. More secrets.

I toss and turn most of the night. I listen to the radio for a while, but all the love songs just make me think about Orion and our date and everything we did in the tree house. Every time I close my eyes, I see his long eyelashes, just inches away from mine, and the texture of his skin, which makes me think about the way he asks me to say his name sometimes. How urgently he held on to me. How amazing his body felt against mine.

I need to see him again.

Like. Now.

But it's after one in the morning, and it's not happening. I reach for my cell phone. Orion texted me our selfies. I flip through them and wish for a miracle. When I see a text notification pop up with Orion's name, I believe in magic.

My thumbs fly across my phone screen, faster than my brain can comprehend.

Me: Can't stop thinking about you!

Too eager. *Delete.*

Away at boarding school, on breaks at Bri's, whenever I get to feeling *some kind of a way,* I text Cory, who lives near her. He doesn't ask any questions. He gives me what I need and doesn't expect any keys to my secret parts. I'd never in a million years message *him* "I can't stop thinking about you." Our thing has never really been about him . . . it's always been about *it.*

With Orion, it's different. He's different.

Curious, I look for Cory's name and scan our old messages—his last text asking me if I was up, sent the night before Bri and I returned to school from Memorial Day weekend, unanswered. He's miles away, but even the thought of him touching me or seeing me makes me squirm in my blankets. I feel like I'm on a train with no stops in sight, flying full speed ahead toward a brick wall. I don't know if I could get off this ride even if I wanted to at this point. I try to think of something that's honest but a little less thirsty to send Orion.

> **Me:** Can't stop thinking about the tree house + you + me.

I wait for several seconds, but it feels like an eternity.

> **Orion:** Hey! Same. What are you doing up?

> **Me:** Thinking about the tree house . . .

> **Orion:** Ok. Now you got me thinking about it too . . .

I chew my lip.

> **Me:** I want to kiss you again. What are you doing tomorrow?

> **Orion:** lol I want you to kiss me again. I'm on lifeguard duty at the Davis YMCA until 3.

Me: I'm coming to see you. Will you take me home after?

Orion: Yeah

Me: Good. I'ma try to go to sleep now so tomorrow can get here faster.

Orion: I don't think I'm going to sleep at all tonight. lol

Neither am I.

NINETEEN

Ray

12 DAYS

The bus stop is right in front of the Davis YMCA. I arrive an hour before Orion's off work. I walk through the pool entry and it's like walking into a Gordon Parks photograph, except in full color. Like most places in Whitehaven, the pool looks like it hasn't been remodeled since the sixties, but is really well-preserved. Three lifeguards are working, all near carbon copies of each other: tall with deep brown skin made ebony by a summer spent in the sun, and mops of wet, tightly coiled hair atop their heads.

I have no intention of actually swimming today, but I'm dressed for the pool. Specifically, I'm dressed for Orion. On a mission. He's conducting swim tests for little kids, all in matching camp T-shirts, near the big waterslide. He hasn't noticed me yet. He's hyping the kids up before it's their turn to swim. He's all high fives, exaggerated tiny splashes, and fist pumps in the air. Something about seeing him this way makes my heart flutter.

I drag an empty chaise into a shaded area beside the pool, spread my towel over it, and sit down. I situate my book and my bottle of water on a table next to me and stretch out on the lounger to get comfortable. I glance over to see if Orion has spotted me yet. He hasn't. I put my earbuds in, and Beyoncé and Luther Vandross sing "The Closer I Get to You." My eyes find Orion again.

It's hard for my mind not to wander into what-ifs. There are girls at school in long-distance relationships with boys back home or boys at other schools. It wouldn't be terrible to be one of those girls, I guess. I open my book to one of my favorite short stories but stare at the pages and daydream while my Beyoncé Every Day playlist runs. Could Orion and I do this? Could we be a real thing? That would mean letting myself get even more wrapped up in him, and we only have about two weeks left together. It's like emotional suicide. Maybe Momma is right.

I look up from my book and Orion is smiling at me from the water.

He waves and I wave back. We spend the next few songs glancing at each other every few minutes and smiling like goofballs. When he has high-fived the last kid in line, Orion climbs out of the water and disappears into the locker room. I fluff my braids and tug at my outfit, making sure everything's sitting right when he reemerges.

He relieves another lifeguard in the high chair overlooking the pool. He mouths *thirty minutes* to me, making a three and zero with his fingers, and I give him a thumbs-up.

A song intro begins and I already know it's "Daddy," a love

song from Beyoncé to her father. Hard pass. I tap my screen to skip it.

Thirty minutes fly by.

"Crazy in Love" blasts in my ear as Orion climbs down from his post and walks my way. I pretend I don't see him approaching. As gracefully as I can, I tug the headphone cord resting between my lips and remove my earbuds one after the other and wrap them around my phone. I pick my book back up moments before he stands beside me. I look up and make sure I smize before blinking into a full smile. Bri would be so proud.

"You changed your hair," he says.

"Yeah. You like it?"

He nods enthusiastically with a big ole grin. He clears his throat. "What, you over here pretending to read?"

"Reading," I say, and hold the cover of ZZ Packer's *Drinking Coffee Elsewhere* up to him, which proves nothing.

"Let me guess: a single woman has various encounters with strangers at different coffee shops around NYC."

"Not even close, but I would totally read that book *and* watch the movie. It's a collection of short stories. The one I'm currently reading is about the only all-Black Girl Scout troop at camp. It's hilarious." I've read this book so many times—never mind if I was just staring at the page in a daze today. "I was hoping I'd get to see you be a hero." I try not to ogle his body, but he laughs and his chest flexes and I almost drop my book. He was shirtless the entire time we were at his pool party, but something about seeing him in his official red lifeguard shorts and knowing he could totally save my life if I was drowning makes him ten times hotter.

"There's plenty of day ahead of us. I'ma save you later . . . give you all the mouth to mouth you need."

"You just said that with a straight face. Um, wow, okay. Smooth," I say, cool as a cucumber.

He slides a chair over next to me and sits down in a spot that gives him a full view of my stretched-out body. I'm wearing a turquoise tank suit with a white zipper down the front, which I know makes my melanin pop. He very deliberately gives me the once-over. He wants me to see him look.

"Nice swimsuit," he says.

"Thanks. I'm glad you like it." He reaches for my hand and I give it to him. He caresses my palm with his fingers, drawing circles. I'm melting into a useless heap when a group of kids cannonball at the same time across from us.

"We should take a selfie."

This guy and selfies, I swear. He runs into the locker room to get his phone.

He kneels beside me and flips the camera around. With our faces pressed together, he counts down, and on three he kisses my cheek.

"You know what I liked the most about the other night?" he asks.

I shake my head, dazed.

Orion's smoldering face morphs into a toothy grin as his eyebrows dance up and down. A laugh escapes me that is way too loud, because every nerve on the surface of my body is tingling. I slap his shoulder playfully, and my abs ache.

"So, *Jupiter*"—Orion playfully draws out my name—"have you talked to your mom about me?"

"That's random, but yes. Why?"

"Did you tell her I'm about to be her future son-in-law?"

I roll my eyes. "Boy, you wild."

"Seriously, just wondering. My parents saw you on my IG . . . our selfies. My mom said you cute. My dad, though . . . I don't know. He's weird about swim all of a sudden and thinks you're distracting me."

Well, damn, Pops. "Am I distracting you?"

"No."

"My mom was actually kind of weird too after I told her that I like—that I met a boy. She knows you're leaving for Howard soon, though. So I think she just wants to make sure this summer fling doesn't end in heartbreak."

Orion raises his eyebrows. "'Summer fling'?" He appears pained, but I can't tell if he's serious or joking. "I peeped you about to admit you like me. It's cool, Ray, you can admit it now. Especially after how you was all up on me in that tree house. Matter fact, you don't have to say it. Actions speak louder than words." He squeezes my hand, and a mischievous grin creeps across his face.

"Weirdo," I say, giggling.

"You like me." He leans forward until his lips are a few inches away from mine. He smells like sunscreen, sweat, and boy, and something else . . . something sweet. His eyelashes are impossibly long. I know he wants me to kiss him, but I wait just to see if he'll come closer to me. I lean back just a little. He glances at my lips, grins. This tug-of-war or whatever we're doing is hot. I need him to be off work . . . *stat.*

"Isn't it almost time for you to go?"

He checks his watch. "Yep. Let me shower right quick; then we can head out."

Orion walks off, and my insides are all fire. And I have no desire to be cooled down.

A few minutes later, he's walking toward me in a white T-shirt and gray sweats and it's like I've never seen a cute boy before. I'm glad I'm sitting down, because my knees would definitely go weak if I were standing. I slip my sundress over my head, and it falls over my hips just as Orion strolls up.

"Hi," I say.

He takes hold of my hand. "Hi." He smells like soap and mouthwash. I want to kiss his cheek, so I do. He smiles and kisses my cheek, which aches from blushing, in return. I take a deep breath.

"You smell good," I say.

"Thanks. I used soap," he says, mimicking me, and grins.

"Take me home, Orion," I say, and we walk through the pool exit holding hands.

TWENTY

Orion

I pull my car into Ray's driveway.

"My mom is working until late tonight, so we have the house to ourselves," she says without looking my way. I haven't stopped thinking about her tree house and the way our bodies touched since I left here Friday, and now that I'm back here with her, alone, I'm freaking out. I try my best to recapture the confidence I had at the pool. My lifeguard uniform was like my cape. Now in street clothes, I'm back to being Clark Kent.

"Yeah, I don't have anywhere else to be," I say, trying to appear laid-back. I can tell she knows this is a front.

I follow her into the house and kick off my slides. She locks the door. I walk to the patio door and look at the backyard, too anxious to look at her.

"Do you want anything to eat?" Ray asks.

I'm starving, but I shake my head, still afraid to meet her eyes. My thoughts are going haywire. She joins me at the patio door, looking at the tree house. She weaves her fingers in between mine.

"Reminiscing?" She leans her cheek on my shoulder.

"Yeah," I basically grunt, because suddenly my brain is not cooperating with my mouth. "It's all I can think about," I say, sounding more like myself.

She lifts her head and grins. I can't take my eyes off her mouth. Her smile widens.

"Do you want something to drink? Water?"

I force myself to meet her eyes. "No, but thanks." If I drink anything, I'll puke from sheer nerves.

"Do you want . . . anything?" The way she asks makes my breath catch in my throat. I nod and then try to kiss her, but she moves her head back, just out of my reach. For a second, I worry I've made a mistake, but she smiles.

She walks backward, pulling my hand, leading me down the narrow hallway. Oh god. My legs tremble, but I follow her. When we are inside her room, she closes the door and leans her back against it. She's so comfortable, so confident. I love that about her. I love everything about her.

The blinds are closed, but daylight filters through the edges of the window, casting a dim light over the room. She turns on a small radio, and Bon Jovi singing "Livin' on a Prayer" fills the air. Like an idiot, I drop her hand, wipe my sweaty palms off on the sides of my legs and begin a walking tour around her cramped room. I'm stalling.

The walls are light purple. I can only walk the L-shaped path around her bed, which takes up most of the room. She says nothing, just watches me and my ridiculous nervousness. I make my way around the room and back, running my fingers along the edges of her white furniture. I peek at framed photos of her and her friends from school, stacks of books, magazines, and CDs, walls full of her paintings and drawings, and clusters of lotions and nail polish and things like that.

I turn around to go back, but just stand facing her from across the room and stuff my hands in my pockets. An ancient stuffed giraffe is planted between her pillows in the center of her bed. She looks at it. I do too. I know my way around some of the bases, but I've never hit a home run with a girl before. My heart is racing and now my armpits are sweaty. *Relax, Orion.*

Without saying anything, she pulls her dress up over her head and drops it on the floor, then raises her eyebrows. I take the hint and remove my shirt. She unzips her swimsuit and I think I might cry. She's so beautiful. I mask the sound that comes out of my throat by pretending to clear it.

By the time she steps out of her swimsuit, I'm stepping out of my sweats. As my pants hit the floor, the voice on the radio— Tom Petty now—sings "free-fallin'" and we burst out laughing. Ray switches the radio off, puts a CD in, and presses play. Then she faces me again. She's not covering herself, so I fight the urge to cover myself. I've imagined being here with her like this so many times since the first night I saw her. My emotions are all over the place, and I don't know where to begin.

"Sade," I say. It's the only thing I can think to say after watching her put a CD in naked.

"Yes, Sade. *Love Deluxe.*" She tilts her head sideways and watches me curiously.

"I put the album on repeat," she says, and bites her bottom lip. Not in a nervous way, but in the way she did in my room before I ran from her.

I don't want to run from her this time.

My heart is beating out of my chest. I start to get hard. Embarrassed, I grab the nearest thing I can reach, which happens to be an orange blanket folded at the end of her bed, and hold it, strategically, in front of myself. She giggles.

I'm mortified, but force myself to chuckle. I shake my head and shrug. "Your body is so . . ."

"Come here," she says, in a way that tells me she knows how lost I am. She leads me by the hand to the side of the bed and pulls the covers back. I discard the orange blanket once I'm waist down under the covers. We lie facing each other. Dumbstruck, I go to kiss her, and she stops me again.

"Orion, I need you to know that you don't have to do anything you don't want to do. I have condoms, but seriously, if you just want to—"

"I want everything!" I practically yell. *Idiot.*

Immediately, I regret cutting her off. I prop myself up on my elbow, about to explain, but then she laughs and covers my mouth with a finger. I laugh too. I'm relieved and embarrassed and excited. I close my eyes and bring her hand to my face. It is warm and soft against my cheek. She smells like cotton candy. I kiss her palm, then press her hand to my chest.

"Say my name, please."

"Orion." Her whisper is softer than the wind.

She kisses me and my insides melt. When she pulls away, I search her eyes for answers, because why did we stop?

"Say my name," she says. Her smile makes me feel like I'm flying.

"Jupiter," I say.

I would do anything she asked me to right now. She presses

my chest until I'm lying on my back and nestles against my side, facing me. I'm painfully aware that every inch of her skin is about to be touching every inch of mine. I want to stop looking at the ceiling, but I'm frozen with anticipation and excitement and fear. I want to kiss her again, but I know I won't stop this time, and I'm nervous that it won't be how she expects.

She turns my face toward hers and runs her thumb across my lips. Her mouth curves into a smile, and I am radioactive.

"I want everything," I whisper.

We don't laugh this time. Her eyes urge me forward.

She kisses me—really kisses me. The music from the CD player and our hushed words and laughter are like a new, intoxicating symphony that I never want to end. After a while, she pulls me down on top of her. She smiles and our eyes lock. I resist the urge to look away, because I want to see Jupiter's face the moment I become hers—the moment we become everything.

"So he waited, listening for a moment longer to the tuning-fork that had been struck upon a star."

— THE GREAT GATSBY

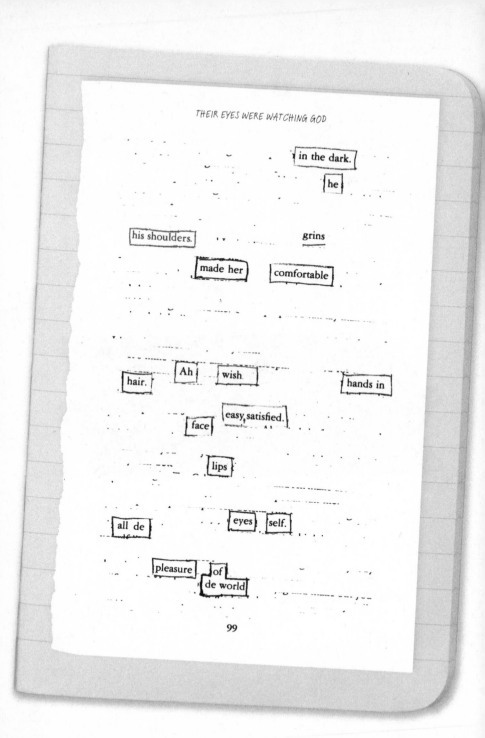

in the dark.

he

his shoulders.   grins

made her   comfortable

hair.   Ah   wish.   hands in

easy, satisfied.

face

lips

all de   eyes   self.

pleasure   of
          de world

In the dark, he, grins.
his shoulders, made her,
comfortable.
A wish,
hands in hair.
Easy.
satisfied.
Face, lips, eyes, self.
All the, pleasure, of the world

TWENTY-ONE

Orion

11 DAYS

I blink myself awake.

It's dark outside now. Ray is asleep on my chest, and as much as I want to lie here with the weight of her head resting on me, I really have to pee and I need food. I'm exhausted and sore and hungry.

I slip out of her bedroom and take a shower. Lavender body wash is the only soap option, but it smells more green than flowery, so it's cool. I dress, and Ray sleeps through it all. Since she's still asleep, I go into the kitchen in search of food and settle for a banana and some water. I can eat at home. I fill a glass with ice and water and take it back to her room. She'll be thirsty when she wakes up.

I sit beside her on the bed.

"Hi." She bats her eyes open a moment and closes them again.

"Hi." I kiss her forehead. "I took a shower. I'm about to head home."

"Okay," she says, words laced with sleep as she moves to get up.

"You don't have to walk me out."

She's probably even more exhausted than I am.

"Today was amazing," I say.

"Was it *everything*?" She squints her eyes open again, and her lips curve into a smile. I lace my fingers into hers and kiss her face.

"You joking, but yeah, it *was* everything. I'll make sure the door locks behind me when I leave. You stay and sleep."

She rolls over and dozes back off. I kiss her hand and let it rest on the bed.

In the car, I tune the radio to the station with the love songs and turn it up.

———

When I got home from Ray's last night, my parents weren't home. My dad, no doubt, would ride me about being out all day, especially if he knew I was with Ray. So I made sure to eat and be in bed by the time they got home. When they did, I pretended to be asleep. I barely slept. Every time I closed my eyes I replayed the night with Ray over and over again. This morning, I made sure to be up, dressed, and ready to leave for training before my dad even woke up. He wasn't gonna catch me slippin'.

I had a pretty solid practice, in spite of constantly thinking about Ray. I always wanted my first time to be with someone that I loved. I can't tell her that I love her—it would probably scare her away. She dances around even telling me that she likes me. But I love her. I can't stop listening to love songs. I made a playlist the other day of just love songs by my favorite singers like MJ and Drake. I even added "Sweet Caroline" because that was one of the first moments I felt really connected to Ray.

It's late in the afternoon and I'm sitting on the patio next to the pool, practicing a new song on my favorite guitar and humming along with the melody. The sound of a bouncing basketball interrupts my thoughts.

"Hey," my dad says. "Shoot some hoops?" He dribbles past me toward the goal behind the pool as if he expects me to just drop everything and follow him. When I don't, he stops and points to the basketball he's no longer dribbling.

I point at my guitar and gesture toward my whole situation—shirtless, shoeless, stretched out on a lounger. "No thanks. I'm in chill mode right now. I can almost play this whole song from memory—I'm in a zone. I'm not even wearing shoes."

"What you in is a daze—playing them songs and always off somewhere chatboxing or whispering into that phone. I see you. Heads up."

My dad chest-passes the basketball to me. I ditch my guitar with a split second to catch the ball before it smacks me in the face. Luckily, there's a lounger next to me, and my guitar isn't in pieces.

"Dad, I could've dropped my guitar . . . you could have broken my face!"

"Coulda, but didn't. You was quick, too. Reflexes like them cats of yours. Come on, let's play. First one to twenty-one wins."

My dad is in one of his annoying moods where he has to measure my manhood through physical challenges. When I was little, he'd make me race him all the time—on land and in the pool—until I started beating him. He taught me how to play basketball, and I'm actually really good at moving the ball around. I'm terrible at shooting, though, which is probably why he wants to play a game of twenty-one. I size him up. I have about an inch over him, but he is still in really good shape. Then again, I'm younger and faster and could probably get past him and to the basket enough to win this.

"What are we playing for?" I scoot off my lounger and glance around for some spare shoes. Nothing.

"Bragging rights. If I win, I get to say I beat a young, strapping buck. If you win—"

"I get to invite Ray over for dinner."

My dad's jolly bravado cracks, and he stares at me like he's trying to make sense of what I just said. He nudges his glasses up on his nose and blinks at me.

"Hear me out," I say. "You keep saying she's a distraction and bad news or whatever, but if you meet her, you'll see that she's great, and you'll see why I'm so into her."

"Oh, I know why you so into her. I was seventeen before, you know."

"I'm almost eighteen now, and it's not . . . it's not like that. It's not . . . just that."

My dad squints at me and takes the ball out of my hands. He spins it and looks off into space. "Wow . . . my boy. Guess I should say *my man* now, huh? You being safe?"

I'm surprised I'm not more embarrassed. I'm not surprised my dad seems so cool about this. A couple of years ago, I overheard him tell my mom that he was worried I was gay because he never saw me with any girls—and because of the cats. He really doubled down on me doing sports then. As if that made any sense. I told my mom what I'd heard and how messed up it was. Because what if I *was* gay? My mom agreed that the way my dad was moving was wack, and that she thought he was being absurd. After that, I never really shook the feeling that his affection for me was conditional.

"Yes, sir," I answer.

"It's real out here, son. I mean it. Say it with me. *You don't strap it . . .*"

". . . you don't tap it. I remember, Dad—can we not right now?"

When my mom had the sex talk with me in middle school, it was very scientific and straightforward. My talk with my dad, years later, consisted of cliché phrases and rhyming one-liners. This one was the hallmark.

"And, so we clear, now ain't the time to be getting into anything serious. You got nationals coming up, and about to head off to school. Have your little summer fun, but don't get in too deep. It's plenty of girls ahead of you. Summer's almost over. More like that girl will come around, trust me."

"Ray," I correct him. He doesn't respond. "And this isn't like that . . . this isn't just some girl. . . . I think she's *the* girl."

My dad's creased forehead softens.

"Anyway, Dad, those are my terms and conditions. You still want to play? Wait. You ain't scared, are you? You know I can't shoot for nothing. Just keep me out of the paint and you good." I stand a little taller to make the inch I have over my dad count. He squares his shoulders to remind me of the hundred pounds he has on me, fifty of which are probably in his arms and chest alone.

"Scared? Boy, come let me take you to school. Here, I'll even take my shoes off to make it fair." He tosses his shoes aside and then bounces the ball to me. I take it to the top of the key and he positions himself at the free-throw line.

"Check." I pass the ball to him. As soon as he touches it, he passes it back, hard, and gets right on defense. He took my advice to heart. He's a mountain, and forces me to take a long shot, which I miss.

He snatches the rebound and dribbles to the top of the key. My turn on defense now.

"Don't worry. I been doing it a lot longer than you, boy. That's all. Let's go." He passes the ball to me before I'm ready. I pass it back, but before I can even get into position to play defense, he's already barreled past me for an easy layup.

"Come on, son, I thought we was playing ball."

This is pretty much how the game goes. I keep putting up air balls and my dad keeps scoring on me. He scores the first twelve points of the game.

"Orion, this girl sucking the life out of you. Play some defense, boy."

"Time," I say. I'm tired of getting scored on, and I'm not about to let him get on me about Ray again.

"We can quit if you need to. You look like you could use a break from this humiliation. Go listen to rap or something, get some aggression about you. Man up."

"Really, Dad? Only one of us is out of breath and it's not me. I'm just going to get my shoes." I spring into the house and up the stairs, put on socks and shoes in no time, and hustle back out to the court.

"You booted up, old man? All right. I'll make it quick so you can go soak your knees. Check." I pass the ball inside to him and slap the ground with both hands. He passes it back. "You better D up, Dad." I'm ready for this to be over.

I bounce-pass the ball between his legs, fake right, then run left around him. I recover the ball and make an easy layup. I do a small victory dance to rub it in a little.

"Two. Check it up." I pass him the ball. I'm more aggressive on my defense now, and I also have something to prove. My new vibe throws my dad off. I'm with him toe to toe on the trash-talking, too. He smiles every time I come back on him, and I'd be lying if I said I didn't love every second of it.

The closer I get to winning, the less he smiles. He seems really scared about losing this game. I can't tell if it's because he's losing to me, or because he'll have to meet Ray, but I don't care.

"Game point, Dad. You can stand aside. I'll make it quick." My exhausted dad just nods his head and assumes a defensive position. This time I dribble straight toward him. He does his best to try to steal the ball and to keep up with me, but I shake him, excessively and on purpose, with a quick fake and a shoulder to his chest. He loses his legs and hits the ground. I dunk the ball this time and hang from the rim. "Game!"

I walk over to my dad, who is sitting up, holding his knees, and help him to his feet.

"Good game, son. You better than I remember." He shakes my hand before dropping it.

"See? She's not sucking the life out of me. She's *giving* me life." I pick up the ball, dribble, and shoot it from three-point range. It actually goes in. Just plain showing off now. "Aye, Pops, try to find a chicken curry recipe. That's Ray's favorite." I grab my guitar and walk into the house without looking back.

TWENTY-TWO

Ray

10 DAYS

Sunlight floods my room. I sit up and scoot back against my headboard. Squinting, I think maybe I'm dreaming because Orion is standing in my bedroom. Then I scream when I realize I'm very much awake and it's Cash beside my bed.

"Whoa, hey, chill, Moonray," he says, laughing. "I knocked, but you knocked out. I didn't want to wake you up in the dark to see some big dude standing over you, so I opened your blinds first. So much for that."

"You think? You scared the shit out of me!" I tuck myself back in and face Cash. He's dressed in black pants and a white dress shirt, looking like a celebrity.

"What are you doing here, Big Head? Where's my mom?"

"She let me in. She told me to tell you she'll be back later than she thought, but soon enough to see you before you go out. I'm assuming you seeing ole boy again. He out the dog-house now?"

I roll my eyes and ignore Cash's question.

"What time is it?" I ask.

"Time for you to get up," Cash says, and tosses one of my pillows on top of my head. I grunt and push it away.

"Why are you so dressed up?" I ask.

"About to go to a funeral . . . one of my mom's coworkers."

"Damn. Did you know them?"

"Nah, I'm just going because my folks want me to go."

"Cash, why are you here?"

"My whole life, you never asked me why I'm here, now this the second time in a week. You only got time for New Friend now?"

"Whatever, Cash. My whole life, you never woke me up out of my sleep dressed for a funeral. What's so urgent?" Cash pops his knuckles and bows his head. Whatever it is, it's serious.

"It's Mel. I don't know. I'm starting to wonder if it's really forever with us." I watch Cash's face and wait for what he said to somehow make sense.

"You're breaking up with Mel? Why? Did she cheat? Did you cheat?" I swear the earth shifts just a little.

"Naw, mane! Why somebody gotta cheat? I'm not tryin' to break up. It's just that she's making all her after-high-school plans based on where I'm going to school. When I think about college, Mel is like the last thing I see. Shouldn't I want to plan with her too?"

"Damn, Cash. What's the reason? Y'all been together since fifth grade. Now you're talking about not seeing a future with her? Y'all are the only reason I marginally believe that love actually works for some people. I need to hear why and I need it to be good."

Cash worries his knuckles quietly for a moment.

"The weird thing is I can't even really say exactly why. I don't know. I just feel like we've always been together because we've always been together. She's fam, but I don't think she's it."

"Shit."

"I'm just saying, you hear all the time about guys who *know* . . . love at first sight . . . homie-lover-friend type stuff. I want that."

"Have you met somebody?"

"I wish it was like that. Then it would make more sense. I've always been faithful . . . you know . . . except that time you and me kissed, but that was dumb anyway and it didn't count."

"Correction, *you* kissed *me,* but no, it didn't count at *all,*" I add with a *yuck* face.

"I got blinders on—I don't see nobody but Mel. I just feel like I'm missing out on something . . . else."

"Poor Mel. Are you gonna talk to her about it?"

"I don't know, but if I break it off, I want to do it before school starts back—give us a chance to transition into just being friends with no drama."

"You think she'll want to be just friends?" Orion and I are only barely together, but I know I'm not trying to go from whatever we are to just being casual buddies. I can't imagine Mel being cool with that after all these years.

"She wouldn't be surprised. You should see how we just be going through the motions. I think we both know it's time." We look at each other and let the truth of what he's just said sink in. He sighs. "That's enough about me and my relationship drama.

What about you? I seen ole boy over here again. I guess y'all kissed and made up."

"That was all a misunderstanding—what I was crying about the other day. It's all good with him now. My mom is trippin' about it, though. She's trippin' in general these days."

"Good about your boy. What's up with your momma, though?"

I reach over and pull the framed photo of me at my father's grave out of the top drawer of my nightstand, as well as the larger photo with the writing on the back that I found in my mom's box. I lay them out side by side on my bed between us. While he examines the pictures, I tell him about the journals and how shady my mom has been about it.

"So when I couldn't find the journals, I went back in and found this picture. Turn it over."

He does.

"One, why would someone take this picture and give it to her? Two, why make a cropped copy and give it to me nearly a decade after the photo was taken? Why would she let me believe that she took this picture? Why hide the original?"

"Damn, so who took it? Who gave it to her?"

"That's exactly what I'm going to find out. I bet this has something to do with whatever she won't tell me about those journals."

"What does your boy think about all this?"

"Orion? I haven't mentioned any of this to him. There's no reason to pull him into it."

"Does he even know about your dad?"

"Yeah, I told him about that."

Cash seems surprised. As he should be. He knows that I don't talk to anyone about my dad. He shifts his weight on the bed so that he's facing me directly.

"Did you tell him your real name?" He narrows his eyes, more amused than accusatory. Even though Cash knows me better than anyone, a wave of agitation washes over me. "Uh, yes, why?"

He purses his lips.

"And why are you looking at me like that?"

"I seen his car parked over here 'bout half a day last time. It must be serious."

"You spying on me now?" I playfully shove him.

He laughs. "Naw, fam. Just being a concerned friendly neighbor. So wassup?"

Cash is the only real friend I've ever had. I mean, I've had other friends, and there's Bri, but he's the person I've always felt safe keeping it one hundred with. I told him my real name right away in fourth grade and swore him to secrecy. I invited him to the tree house right away and told him all about my father. In sixth grade, out of curiosity, we awkwardly kissed, then swore we'd never do that again. Not just because of Mel, but because we were like family and there was nothing there. Sixth grade was also the year I started to really feel the loss . . . not having a dad. That's when, I guess, my walls went up, and I started keeping more to myself. I can't front with Cash, though.

I start at the beginning and I tell him everything, like how Orion fumbled all over himself the first time we met and how I knew from that day that he was gonna be different from other guys. I tell Cash how Orion and I took turns running from this and then kinda getting comfortable in it.

"Out of all the guys I've hooked up with, Orion is definitely the coolest." I finish talking, and when I don't hear anything from Cash, I realize that I've been locked in a daydream staring at my ceiling. He watches me, half grinning.

"What?"

"See, that's what I mean. You can't even talk about dude without getting all weird in the face and staring off. I want my girl to be so in love with me that she gets like that. I want to want to be with a girl so bad that I'd get beside myself and do anything to make it happen."

"Back up, friend. I'm not in love with him. He leaves for college in like two weeks and I leave for school before that. It's just a summer fling . . . an exceptional summer fling. Nobody said anything about love."

"Moonray. C'mon, son. I know you. And I ain't never seen you like this before, even when that light-skinned dude from across the street used to come around. Exceptional summer fling, my ass." He snorts.

I roll my eyes. "You sound like Bri. Orion's just different." I definitely feel things with him. But love? "Cash, I'm not in love."

"You sure about that?"

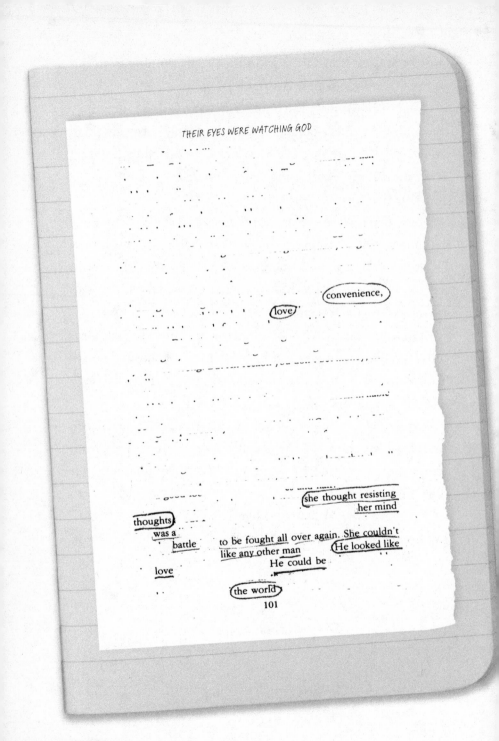

convenience,

love

she thought resisting
her mind

thoughts
was a
battle   to be fought all over again. She couldn't
like any other man   He looked like
love   He could be
the world
101

Convenience? Love?
She thought resisting thoughts.
Her mind, was a, battle.
To be fought over, over again.
She couldn't like any other man.
He looked like love.
He could be . . .
The world.

His gold chain.

TWENTY-THREE

Orion

7 DAYS

I've been restless for the past few days. I'm excited about Ray coming over tonight. She won't admit that we go together, but when she accepted my invitation to dinner, I knew she knew that she was coming as my girlfriend. I woke up early this morning out of habit. We leave for nationals tomorrow, and I was supposed to rest today, but I still swam some laps this morning.

The idea of spending more days away from Ray when we barely have a week before she leaves sucks. But I'm not sure what I can do at this point. Making tonight great is my best hope. I just know my parents are going to love her.

I check my watch. Dinner's in an hour. I finish my last set of plank holds and collapse onto my bedroom floor. Jinx takes this as an invitation but I nudge her off me. Eminem is blaring from my wireless speakers, but I'm cooling down now. So I swipe my cell phone off the edge of my bed. I select the playlist that I named Jupiter and Orion. It's all love songs that remind me of us. I hit shuffle, and "Total Eclipse of the Heart" by Bonnie Tyler plays. I remember hearing it the night we made out in Ray's tree house. I googled the lyrics to find it. The way our bodies were touching, and how she'd stop kissing me to look into my eyes . . . it was like in the movies.

A knock on my door startles me, just as my trip down memory lane was about to get me hype. I sit up.

"Come in."

My dad swings my door open. "Boy, what are you listening to?"

Before I can stop my playlist, he turns my speakers off and shakes his head. He surveys my swim wall of fame, and I take advantage of his inattention to put on a long shirt and plop onto my bed. Jinx climbs onto my lap.

Dad is still studying the Junior Olympics section of the wall with intense focus but somehow a faraway look on his face. I think he expected those ninth-grade moments to be my breakout year. He thought I was headed straight to the Olympics after that. I don't have Olympic dreams like him. I'm always striving to cut time, but I know my end goal is just to make him proud.

"You feeling ready for nationals?" he asks without looking at me. And the lilt of his voice says this conversation is going to be a serious one.

"We're heading there tomorrow, whether I'm ready or not." I laugh, attempting to lighten his mood. "Nah, but I'm ready, though . . . and you don't have to worry about Ray distracting me at dinner or whatever, so please don't even go there."

"About dinner . . . that's actually why I came up here." He turns to me then, staring hard. "This isn't a good idea, Orion."

"I knew it."

"I know you won the game and all, but meeting the parents just seems kinda serious, and I don't think you need to be getting serious with anyone right before you start college. Your whole life is ahead of you. . . ."

He doesn't get it. Maybe he just doesn't want to. My dad won't keep eye contact with me, but I look at him anyway. "The other day, you said you remember being seventeen. Do you really? I love her, Dad. I don't even understand fully, but when I saw her, I knew. Like the universe put her in front of me. And I think she probably loves me too—she's just very guarded about it. . . . Whatever . . . my point is, this is what is happening in my life right now. Regardless of how you feel about it. You said my whole life is in *front* of me, but my life is happening right now."

He stares now, eyes full of pity. "Son, out of all the girls . . ." His sigh is real heavy.

"You don't get to choose who I love, Dad," I say a little louder than I mean to. "I never ask you for anything. My entire life, I've only tried to give you what you want. I work hard at school; I go to church without complaining; I work hard at swim. I do all that stuff to be a good son—to make you proud."

Shock registers on his face. I'm shocked, myself, at how real I just got, and continue while I still feel courageous.

"Mom told me you blame yourself for what happened to Nora. We never talk about Nora and I never ask you to, even though I've wanted to. Losing her was the worst thing that ever happened to me, but I feel like I lost a big part of you that day too." I feel a tear coming, but I swallow it back down. Not here. Not with him. He wouldn't respect that, or see strength in it like Ray does. "It's like you closed off the part of yourself that made me sure that you love me. Do you know what it's like to be a near-perfect child and not be sure your dad even really *likes* you?"

I've never seen my dad cry before, but for the first time, his eyes water. It's like a punch to my gut. I don't want to hurt my dad's feelings.

"You're a great dad. You treat me well and you give me great advice. . . ." His face cracks into a hint of a smile at this, and I'm relieved. "But when Nora died . . . You have another child, Dad. We didn't deserve to lose Nora, and I didn't deserve to lose you. I've never asked you for anything, but right now, I'm asking you for something small. I'm just asking you to meet the first girl that I ever loved."

"Son . . ."

I'm not used to my dad being at a loss for words. I'm not used to spewing out so many feelings to my dad either. I need to lighten the mood.

"I mean, I'm also asking you to cook for her. But I did get your favorite banana pudding for dessert from that place you like so much. It's an easy yes, Dad."

His face softens, and he sighs heavily. But I know I've won. He musses my hair and joins me sitting on my bed. We've never sat on my bed before. I've never communicated so frankly. I feel grown-up and also really happy to be with my dad like this.

His barely there smile fades, and I get a weird feeling in my stomach.

"That was a mouthful," he says with a hushed gravity. "You need to know that I love you, son . . . more than anything. You gotta know that. I know I give you a hard time about being sensitive and with your cats and all that. . . . Your momma always talks about how happy she is that you're not afraid to show your sensitive side. That takes . . . something, I don't know . . . but I've never had it. I came up in a different time." He sets his hand on my shoulder.

Good thing he just complimented my sensitive side, because I'm pretty sure I'm about to cry.

"And as far as your sister . . . I got my own demons to fight regarding that. As long as I live, I'll regret the way it's affected you."

"I'm fine, Dad. I understand—"

He shakes his head no, so vigorously that I stop talking. I think I stop breathing.

"No, son, you don't understand." He stares at his hands. "Listen . . . I'm trying to figure out where to . . . About your friend . . . Jupiter. It's not about any kind of distraction or none of that. It's about who she is, son."

When did I tell my dad Ray's real name?

He gets up and closes the door. Everything that was warm between us dissolves. He sits back down beside me, but it's as though we're in different worlds.

"Let me start at the beginning," he says, all the color drained from his lips. "You deserve to know the truth. I was the reason . . . I was there . . . on the road that night. I killed Jupiter's father."

He goes on talking, but all I hear is *Jupiter's father* on repeat in my head. Later I'll have questions, but right now all I can think about is her. I have to tell her. Tonight. Even if that means we are over.

We are so over.

TWENTY-FOUR

Ray

I'm still a little wound up after the talk with Cash the other morning. What he said about my thing with Orion being love has got me all in my head. So I walked to the library this afternoon to get my mind off him, only to end up checking my phone a million times to see if he'd texted me. When I saw that he hadn't, I pulled up our texts and looked at our selfies . . . over and over again. I love that he texts them to me without me even asking. When I got back home, I didn't bother going into the house. I came straight up here to my tree house and turned on the radio.

I'm not focused enough to try to create poetry or art, so I alternate between flipping through a stack of recently finished pieces, and pacing around the porch, and stretching out on my blanket, daydreaming. Nothing takes my mind off Orion. I think about our first kiss and everything that followed. I'm in the middle of a steamy flashback when my mom's head pops above the landing at the top of the ladder, startling and also annoying me.

"Knock, knock."

"Really, Momma? You're supposed to wait to be invited up the ladder. You're trespassing." I try to temper the agitation in my voice.

"Too much space between us lately. I'm the mom— I wouldn't be doing my job if I didn't trespass every once in a while." There's a cheesy grin plastered across her face.

I look at her and try to remain expressionless.

"May I come in? I have lemonade."

"Is that a bribe?"

"Maybe."

"You can come up. Just sit on the porch, please."

"I'm honored." My mom climbs onto the porch, reaches across the threshold of my tree house and passes me a thermos of lemonade, and then just stands there, leaning on the door frame.

"What are you up to?"

"Just looking through some of my pieces from *Gatsby*. There's a definite theme."

"Really? Do you want to share?"

"You know what? Yes. Most of these pieces are about a sad girl who will never meet her dead father. How crazy is that?"

Her forehead creases. "Baby, I didn't come up here to—"

"I didn't invite you." I'm instantly sorry for my insolence.

If it upsets my mom, she does a great job of hiding it. Her face smooths over and she just holds my gaze with soft eyes.

"Okay," she says. "Yes, I know more about your father's death than I've told you, but, baby, it just doesn't make sense to load you down with pointless information that would only hurt you further. You lost your father. That's the worst of all of this. There's no reason to pile on more potentially painful details."

"What could possibly be more painful than the actual death of my dad? If there's more to know about that night, I deserve to know it."

"Jupiter Moon Ray Evans, you don't even want to go to his grave—you give me attitude about going whenever I ask. It gets you in the worst possible mood. Does Bri know when and how your father died yet? Obviously, you're still healing . . . why would I ever want to add to your pain, baby?"

"Obviously, we're *both* still healing. You still have y'all's wedding picture up. You've never been close to marrying anyone else in seventeen years. If we're not going to talk about this for real—"

"All right. Listen, I'm sorry for raising my voice. I'll tell you what you need to know about that night. But first . . . may I come in? Like, all the way in?"

I gesture for her to. "Fine."

She pauses after she steps across the threshold.

"I haven't been in here in a while. Full disclosure: I come up here sometimes when you're away at school. It's empty and there's no sign of you, but your father is all through this place. His hands touched every piece of wood, every window, every door. He poured so much love into building this tree house for you. When I'm in here, sometimes it resonates. I can feel it . . . the love. I can feel . . . him."

I feel a twinge of envy when she talks about him. Sometimes I imagine him so hard that I think I feel his presence here too.

"You want to know what else he loved?" My mom pulls a bundle of lavender from the vase on the desk. A silver velvet ribbon is wrapped and tied around it. "Lavender."

She unravels the silver ribbon, its sheen catching the sunlight from the window. She pulls the bunches apart and starts weaving them into one another.

"I'll make you a flower crown. When you were little you loved these." She pats the desktop for me to scoot near her and I do.

"Is that why you grow so much of it? Because he loved it?" One more thing she holds on to.

"Mm-hmm. You were so fussy at the hospital. I didn't know what I was gonna do with you when I got you home. You were inconsolable that day. We both were. I took you into my bedroom and laid you next to me on the bed. Your father kept a sachet of dried lavender buds under his pillow because he said they helped him sleep. I think you and I had our first good sleep right there that day." She and I made sachets all the time growing up, and still keep them by our pillows. "That's when I decided to learn everything there was to learn about lavender, which led to me learning about other medicinal plants and gardening and so forth."

Her fingers work deftly as she knots the silvery ribbon around the stem of lavender, then adds another, repeating the steps. Silence hangs there as my mother finishes weaving in bits of my dad around twigs and velvet ribbon.

"You and lavender . . . the two gifts he left behind for me. For you, he left this tree house." She holds the finished crown up to me. It's such a simple thing, yet it's so beautiful. I turn around so she can tie the crown into place on my head. Why hasn't she mentioned my father's love of lavender before? That's a simple thing to have shared. Why has she kept even that part of him all to herself?

"He really loved you, you know? Even though he never met you, he loved you."

"Don't you think I know that?" I yell, but I don't mean to. I'm just on edge. I'm somewhere between angry and grateful for her making me believe he was in the stars . . . for giving me hope. Bringing me to his graveside as a kid never sat with me the way she hoped it would.

Being in the tree house, on the other hand . . .

Maybe that's been the difference this whole time. I wonder what it would be like—going to see his grave on my own without childish hopes. Could that do anything? Maybe being there will be as meaningless as before. I turn a piece of lavender in my hand and look around at the smooth wood floor.

I should probably go. Just to see.

"I'm sorry I yelled, Momma. I need to go. Are the keys on the hook?" I pack up my art journal, a few loose pages, and the thermos of lemonade.

"Yes, but . . . it's so early. . . . Your dinner isn't until much later. Ray, we need to talk. . . ."

"I know—I just need to make a stop first. We'll talk in the morning after your shift." I climb down the ladder.

"Ray, the crown . . . ," she calls down.

"I'm wearing it. Thanks!"

I rush to my room and grab my cell and headphones, then toss them into my bag along with some lip balm and mascara.

I grab extra batteries and spot the graveyard photo with the writing on the back. I toss it into my bag as well. I grab Mom's quilt from the closet, and I'm heading for the front door when I catch my reflection in the mirror. *What am I doing?* Sure, I could stay, especially since my mom is finally ready to talk. But what she said . . . unlocked something. I don't know why it feels so urgent, but I have to follow my gut and go see my dad right now.

The flower crown that my mom made is so delicate. The lavender is a deeper purple than the lilac tips of my shoulder-length braids. The white linen tee and sky-blue skinny jeans I'm wearing make me feel like summertime—like a fairy. I glance into the backyard and my mom is just climbing down the ladder. I grab the car keys on my way out the door. I will ask her about the photo when she gets home in the morning.

After tonight, no more secrets.

━━━━━

The cemetery is pretty quiet for a Saturday afternoon. I make my way downhill to his grave. The flowers next to his headstone are dead or dying. I've never seen the honeysuckle dead before. Someone started leaving it around the time I was six or seven. We never discovered who. But I liked tasting the nectar, and used to look forward to that part of our visits. The lavender and ribbon my mom left look practically flamboyant next to the dry bouquet. I touch the silver binding.

"Look, Dad, we match," I say, smoothing the silver ribbon on the back of my flower crown.

I make quick work of setting out the blanket and getting comfortable, cross-legged with my lemonade. I place my cell phone and my art journal in front of me, between me and my father's epitaph: *A star shining brightly.* I sit quietly for a long time, trying to figure out why I'm even here.

"So . . . I make this art." I hold the black leather journal, bursting with stuffed pages, up to the headstone as if it has eyes. "I find poems in the pages of fiction. This summer, on my birthday, I found one about you. Then, for whatever reason, all the others seem somehow connected to this boy." I flip through the pages until I find the one I'm looking for.

"Here's the one I made on my birthday." I look at the page: my words and the drawing of a lone girl standing in the middle of a road. Is it weird to read poetry to a headstone? I glance around and begin. "'Smiling faintly, I'll wait desperately to please Mr. Nobody. Me, with him, standing alone.' That's from *Gatsby.*"

I take a few sips of lemonade and scan the cemetery grounds. "How sad is that?" I'm still the only person here, as far as I can tell.

"Momma thinks whatever she's kept from me about the day you died could hurt me, but I can't imagine what could be worse than finding out your dad died a few yards away from you minutes before you were born." I unravel the silver ribbon that binds the sprigs of lavender and tie it right back up again.

I feel like I've been holding my breath for ten thousand years, and these words to my dad are my first breath of air.

I set the lavender back on his headstone and kick my shoes

off. I'm more comfortable now, and words . . . feelings . . . things I didn't even realize well up like water in a dam, near bursting.

"Most of the poems this summer are about a boy I met, Orion. You'd like him, I think. I hope. I have no way of knowing what you'd like in a boy. Orion's the kind of boy I imagine dads would like." The words rush out of me, the dam shattering.

"I like him. Too much, I think. It's hard for me to feel . . . to like someone so much and not really know how things will turn out. You know? L-like what if I . . . I mean, like, I wanted to meet you really badly and I—I couldn't. When I was old enough and finally understood you weren't going to just appear from the grave . . . it . . . I left here with a gaping hole where hope once lived. I might as well have plugged it with stones."

I decided hope was foolish.

I was determined to never experience the simmering pain of destroyed hope ever again.

"Before, I told myself it didn't hurt, you know? Like I didn't care that you died. Like . . . I felt nothing, but nothing is its own kind of pain, you know?"

I look up into the branches of the oak tree. "That's how things come to me—in poems. Words and pictures in my head. I don't even fully get them, but poetry just pours out of me or plays on repeat in my head. That's how I found the 'nothing' that I was sure I felt. On the pages of my journals. Momma was putting this crown in my hair, and finally it just clicked. The whole time, the void, the nothing, the piece of me that I can't give to anyone has been *you*."

Tears come, and a breeze rushes past, cooling my cheeks. I picture my dad wiping my tears.

"Orion stumbled into my life and chipped away at the stones that walled up my heart. It's the way he looks at me, and how his compliments make me feel adored. And when we make love . . . I . . . I mean—" I bar my mouth shut, grossed out. Even to a headstone, talking to my dad about sex is not happening.

I picture my confession here stitching me back together. I know he's not here, but the longer I talk, the more I understand why people believe they can talk to the dead. Maybe some small part of me hopes it's true. Maybe I haven't given up on hope completely.

"I like Orion. I more than like him. I probably love him. I think I do love him. I knew it way before now, I think, but I've never been honest with myself. It scares me. Momma loved you and look what it got her." A hard truth. Maybe that's what I'm here for.

My eyes sting with the threat of a new round of tears, but I take deep breaths until the urge to cry goes away, imagining my dad holding me.

"I'm tired of being scared. I want to know what it feels like to be in love with somebody and to let them love me back. I'm going to see him tonight. Meet his parents. What if they hate me? Or think I'm not good for him? Or—"

Branches overhead rustle loudly, drowning out my words. It looks like it's going to rain today. I check my phone.

"I should get going. But I'll come back before I leave for school and let you know how it went. Promise." I stand and rest a hand on the headstone, my chest lighter than it's ever been. My head and heart clearer somehow. "Thanks for listening."

I unravel my earbuds from around my phone and pop them in, and I'm starting back for the car when I remember the photo in my bag. I take it out and study it. I peer around, wondering what direction it was shot from. Where the photographer must have been standing at the time. There's no way of knowing how close they may have been—they could have zoomed in.

I stuff my headphones and cell back into my bag and hold the photo up. In the foreground, there's a tall monument and what looks like a cherub just to the left of it. Whoever took the photo was standing near those two graves. I scan in that direction and spot the monument and the angel.

I walk across the cemetery, slowly, in quicksand, maybe twenty or thirty yards.

There's a stone cherub on top—it's a child's grave.

As I get closer I see a bundle of dried lavender tied with silver ribbon—Momma's silver ribbon. I touch my flower crown reflexively. My mind races back to my birthday. She started a second bundle as I was leaving. I thought she was doing so absentmindedly, but she wasn't. She intended to bring it to this grave. When I can finally tear my eyes away from the lavender, I find the name carved into stone.

Nora Leigha Roberson

What the hell? Why would Momma be putting flowers on Orion's sister's grave?

TWENTY-FIVE

Ray

I slip the picture into my back pocket and ride in silence to Orion's. Momma has a lot of explaining to do. Did Orion tell her about Nora? Did they talk that long when he was waiting on me before our date? No, she'd tied the extra lavender bundle before we even met. Maybe my mom saw it on the news, and with the dates . . . maybe she felt compassion. Who took this picture and gave it to her? I don't understand. I feel like I'm tiptoeing on the cliff of something, and it feels huge. Bri's phone goes straight to voice mail.

I pull up in the driveway and Orion is at my door before I shut off the engine. He's smiling, but his eyes are full of worry. I'm overcome with the need to wrap my arms around his neck and hug him, but I can't shake the feeling that something is wrong here. He pulls me into a hug and grasps my back cautiously at first, then wraps me up in a sweet embrace. Instantly, I melt and hug him back. When he releases me, I kiss him more deeply than I intend to. Somewhere deep in my gut, I feel like these moments—holding him and kissing him—might be the last. I was so hopeful before I saw Nora's grave. Now I'm just . . . not.

"Whoa. All that?" He's surprised.

"Yep. All that," I say, and suddenly wish we could just be alone tonight.

I grab the hostess gift I made for his mom and hook my arm into his. I watch his face as we walk toward the house. He looks away from me, skittishly, when our eyes meet. He's more nervous than I am.

"Hey. Um. Ray, after dinner, I was thinking we could go for dessert. For ice cream. We can walk. Just us. I want to . . . I want some time with you. To talk."

"Yeah, okay." I give his arm a squeeze. "Yeah, I actually need to talk to you, so that's perfect."

Orion's mom is model pretty. She carries herself like a queen. Her posture is a little too straight, chin held a little higher than most. The wind catches her hair with every step she takes toward us. She's like the perfect Black TV mom.

"Ray! It's so nice to finally meet the girl who has Orion all smiles these days." She hugs me, then squeezes. Pulling back, she takes me in. There's a warmth nestled in her gaze, and I wanna hug her again. Orion must get all his sweetness from her. "Aren't you easily the most beautiful girl in Memphis?" Something about her makes me happy that she's pleased with me. I think I'm blushing.

"Hi, Mrs. Roberson," I say, and hand her my hostess gift. "Thank you. It's nice to meet you, too. I made this for you. It's a lavender sachet."

She pulls out the pouch and her eyes light up. "How thoughtful of you. It smells wonderful. Thank you, dear." She notices my flower crown and beams.

"M-my mom made this for me."

"It's so pretty. Orion told me you were an artist. It looks like you come from a very creative family." She touches my flower crown and the tips of my hair. "Aren't you a beauty. I was just about to carry the food out to the patio. Rain is threatening, but I think it's a ways off. The weather is too perfect right now to be inside. Come along, dear."

"Yes, ma'am." I set my keys down on a bookcase near the door and stick close to her heels. Mrs. Roberson's face contorts into the cutest impressed face as she looks at Orion. "Son, you picked good," she whispers to him, but I hear and grin even harder.

The kitchen is beautiful, with lots of natural light. There are tall, slender brown cabinets and floral wallpaper in the breakfast nook. I didn't notice these details when I was here before. White rice, curried chicken, and veggies are spread out on the island counter, and it looks absolutely delish. Orion's smile is gone. His eyes are shut and he's taking a deep breath, rubbing his hands together. Why's he so nervous?

"I love her," I whisper to him. He plasters on a smile.

Mrs. Roberson hands me a large covered dish piled with rice. She picks up the pot of curry and leads the way to the patio.

"Orion, get Miss Ray something to drink and come outside," she says. "Your father is turning the corn on the grill, so we'll be eating real soon."

Orion's toothy grin is back, and it coaxes a real smile out of me. The butterflies in my stomach remind me that I'm not just here to fall into instant mom-love with his goddess-fairy of a mother. I need to impress his dad, too. He's the skeptic. I keep thinking about my mom's bundle on Nora's grave. Someone in this house must know her . . . or something. Orion said his dad used to take lots of pictures. Maybe he—

"Hey." Orion startles me. "Is everything okay? Is meeting my parents too official or anything?" *No, everything is not okay. My mom's putting flowers on your sister's grave.* "I'm good. I just . . . let me get this rice to the table." I do my best to give him a convincing smile.

I walk to the patio door, and Orion's tall twin from the future steps into the house. There's a salt-and-pepper shadow of a beard on his deep brown face, and his hair is cut close to his scalp. He's a work of art. He raises his eyebrows when he sees me, and his expression is friendly.

"Hi," he says, wiping his hands on his apron. "*You* must be Ray!" He reaches his hand out and I shake it.

"Yes. Hi, it's nice to meet you, Mr. Roberson."

"Nice to finally meet you too, darlin'. How's your summer going?" Mr. Roberson gestures for me to follow him. He sure is friendly to not be so sure about me and Orion.

"I can't complain," I say, setting down the dish. The setup outside is beautiful. A white tablecloth printed with deep green banana leaves covers the table, and a white porcelain pineapple is the centerpiece. The pool lights and all the solar lights in the yard have flickered on, and orange citronella candles are strategically placed around the patio. Cicadas hum in the background, and glow lanterns hang around us, lighting up the outdoor eating area. The perfect summer evening.

"Good," Mr. Roberson says. "Well, if y'all hungry, let's eat."

There's a little small talk as we all load our plates with fragrant curried chicken legs, rice, and green beans. Mr. Roberson uses tongs to distribute corn to everyone's plates. The end of a forearm tattoo peeks out from under his sleeve. A fish of some sort. Just as I'm about to ask him about it, he jerks his sleeve down. I look up at him and he's busy loading the corn as if he didn't just see me notice his tattoo and then rush to cover it. I get a sinking feeling in my stomach.

"The chicken is so good," I say, to get a conversation going with Orion's dad.

"Yeah? Orion told me it was your favorite. Glad to know I did all right. I googled a recipe."

"You did great."

Dinner is awkwardly quiet. Orion is sweating bullets, and every time I glance at him, his smile looks forced. I start a conversation about Orion's swimming and Howard, and that gets everyone going, but Mr. Roberson hasn't made eye contact with me since we sat down.

Orion mentions that I'm returning to boarding school and Mrs. Roberson lights up. Mr. Roberson simply looks down at his plate. He doesn't meet my gaze. His wife fires off questions about life in boarding school; Orion talks about his hope for the upcoming national swim meet, and even brings up his dad's time in the Navy, and how as soon as he was discharged, he'd grown dreadlocks and a beard in defiance of his clean-cut Navy requirements. I joke about their horrible sailor outfits. Orion's dad has a great sense of humor and laughs at my jokes, looking my way, but never once looks directly into my eyes. I get more brazen in my attempts to get him to meet my gaze.

"Did you get your tattoo when you were in the Navy?" I ask, as soon as the conversation wanes. His eyes lock onto mine, *finally*. "I saw a little of it earlier when you were serving the corn."

He shifts in his seat, and his eyes dart to Orion. "North Carolina, where Ann's folks are from"—he nods toward Mrs. Roberson—"after I was discharged."

"Can I see it?" I ask, in my most upbeat voice. He just forks rice into his mouth, and doesn't answer me. When he swallows, he sits there for an awkwardly long moment, looking at his plate.

"Douglas?" Mrs. Roberson nudges his arm, but he just sits there.

"Dad?" Orion chimes in with a nervous chuckle. "What's up, did you hear her?" Now part of me regrets being so direct.

"It's okay," I say. "I'm sorry. I didn't mean to . . . if it's personal or . . . I didn't mean to pry."

"No, baby," Mrs. Roberson says, then she turns to her husband. "Douglas, you're shy all of a sudden after all these years? You're being rude to our guest, honey." Her voice is playful, but also tentative. Orion chuckles again, and this time it sounds forced.

My heart is beating wildly. If anyone looked close enough, they'd see my heart pulsing at the base of my throat. The way Mr. Roberson looks at me, into me, as he slowly raises his sleeve causes goose bumps to sting my arms and legs. I don't know when Orion put his arm across my shoulder, but his closeness suddenly irritates me.

I brace myself for I don't even know what. Mr. Roberson breaks our gaze and I follow his eyes down to his arm. Orion leans over the table, and Mrs. Roberson leans just a little closer to her husband. It's a mermaid, a Black mermaid with an Afro, perched on the top of a giant fishing hook—no, an anchor—with her tail wrapped around it. She's topless.

My head is swimming from adrenaline or nerves or both. I don't know what I expected to see, but the anticipation has nearly exhausted me. I play it cool. "Wow, I don't think I've ever seen a Black mermaid before."

Mr. Roberson quickly pulls his sleeve back down.

"I'm okay with nudity if that's what you're worried about," I say in an attempt to shift the energy around the table. Orion chokes on his drink, and we all have a laugh.

"It was a long time ago," Mr. Roberson says, looking more relaxed now.

I look from one face to another, trying to decide if and how to bring up the graves and the photo and everything. Mrs. Roberson says something to her husband, who's smiling back. He chuckles at whatever his wife just said. Orion is wolfing down his food, starved as usual. Probably thinking about how perfect everything in his world feels right now. Meanwhile, I don't even know what my real world is. I'm in a fucking fishbowl—I can see everything, but it's all distorted, and I only know half of what is really happening around me. But someone here knows everything. The answers are in the smiling face of someone or everyone at this table . . . and my own mother. I refuse to leave here still in the dark. All I have to do is casually bring the conversation around to the graveyard. But even when I leave here, I'll still have my mom to deal with. I'm emotional. I need to move.

I scan the space around us, and my eyes land on lush vines jutting out from the fence beside us. Honeysuckle. It covers the lattice on the entire perimeter of that side of the yard as far as I can see. How did I not notice that before?

A drop of water cries down the side of my glass. *Deep breaths.* I inhale to soothe my nerves. *Just ask. You think something's up . . . just ask. If you don't . . . how can you even be around Orion?* Honeysuckle grows wild everywhere in Memphis. And maybe Momma brought too much lavender that day? *Inhale. Exhale.* Something about all of this feels wrong.

"Excuse me. I need to use your restroom," I say to nobody in particular. I press my lips into a polite smile, and my eyes land on Mrs. Roberson as I scoot back away from the table.

"Okay," I hear Orion say, but can't bring myself to look at him before turning and walking away. The closer I get to the bathroom, the closer I get to crying.

I lock the door behind me and stare at myself in the mirror. The last time I was in here, I was scheming on ways to hook up with Orion. Thinking back to that night only brings me closer to tears. I turn on the cold water. I let it pool in my cupped palms and raise my hands to my face, grateful I chose waterproof mascara. I do this several times until my eyes stop stinging as the urge to cry subsides. I look back at my reflection in the mirror. My face is dripping onto my shirt, but I don't bother drying it. I close my eyes and take deep breaths to steel my nerves. *Inhale. Exhale.* In my calmness, I picture the honey-suckle vines, green and white and fragrant, then brown and de-composing on the grave. *Inhale. Exhale.* The stone cherub with its blank eyes. *Inhale. Exhale.*

My eyes spring open. I gasp, and a catch in my throat causes me to cough until I can breathe again. The pages of Momma's journal—the flowers, the mermaid tails with the long, exag-gerated fins—the way they curved like an *S* that coiled into a figure eight. The faceless man. The white loc of hair.

My ears are ringing. I'm blinded by tears. I think of all the smiling faces I left at the dinner table, and anger wells up in-side me. If he's the man who helped them at the accident, why so much secrecy? Does Orion know? Did he know who I was this whole time? Is his perfect mom pretending too? Well, *I* can't pretend anymore. Without hesitation, I swing open the bathroom door. I turn the corner into the kitchen, and Lotus springs across my path, scaring the shit out of me. I stop short. He bounds up the first flight of stairs and disappears into the study off the landing. The last time I was here, Jinx was the one who startled me when I was snooping. *The study.*

I run up the stairs, throw the door open, and turn on the light. I don't care who hears me. I don't care who sees. The last time I was here, I thought I saw something on the desk. It seemed ridiculous at the time, but now I wonder. Nothing makes sense, so anything is possible. I very well could have seen a Crestfield envelope. Scan the room frantically, but there's nothing here. The piles that were here before are gone. The study is spotless.

Just as I'm about to turn and leave, I see a photo of Orion and Nora when they were children. Orion's holding her, her toddler legs flopped over the side of his lap. Something about the framed photo feels familiar. The sepia tone. Just like the photo of me at the grave.

I search the room again for mail, anything that won't make me feel like I'm insane. I spot a bin stuffed with papers.

"Ray?" I turn around at the sound of his voice, and Orion's face folds into near panic. "Ray! What happened—are you okay?" He wipes tears from my face and holds my shoulders and looks me over as if he's checking me for injuries.

"What happened? Why are you crying?" He hugs me to him and I let myself cry. "It's okay. It's okay. I'm right here," he repeats over and over again.

But it's not okay. I wrap my arms around him and squeeze him so tightly that my arms ache. I hate how much I need him right now. I hate how much this feels like goodbye.

"What's goin' on in here?" Mr. Roberson stands in the doorway. I release Orion and step around him to face his dad, whose forehead goes slack with realization.

"Ray?" Orion touches my arm and I shrug him away. Slowly, I walk toward his father. The fire and fight in me cool to ice the closer I get to him.

"Dad?" Orion sounds frantic.

I reach into my back pocket and pull out the photo of me at my father's grave. I hold it up to Mr. Roberson's face. The longer he studies the picture, the more rage wells up inside me. Eventually his eyes find mine again.

"Who *are* you?" I ask. I shake my head. "Who *are* you?" I repeat in a whisper, because it's all I can do. "You know my mom." Did they meet at the graveyard? Are they having an affair?

"Dad?" I hear Orion say.

Mr. Roberson tears his eyes away from me and glares at Orion. "See? I told you this was a bad idea."

I turn to look at Orion, wishing he wasn't in on this . . . whatever this is. "Orion. What is happening? *What was a bad idea?*"

He doesn't shake his head. He doesn't tell me it's not what it looks like. He doesn't say that everything we shared was all a lie. He doesn't have to. He won't even look at me. If he doesn't look up from his feet and face me right now, I'm going to rage. When his eyes, full of anguish, finally meet mine, that's when I know. Everything was a lie. Every part of myself that I shared with him, that I gave to him . . . the pain inside me is too much to survive. So I go numb.

I don't know what twisted situation I walked into the day I met Orion or how much he must have already known about me. Nobody's answering my questions and at this point I don't even care. I just need to get out of here.

I release the photo and let it fall to the floor. My feet are in quicksand, but I square my shoulders and will my body to walk out of the room. When I'm on the landing, I run.

TWENTY-SIX

Orion

I follow Ray down the stairs out of desperation, not knowing what to do or say. I follow her around the foyer as she frantically searches for her keys. My legs are cement. I look around and see her keys on the bookshelf next to me, and grab them. She snatches them from me. Reflexively, I try to hold her hand, but she yanks it away too fast.

"Jupiter . . ."

"Don't you say my name. Don't you say anything to me." It's barely a whisper—like she can hardly breathe. The pain in her face churns my stomach. I want to tell her she's wrong . . . that I didn't know . . . that I'm just as shocked as she is. I want to tell her that I just found out today, but words won't come. Her gaze hardens. Her words are daggers of ice, straight through my chest. "Lose my number."

My stomach . . . I think I'm gonna puke. I look around for my dad. He has to do something. This is his fault. My mom calls after Ray, but it's too late. The door slams shut.

The night air is chilly on my skin, the asphalt firm under me. I don't even remember coming outside, but I'm standing in the middle of the street watching as Ray drives away. As if on cue, rain begins to fall. Someone pulls me by the arm and I'm back on my doorstep, out of the street. Somewhere horns are honking and all I see is Nora's face.

If we are the stars . . . I'm some sort of supernova, exploded in a million pieces.

All that's left are fragments of who I used to believe I could be—Ray's.

My mom's hand is on my face. Her eyes are red from crying. She always cries when I cry. "Baby, you're going to be okay." She's warm, but I'm still shaking.

"I'm *not* gonna be okay." The words hurt coming out. "Ray is not going to be okay. None of us . . . we are not okay, Momma." My legs are gone from under me. I'm sitting on my heels, in a heap on the floor, holding on to my mom. I blink tears down my face, letting it all out. I hear heavy footsteps and will myself to get up. To wipe my face. To man up, as my dad would say.

My dad shuffles to a stop beside us, his red eyes shifting between my mom and me. We wait for him to say something, anything. But he just stands there, wringing his hands. "Why, Dad?" I ask with what feels like the last breath I have in me. "Why didn't you say something when you knew? Why did you let me love her? I sh-should have told her . . . as soon as I knew. I shouldn't have let her walk into this. . . ."

My dad grunts as he moves past us, out the door. My mom calls after him, but she doesn't leave me. He doesn't come back.

After a while, my mom's lips press against my forehead. "Let's get up. We all have a long day tomorrow."

How can she even think about tomorrow when the world just shattered?

"Mom, did you know?" I can't bring myself to look into her face.

"I knew about the accident when it happened. Dad told me about Ray before I came outside to get you. I had no idea he had kept in touch with the family. I'm gonna have a long talk with him about all of this when he comes home." She sniffs, and I think maybe she's still crying. "Come on, son. Maybe take a shower to settle yourself before bed. I'll sit up with you for a while if you need. Early morning—New Jersey for nationals tomorrow. You need to rest."

I don't want to swim. That feels too much like living.

I release my hold on her and slink off to take a shower. I stand under the hot water, letting it beat down on me until it runs cold. Until my eyes are out of tears to cry. I towel off, and in my room, my fingers graze my phone. For a flicker of a second, I think of texting Ray, then remember she asked me to lose her number. There's nothing I could possibly say that she would even want to hear right now anyway.

I had reached her. I was so close. When she arrived . . . the way she kissed me . . . something was different. And now she's gone.

I bury my head under a pillow, and Jinx curls up right next to me. "Jinx, how do I fix any of this?"

I can almost hear her answer: *You can't.*

TWENTY-SEVEN

Ray

And to think I let myself love him.

Too blinded by tears to drive, I pull off Orion's street and stop by the curb. The road is narrow with trees that create a canopy overhead. I'm alone except for a couple running with their dog and laughing to get out of the rain. I dig a nail into my palm until it stings.

Killing the engine, I try to stop crying. "Breathe," I whisper. But my brain won't quiet long enough to think. I exhale and a scream comes out instead.

I have an impulse to get out of the car and run, but run where . . . and from whom? My father's headstone comes to mind, the grass between my toes.

I can't run from myself anymore.

No more tiptoeing around Momma's feelings. I deserve to know the whole truth . . . so I can fully free myself from this bullshit.

My father's grave site plays in my mind and blurs into Orion's face.

I shake off the thoughts of Orion. His touch. The sweetness of his love. Was any of that even real? If he could hide his dad's connection to me and my mom—whatever it is—could he have faked his interest in me too? Was this some kind of twisted curiosity of his?

My hands shaking, I start the engine and drive toward the hospital where Momma has just started her night shift. She should have told me. Those flowers on Nora's grave . . . she *knew* who Orion was and said nothing. Just let me fall for him. The anger simmering in me boils as I park.

In seconds I'm walking through the hospital doors. I don't wait for the elevator and take the stairs to her floor. The nurses' station is steps ahead when someone gently grabs my arm.

"Ray? You're Rosalyn's girl, right?" An older Black woman in scrubs who looks vaguely familiar is caressing my arm now like I'm some kind of wounded bird. I look over at my reflection in a glass interior window beside me. I'm soaked to the bone and my eyes are swollen. My flower crown is sideways, and bits of lavender dust my shoulders like snow.

"Yes," I say, looking at her badge. "Ms. Davis, can you tell her that I need to see her, please?"

"She's tending to a birth right now, sweetie—is it an emergency? Are you all right?"

"No. No, I'm not all right. But I can wait until she gets home." I take off my flower crown and offer it to the nurse. "Can you please give this to her, and let her know I stopped by?"

Ms. Davis nods. I head down the hallway and don't look back.

Part of me is glad Momma was busy, because I probably would have started to cry all over again. I walk into my house and don't bother turning on the lights. I find my way through the dark into the den and crash onto the sofa. Suddenly, I'm exhausted. I close my eyes, but sleep doesn't come. I'll just get in my bed— deal with all of this in the morning. I head to my room as questions flood my mind.

How could she let me walk into Orion's house tonight, knowing whatever it is she knows . . . knowing that I didn't? Why did Mr. Roberson take that photo of me? Why did he give it to her? How long have they—

I jump when the house phone rings.

I blocked him on my cell, but now Orion is blowing up my house phone. My heart is racing. Twice more, he calls without leaving a message. It rings again and my fingers flinch. What could he possibly have to say?

Brriiiiiiing.

Ugh. I rush over, hand hovering over the receiver.

Brriiiiiiing.

But what would it change?

The ringing stops, and I bite my lip. I just want . . . I don't even know what I want. I'm so confused. I'm heading back down the hall when the phone rings a fifth time. *Ugh! Fine.* I dash back and reach for the phone, but before I answer, the voice mail picks up.

Beeeeeeep. It's my mom.

"Ray. If you're there, baby, pick up. I'm so sorry you found out this way. I heard from Douglas—Mr. Roberson. I was gonna tell you in your tree house, but you ran off. I really messed things up. So many things should have gone differently. You don't deserve any of what's happened to you. Are you there?"

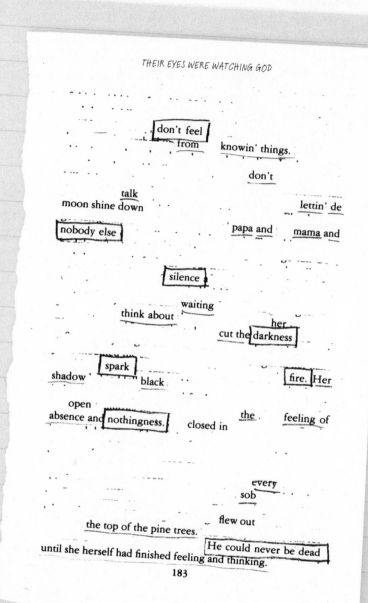

don't feel
from   knowin' things.

don't

talk
moon shine down   lettin' de

nobody else   papa and   mama and

silence

waiting
think about
her
cut the darkness

spark
shadow   black   fire. Her

open
absence and nothingness.   closed in the   feeling of

every
sob

flew out
the top of the pine trees.
He could never be dead
until she herself had finished feeling and thinking.

don't feel
from known things.
Don't talk.
Let the moon shine down.
Papa and mama and nobody else.
Silence. Waiting.
Think about her.
Cut the darkness. Spark a fire.
Her shadow, black, open.
The feeling of absence and nothingness.
closed in.
Every sob flew out the top of pine trees.
He could never be dead until she herself had finished
   feeling and thinking.

TWENTY-EIGHT

Ray

6 DAYS

It's almost six a.m. when my mom comes home from work. The house is dark, but I've turned on a lamp in the den. She closes the door behind her and sets her bag down. She freezes when she sees me awake and waiting on the sofa.

She retrieves the flower crown from her bag and sits on the sofa next to me. The flowers and tattered stems fill the space between us. If I look anything like I feel, I'm a colorless hag with eyes red and swollen from hours of crying and restless sleeping.

"I need answers, Momma." My throat is sore from sobbing, and the words come out in a whisper. She closes her eyes. "Please. Don't make me ask any questions. Just . . . tell me." By the lamplight, I can see tears wet her face. "Please, Momma. No more silence. I can't take it anymore." Inside I want to yell, scream, demand. All the things. But I'm so tired, I don't have any more fight in me.

"My Jupiter. I wish there was some way . . . someplace to start that would make all of this . . ."

As angry and as confused as I am right now, I still need her to comfort me. So when she extends her palm to me, silently asking for my hand, I place mine in hers reflexively. It takes everything in me not to fall into her arms.

"Let me start at the beginning." Her hand tightens around mine. "The night your father died, I was exhausted and about to pop. I hadn't wanted to go, but he'd insisted since it would be our last time going anywhere, just the two of us in the world. We went to our favorite spot about an hour outside the city.

"On the way back, I was supposed to talk to him. . . ." She closes her eyes, and a tear slips down her face. "I—I was supposed to keep him company, b-but I fell asleep." She takes a big breath and I squeeze her hand.

"The next thing I remember are labor pains, staring at the sky, praying that Ray would answer me when I called his name, and praying that help would come soon. Then I woke up in the hospital. And everything in between has always been a little fuzzy. But in therapy I did remember a man."

"Orion's father." Of course. He was the angel from her journal.

Her eyes widen. "Yes, but there was so much going on—so many details. I didn't put it all together until years later." This doesn't comfort me.

I take a deep breath. "Go on, Momma."

"The next year, on your birthday, I visited your daddy's grave. His presence was so powerful there, and you were so peaceful when I laid you down on the grass. I left a bundle of lavender that year and every one since. The year you turned seven, the honeysuckle showed up." She wipes another tear. "F-from Douglas, Orion's father, even though I didn't know it yet.

"I met Douglas for the first time when you were in middle school. He'd seen the news about that mural contest you won for City Beautiful. He wanted to offer a gift to you, for your future . . . for college. A city bus had struck and killed Nora while he was away, and he'd seen it as his karma—for causing the accident that killed your father. Seeing you, all those years later, felt like his opportunity for redemption.

"He gave me the photograph of you at the grave and assured me, quickly, that he wasn't a stalker. He confessed that he'd been there that night. He knew details, like the way your father's cell phone had been wrapped in silver duct tape. He knew, because he'd used it to call nine-one-one. See, Douglas had been driving a long distance on too little sleep and drifted over the double lines—*just* enough to see the car in the oncoming lane swerve out of the way. We crashed . . . flipped."

Tears well in my eyes and I try to swallow them back down, but they come anyway. My daddy didn't live to call the ambulance. He died . . . he died right then.

"I don't have to tell the rest, Ray. Really we don't have to do this."

"No, please, I need to hear it."

She tucks a hair behind my ear and laces her fingers back between mine. "He kept driving initially. He was terrified. He had a family at home. Orion needed surgery. He didn't want to lose his job—go to jail. But his conscience wouldn't let him leave. So he pulled over and ran back to us. Your father was taking his last breath when he reached us. He said he still wasn't sure he would stick around. But he did. He thinks his hesitation to help caused your father's death. He believes if he had stopped sooner he could have saved him. That's why he thinks losing Nora was his karma."

She's talking to the flower crown resting between us. "Your tuition. Douglas asked if there was any way he could do right by us. At first I didn't want anything from him. We weren't going to get your father back. But you wanted to go to Crestfield so bad. Your school counselor had said you, more than any other student she'd seen, were ready to thrive. So I told Douglas about Crestfield and he insisted on paying for all of it. I couldn't have afforded to send you there without it."

"So the scholarship wasn't really a scholarship . . . and the journal. You did remember. Why—"

"Until I met him, I thought those images were hallucinations. By then you were so detached from the graveyard visits, I didn't think it was worth opening the old wounds again."

"But Orion. You knew who he was. You knew I was about to . . . you watched me fall for him, and you said nothing." I pull my hand away from hers and find the window. The sun has just started to rise, casting a gray light over everything. "Only you *did* do something. You erased his messages."

I wait for her to deny it but she doesn't.

"Why do that, instead of just warning me? Why did you let me walk into this situation that has wrecked me, Momma?

Orion's dad killed your husband and left you—left *us*—to die, and you made a deal? You put flowers on his daughter's grave? You took care of his feelings, but what about mine?"

I don't wait for her to answer. I run to my room, but stop myself from crashing onto my bed. She would just follow me in here, and I can't hear her voice one more second. I grab my bag, check it for my cell, and dart back down the hall, out the patio door, and up to my tree house.

I can't believe I'm here. After all that I go through to avoid drama.

"What the fuck?" I ask the empty walls of my tree house, and sob.

TWENTY-NINE

Orion

4 DAYS

I slam my swim locker closed. Heads snap my way, but I ignore them and find a seat on a bench in the corner of the locker room, far away from everyone else. A swim locker room: the smell of chlorine, the echo of everyone's voices, and even the far-off sound of the announcers calling the races over the loudspeakers fry my nerves. My jaw is sore from grinding my teeth. I usually have to listen to music through my headphones to drown out the noise and stay calm. When I'm in a locker room, it's about to be showtime. I'm about to be at my best. But today, no matter what I do, I still feel on the verge of screaming. Everything rubs me the wrong way.

"O-Dog, bro, save some of that for the race," Hollywood yells.

I don't look around to see him. I don't answer. I don't respond at all. My insides are wound up so tight, I'm just not in the mood to play around. I thought I would feel better by now. Prelims went well. Our relay team advanced. I'm hoping for a good showing at the 100 freestyle prelims today. I still woke up feeling like shit. All I can think about is Ray. Usually, I'm loose after warm-ups, but I'm restless thinking about how my dad screwed everything up. I raced through this nightmare yesterday. I hope I can do it again today.

My parents and I barely spoke to one another on the flight to New Jersey. My dad had just blown up our family, my relationship with Ray. Mom was livid that Dad hadn't told her the whole story—kept her in the dark all these years. I was surprised that my mom still wanted to come, but she told me that nothing would keep her away from nationals.

Swimmers start filing into the locker room and more eyes move my way. Everyone's being friendly, but from a distance. I guess word got out that I'm not in the best mood. Somewhere deep down, I'm proud of making it here today, but how am I supposed to pretend like things are normal when I just found out that my dad is a liar and possibly a murderer? How am I supposed to race when my mom has one foot out the door? How am I supposed to breathe when Ray is at home feeling hurt and betrayed by everyone—including me? The last place I want to be is in this locker room. I'd rather be with Ray, but she won't even answer my calls.

My watch says it's almost time to report to the pool. I hop into a hot shower to keep everything warm. I take deep breaths until the only thing in the world is the sound of the water crashing against the floor.

The locker room is empty by the time I towel off and put on my team joggers and jacket. A buzzer sounds in the distance.

Ten minutes to race start. I sit and rest my head in my hands. Tears fill my eyes and I let them fall.

I lost her and it's not even my fault. She doesn't see it that way. She thinks I knew. Even if by some miracle we stay together, how can she come around and be in my house knowing that the man who ended her father's life lives upstairs? My tears come faster. He never said anything. All this time. How could he lie to Mom and hide this and—

"Aye, Orion, you good?"

I didn't even hear Ahmir come in.

"Ahmir, hey," I say, swiping my face—unable to hide that I've been crying. Mercifully, Ahmir ignores it.

"Hey. Coach said you haven't been yourself, so I just came to check on you. It's almost time."

"Yeah. Thanks, man. I'm good. Knock on wood." I clear my throat, still trying to pull myself together.

"All right, you sure? Aye, you got this. . . ." He puts his hands on both my shoulders and gives me a shake, raising his eyebrows reassuringly. "You good?"

I stand up straighter and nod. "Thanks, man. Thanks for checking on me."

"Cool. See you out there." He fist-bumps me, then leaves.

I pop on my headphones and cue up my race playlist, hoping it gets me in the zone. The bass pumps through the headphones and energy buzzes through me. It helps. Some. Outside, there isn't a cloud in the sky and it's hot. The stands are packed with spectators, and I'm slowly getting into it.

A horn blares and a group of swimmers dive in, beginning

the freestyle races. My group is up next. I run through a series of quick stretches and warm-up exercises in preparation for my race. I scan the stands for my parents, but finding them here is impossible.

The crowd roars, and I bend down and flick the water. I scoop a bit on my face and hands and inhale the chlorine scent. It usually transports me to the right headspace, where I feel ready to dominate. But scents of lavender are wrapped around my every thought and feeling.

I'm on the block now, about to race. My toes teeter on the edge and I wait for the buzzer. I steady my breath and visualize myself in the water, swimming; then Ray appears in my mind, swimming beside me, her hair wild and beautiful.

I can almost hear my dad: *Focus*. I shove away the images of Ray as best I can.

The buzzer cries and I dive.

Muscle memory takes over. I swish through the water like a shark. Hit the wall and flip. Again. Up for air. Ray's face. I shake it off and reach, arm over arm; my form is off. I can tell. I straighten up and push.

When I hit the wall and the race is done, I know before I check the scoreboard that I blew it.

I didn't hit my usual time. I was the last to the wall, and last out of the water. That's it for me. My shoulders sink and I paint on a smile, congratulating the guys who are going on to compete in the finals. Lifting my chin, I look for my parents. No luck. The crowd's stirring as the next heat of swimmers takes the blocks. I shower, dress, and go to meet my parents at our rendezvous spot near the exit.

"I know you did what you could, Orion," my mom says. "You worked hard to get here, and you competed under some pretty tough circumstances. I'm proud of you." She kisses and hugs me.

"Thanks, Momma." Hard as I try to be cool and chill, something about my mom makes me beam with pride and blush. She's right. I did work hard to get here. I did it. Even if I didn't win. I made it this year; I can make it again. I got full scholarships—academic and athletic—to most colleges I applied to, and I have more medals than I can count. I'm gonna be a Howard Bison, swimming with all bruthas at the best HBCU. I have plenty to be proud of. I gas myself up before meeting my dad's eyes. Hoping it's enough armor for the disappointment I'm sure awaits me, even though he has no right.

"Yeah, good swim, son," my dad says, surprising me with a compliment, "but I can't remember the last time you came last in a heat."

And just like that . . . he's back.

"I don't need this from you right now, Dad," I say, looking him dead in the eyes, shocking even myself. "Not today."

"Watch yourself, son. I'm giving you—"

"I don't need anything from you. I know what this is, Dad. *I'm* the one doing the swimming. I don't need you telling me anything." I'm sweating bricks. I never backtalk my dad, and we're in public: a double sin. People are walking around us, oblivious that our family is falling apart.

"Orion . . . ," my mom starts.

For a split second I feel a twinge of guilt. But I'm not apologizing, not to someone who has yet to apologize for so many things that I've lost count. No. I snap. "And, you know what, I'm not sorry for speaking the truth. Maybe speaking the truth is what we should all be doing more of." Dad looks both pissed and shocked.

I rarely say what I need to say—to my dad or to anyone. Except when I'm with Ray. Being with her was the only time I really went for what I wanted, did what I needed to do, said what I wanted to say. I lived.

I'm not being quiet anymore.

"Dad, I love the water. I love to swim, but all this competitive stuff I've done? All these years have been for *you*. But you're never satisfied. I made it here, among the top swimmers in the country. And even after the wrecking ball you drove through our family . . ." My eyes are stinging, but I don't care if tears fall. I'm not wiping them. Let him see me. Let him squirm in the face of my pain. I'm not hiding myself anymore.

My dad looks dejected, his face slack and the corners of his mouth turned down. If his feelings are hurt, good.

"You wrecked everything. Literally! My meet. Ray. And look what you did to Mom. She hasn't been the same since the other night."

She tugs on my arm. "No, Mom, I'm not finished. Dad, you only care about yourself. Nothing I do will change that. So I quit swimming for you, Dad. Living for you. From now on I'm doing all this for me."

It's a standoff between me and my dad. He doesn't say anything, so I turn to my mom. "I'm sorry, Momma. You guys go ahead. I'm gonna hang out here. I'll get a ride to the hotel." I look over at my dad, who still watches me, stone-faced. "I'm gonna go find my real coach and get notes on my race. I'll text you when I get back to my room."

There will probably be hell to pay when I see my dad again, but I don't care. I don't even know who he is. I guess I never did. He parts his lips to speak but nods instead.

⬛

When I get back to my hotel room and crash onto the bed, I check to see if Ray has texted me. Nothing. There's so much I need to say to her, just not in texts. I need to talk to her. But I want her to know I'm thinking about her.

I attach my favorite selfie of us, the one from when she came to see me on lifeguard duty—the sweetest day of summer. I hope it helps her remember where we were before all the mess with my dad. I hope it makes her remember what we were building. We look so happy—blissfully ignorant that everything was about to go up in flames. I hope some piece of her remembers who we wanted to be. I type *Us,* then hit send.

THIRTY

Ray

If art is an expression of what's inside the artist, or what the artist sees in the world, whatever I create this morning will be black. Void.

I take a random loose page from my bag. It's from *Their Eyes Were Watching God*. Janie stands in judgment by townsfolk who never really loved her. I scan the page for words to circle, hovering my pencil over each line, until words eventually call out to me.

storm, wind, sudden, boy
never, good, dangerous, neglected, no

The words I find are disjointed and lack color, reason, and light. I guess I shouldn't be surprised that dark words are the only ones I see. I keep scanning the page, starting over again each time I reach the bottom, in search of words that say . . . something.

took, move, fever, couldn't rest, anonymous

Maybe I'm not supposed to find art today. Maybe beauty isn't what my spirit needs. Maybe my spirit just needs truth. I put the pencil down and pick up a black Sharpie. I start at the top of the page again.

This time I find the words quickly, and where there are no words, letters present themselves. I blacken every syllable of the remaining words on the page until nothing but the truth remains.

The

boy

was too good.

to

be

177

The
boy
was
too good
to
b, e,   .
T, r, u, e.

THIRTY-ONE

Orion

2 DAYS

It's my first time in a long time coming home from a meet without so much as a heat win, but the best of the best were there. And I'm proud to be able to say I went. The coach at Howard emailed my parents and me to congratulate me on the accomplishment. When I read it, the first thing I wanted to do was tell Ray, but she's still not answering her phone or returning my calls.

Straight from the airport, I settle on my bed and strum my guitar, Drake lyrics floating around in my head. How to get through to her? But also give her space? Do I just let her go? A knock at my door gets me out of my head.

"Orion, it's me and your father. Can we come in?"

I hop up and open the door before sitting back on my bed. My dad steps in first, Mom on his heels.

"That music sounding all right," he says. "You getting real good at picking them strings. Who is that?"

"Drake," I say, and lay my guitar down beside me on my bed. "What's up, Dad—why are you here?"

"This right here. This hard attitude you've been giving me. This is why I'm here." He pulls the chair out from my desk and sits down. My mom hovers by the doorway.

"It's been really hard facing how I hurt you and your mother and your friend. Nothing I can really say can fix none of that, but I do want to say a few things. Your mother, I don't even know how she can still look at me, but she helped me get my thoughts together, so just hear me out."

He's quiet for a long while, like he's working up the nerve to speak. He glances at my mom again before he begins.

"Son, I been thinking about everything you said back at that pool the other day. I know we haven't talked too much since then. It's been real hard watching you be so cold toward me. I can't say I don't deserve it. . . . Listen, you one hell of a swimmer. Nothing I do or say can take that away from you. I'm sorry I haven't celebrated that, above all else, over the years. You set me straight, though. Your team and yourself the only folks you should be swimming for. I'm proud of you when you wake up in the morning—you don't need to do nothing to earn that, it's just a fact. I need you to know that."

"Okay." Hearing him say it cinches together pieces of me I didn't know were fractured.

He looks back toward the door at my mom, who nods for him to keep going.

"And as far as your friend Ray, I won't rush you—or your momma—to forgive me for what I did and for all the ways

273

I lied over the years. I know a boy in love when I see him, and I know you love that—I know you love Ray. And I'd bet cash money Ray loves you, too. Y'all didn't deserve none of this. Girls . . . women need they space when you mess up. I'm in the doghouse with your momma right now, and I accept it as my rightful place. It's my fault that you in it with Ray, and I wish that wasn't the case. I know what a big deal it was for you to even talk to that girl, nervous as you are—as you used to be. I've watched you grow from a boy to a young man this summer." He sets a hand on my shoulder.

"If you never swim again," he goes on, "I could never respect you more than I do right now for following your heart and speaking your mind—to me and to Ray."

Tears wet my face. My dad flinches, but he doesn't look away. Instead he pats my shoulder and pulls me into a hug.

"Th-thanks for saying that, Dad."

When he holds me, something heavy leaves my body. When he lets me go, I feel sturdier on my feet than I did a moment ago. I've felt myself getting stronger these past few weeks, but my dad's words somehow seem like the last boost I needed to really stand strong. Hearing that someone you love loves you . . . It's one thing to know, but to hear the words . . .

I can't let Ray go without saying the words.

"Thanks for putting him up to this, Momma."

She smiles with sad eyes and nods before walking away.

"All right. I'll leave you to your music, then," my dad says, and follows my mom out, closing the door behind him.

I lie back on my bed and look over at Jinx, who is on the pillow beside my head.

"Hey, Jinx. You think I should keep calling Ray, even though she's not answering? You think my dad is right—that maybe she loves me?" Jinx stops licking her paws and blinks at me a few times before returning to her grooming.

"Okay, well. Thanks. I think so too." I give her head a scratch. I wonder what Mo thinks.

Me: Ray still not returning my calls. I wanna go over there.

Mo: Damn. Look, she not gone make you stand outside. Worst case, she tells you to leave and don't ever come back. At least then she said the words and you know where you stand.

Me: How you get so wise, Mo?

Mo: I was born wise boi.

I lace up my shoes and run.

THIRTY-TWO

Ray

Outside my tree house, the world has come alive around me. The sun is already warming things up. Birds are everywhere; dogs are barking; there's the distant sound of children playing outside and the steady hum of morning traffic.

I've been making poetry off and on all morning. The thing about found poetry—any poetry, really—is that there's no room for fluffy words to bend or soften what's real.

Every word is chosen with purpose.

You get to the point quickly, and the absurdity of the fantasy or the hardness of the truth stares you right in the face, unflinchingly. It's cathartic.

"I'm going out for a little bit," my mom shouts. "I washed some fruit and left a kettle and some oats warming on the stove for you, Ray."

I keep shuffling papers, staring at the words in front of me, until I hear the Jeep roar. She probably doesn't really need to go out. She knows I'm hungry and have to pee. I've been avoiding her since she told me everything. I fell asleep in here last night and am still not ready to be around her yet.

I wait until the hum of the Jeep is far away before climbing down out of the tree house. I scramble to the bathroom, then eat breakfast. As soon as I unblocked Orion's number on my cell, I got a text—a picture of me and Orion. My eyes water looking at our smiling faces.

An incoming video call from Bri interrupts my daydream or nightmare . . . at this point, I'm not quite sure.

"Hey, Ray." Bri looks amazing, as always. She's calling from her bedroom, which is lilac with white furniture, just like mine.

"Hey, Bri." I try to sound enthusiastic and fail miserably. "How was Martha's Vineyard?"

Bri squints her eyes at me and cocks her head. "The Vineyard was amazing as always, but what's up with you? Trouble in paradise? Orion hasn't posted any selfies with you in almost a week."

When you're trying to keep people out of your drama, the worst thing that can happen is that they ask you what's wrong. I close my eyes and say a silent prayer that the tears threatening to spring don't. That doesn't work either.

"Damn, girl. What happened? Do I need to come down? I'll be on the first flight."

"No."

"Did he cheat? What the hell?"

"No, Bri. He didn't cheat. He just . . . he's just turned out to not be who I thought he was."

"Um, that's vague as hell. He got my girl crying—a *boy* got my girl crying. I need details. What did he do?"

More tears burst out of me. I thought I'd worked through these raw emotions in the tree house. Being pressed to say the words out loud is bringing everything right back to the surface.

"Listen, I know it's not your style to get too personal. I don't mind the way you keep me at arm's length, because I know that's the kind of space you need. But, Ray, I'm here for you. No pressure, but I want you to know you can talk to me when you're ready."

Bri knows me better than I thought.

"I know, Bri. Thanks. And I'll tell you everything when we get back to school, I promise. It's just so much to unpack right now."

"Okay."

"Thanks, girl." I wipe my face with my shirt and muster a smile. "So what about you? Same boy at the Vineyard or new boy at the Vineyard?"

Bri starts to answer, but the screen freezes and the audio goes out. I wait a few moments to see if it'll reconnect, but it doesn't. I close the call and send her a quick text.

> **Me:** Thanks for being a good friend. Turns out Orion's family knows mine and . . . it's just not good. It's a lot. I'll fill you in when I get to school.

I hit send and my shoulders sink.

Keys jingle in the front door, and I don't have enough time to make myself scarce before Momma walks into the house. So I sit there and hope that she's still in the space-giving mood and just walks on by.

She's not and she doesn't.

"Hey," she says right behind me.

I stare at the blank screen of my phone.

"You know, it's just the two of us. We are going to have to work through this." The truth in her words causes me to look up at her.

"Come on," she says, extending her hand to me. "Come sit with me under the lemon tree. We can talk about whatever you want. As long as we talk." I stand and lead the way outside without taking her hand.

I wait for her in the garden. She brings her fluffy meditation quilt and an extra pillow. I help her arrange the space and join her, both of us lying on our backs, faceup in the shade of the lemon tree. Lavender settles over me, reminding me of my dad. This is as close to being with both my parents as I've ever felt.

She wraps her arm around mine and I don't pull away. I imagine my dad doing the same on my other arm. There's so much I want to ask her. So many things I want to know.

"You never talk about him," I say.

"You're right about that."

"It hit me the other day when you told me about the lavender. Tell me something else about him."

"He loved giraffes," she says, an easy smile on her voice. "In college, he had these black posters in his dorm room that had motivational quotes and inspirational photos of giraffes looking off into the horizon or in silhouette. He had them on T-shirts and ink pens. And he was unapologetic and unashamed. He said that some people loved cats, some people loved dogs, some people loved NBA teams—he happened to love giraffes."

I roll onto my side to face her. "My giraffe is the only toy I haven't been able to bring myself to part with. I wonder if it's because of him."

"Giraffes. Lavender. Ray Senior is with you. He's all over you." She glances at me, her eyes smiling. She goes on to tell me how he dreamed of taking our family to Kenya once I was old enough to remember it. There's a hotel there that is a sanctuary for giraffes. At breakfast time they poke their heads right through the windows of the hotel and guests can feed them. "He had lots of big dreams for our family. He was an only child. Like you. And just so excited to have someone else in this world who was part of him." She sounds like she's about to cry.

"What else? Before me. What was it like when you guys were . . . falling in love?"

"Mmmm." Her eyes light up in the way I imagine mine have once before. He's been dead for seventeen years, and she still blushes when she talks about him. Maybe that's why she doesn't talk about him. Maybe it makes her miss him more. "Your father was an amazing dancer. I'm not talking about the trendy, popular dance steps you young people do either. He could dance to any music from any era and light up the dance floor. He danced with his whole body—hips, shoulders, even his face . . . he was so expressive. I was just two years older than you when we danced at a frat party off campus, and that was all she wrote." She laughs as if she expects me to laugh with her. I'm just not ready to give her that yet.

She doesn't get to be light and laugh with me after this needless betrayal. She said she was protecting me from the pain or whatever, but she knows how hard it is for me to trust anybody, and she watched me fall for Orion. Knowing what she knew—knowing what I didn't. It takes a lot for me to hold my giggle in, but I stay quiet.

"Loving your father was like loving myself. He loved me so deeply, like it was his life's mission to make sure I knew every day that I was the most important thing in his world. It's easy to love a man like that."

"I think I could have loved Orion. But you guys . . . you ruined any chance of that happening. All the secrecy. It just doesn't make any sense. And look, it didn't help anything. It made everything worse!"

"I'm so sorry, baby."

There's a long silence. My heart is pulsing in my ears. For once, I'm not fighting back tears. I'm done crying. I'm just so disappointed.

"I see how much you miss him," I say, only glancing at Momma. "I've heard you crying yourself to sleep so many times. I see you looking at y'all's wedding photo, and the other photos and bits of him you must have tucked away in boxes and in your heart. I didn't even question it when you didn't bring anyone around. Who would want to go through all that pain again . . . for what?"

"Girl." Her eyes are cast down now, tracing the pattern on the quilt.

"I mean it. I should have never bothered with Orion. I should have followed my first mind and left him alone." Just saying his name makes me feel pangs I'm not ready for.

"Ray." She sits up. "I don't keep men away because I was scared to fall in love, or worried about being hurt. I'm still in love with your daddy. The moment I have room in my heart for someone else's love to grow, that person will just have to be worthy of sharing that space with your father."

She plucks a piece of lavender and hands it to me.

"He's the reason we look up, you know," she says. "Whenever there was a new moon—when the moon reflects little to no light—he'd drive us out into the country to go stargazing. He never brought a book along or even a telescope. He wanted to see the stars as they were meant to be seen by us, from afar." She pauses at that, and we both smile. I can't help it.

"Orion was his favorite constellation. It's the easiest one to find." She takes hold of my hand, stopping me from worrying a loose string in the quilt stitching. "Speaking of Orion, he's been calling an awful lot this past week. When do you plan to talk to him?"

I take my hand back and rest it under my head.

"I don't know. I'm not sure what I'd say. I'm not even sure how I feel. He knew. . . ."

"Maybe you don't have to say anything. Clearly, he has some things he wants to say. You both about to go off to school. Do you really want to leave this unresolved? I can tell he's special to you. And there's no doubt that you are special to him. I can tell just by the sound of his voice that he really cares about you. First love . . . even summer love can be so magical, especially when it's real." She reaches up to pinch my cheek, but I move my face away.

"*Love* is a big word," I say.

"Yeah. It's a big thing. If he calls again, answer. See what he has to say. Whether it's enough to soften your heart to him, who can say. You probably have some things you'd like to say too. Questions you want answered. Just don't let things lie where they are."

"I'm still mad at you, Momma," I say without looking her way. "I'm just so angry. Anybody could have seen that I'd end up getting hurt. Yet you let me . . . it feels like you set me up. You're all I have on this earth, and you . . ." I don't want to cry. I don't want to give her my tears, so I stop talking.

"You have every right to be angry with me. Our love will withstand this and all things. I'll do everything I can to make us whole again. I promise." She rolls onto her back, and we're looking up at the lemon tree again in silence, arms twisted around each other, hand in hand.

Momma's words play in my head like a loop. *Loving your father was like loving myself. He loved me so deeply.* I can't help but think of how Orion made me feel the same way. Like I was everything. How easy it made it for me to fall for him, as hard as I tried to deny it. If a love like that sticks to you long after death . . .

But he knew. He knew what his dad did. He knew who I was. How could he do this to me? How can we ever be anything now?

THIRTY-THREE

Orion

I thought that by the time I got to Ray's house, I'd have a clear plan of what I want to say to her, but I'm almost there and still have no clue what I'll say other than "I'm sorry—please forgive me." There's no way that's enough. The closer I get, the less confident I am that this will work. I have to explain to her that I didn't know—I was going to tell her everything after dinner.

Ray's driveway is empty, but that doesn't mean she's not home. I park on the street in case the Jeep comes back while I'm here. Nobody answers the door when I knock, so I ring the doorbell. Still nothing. Maybe she's in the tree house? I scan the cove to see if anyone is watching before I slip around the side of the house and into the backyard. I walk quickly past the garden and the lemon tree and stop at the base of the ladder.

"Ray?"

Nothing.

"Ray?"

Still nothing. Maybe she's wearing her headphones? When I get to the top of the ladder, it's clear she's not here. I should climb right back down, but missing her and being in the place that is so much of who she is drives me toward her tree-house door, which I expect, and maybe hope, is locked. It's not.

Instantly, I feel like an intruder. My heart is racing because I know she wouldn't want me in her space like this, and if she catches me, my apology won't mean shit. She's clearly been in here today. It looks like whenever she left, she did so in a hurry, because her pens and Sharpies are still lying on the desk, not organized neatly in their corresponding glass jars the way she likes. And based on the pile of blankets in the corner, she probably slept up here too.

Several pages are scattered across the desktop. Most of them just have the remaining words blacked out. Others are totally blacked out, with the words in white seeming like they float off the page. Before I can stop myself, her poetry is in my hands.

She had wanted him so much.
And he was dead.
I can't help what's past.
They're things, you'll never know, Us, can never be.
He, dead, nothing but unfamiliar, and invisible.
She was trying to touch what was no longer tangible.
Unhappily, lost.
He, w,a,s, definitely gone.

Dead? Her father? Damn—or me?

Everything that went down at dinner probably brought a lot of these feelings back up. My stomach knots, recalling the pain on her face when she left. Why didn't I just pull her aside and tell her right then? Or cancel dinner or something? I check my watch. I've only been in here a few minutes, but I shouldn't be here at all. I need to get out of here but can't stop myself from reading more of the poems.

He was a glance from God, then, he was gone.

He promised because he meant to, he could never bore her,
she had to love, so wishful,
She wanted to know.

The trouble is, he didn't tell the truth.

The boy was pain.
And pain she knew.

These are about me.
She's afraid.
Afraid to love.
She loved her dad before she understood that he was dead. She loved me . . . before she felt I betrayed her trust. Just apologizing isn't going to fix this. I need to really *show* her . . . prove to her that I understand and that she really can trust me with all of herself again.

I hurry out of the tree house, shutting the door behind me. I jog to the back gate and close it securely. My phone buzzes.

Dad: Ray was here looking for you.

I read the text over and over again. She wants to see me. What did she say? What did he say?

I tap my screen to call him and my phone dies. *Shit.* I jump in my car, determined to get home to a phone and my charger as soon as possible. She wants to see me.

THIRTY-FOUR

Ray

ONE HOUR EARLIER

I've been parked at the curb outside Orion's house for nearly half an hour. The gate to their carport is closed, which could mean nobody's home or everybody's home.

Momma spilled everything, and now I need to talk to Mr. Roberson myself. Before I can talk to Orion.

I wrote down some notes about what I want to say. I don't know when or if I'll get to fix things with Orion, or whether fixing things means starting over or making a clean break, but if I'm going to be able to move on from this and get on the road to feeling normal again, I have to say everything I need to say.

I raise my hand to knock, but the door opens before I can.

"Ray," Mr. Roberson says, brows cinched. "Do you want to come in? Orion's not home."

"No, sir. I'm . . . I wanted to . . ." The words stick in my throat as I stare at this man's face. The face of the man who killed my father. An accident, sure. But it killed him nonetheless. I turn to walk away. "Can you just tell him I came by?" I can't do this.

"Yeah, sure. I'll tell him. . . . Ray . . ."

His voice is tinged with a note of something: sadness . . . regret. I turn back toward him and force myself to look at him directly. His broad shoulders are slumped, and his eyes are red. He hasn't slept or he's been crying.

"Orion's been trying to reach you."

"I know." I have to do this. If I'm going to have any sort of closure, I have to do this. I step closer to Mr. Roberson, and the shock is written in lines on his face. "Um . . . actually, I have some things I need to say . . . to you as well. I wrote them down, if you don't mind." I pull the paper from my pocket, unfold it, and start reading in spite of my nerves.

"I wasn't there. Well, I was there in the womb, but you know what I mean. I will never know what you were going through in those moments when all of our lives changed. You didn't have to help my mom out of the car. But you did. And you didn't have to reach out to her all those years later or offer to pay my boarding school tuition." I dig a nail into my palm and exhale. "You made some questionable choices that night, Mr. Roberson, but you probably saved my life and my mom's, too."

Tears streak his face, and it's odd, because I'm pretty sure Orion said his father doesn't have tear ducts. He appears like he wants to say something, but the words won't come out, so I keep going.

"Accidents happen. If you hadn't helped my mom out of that car . . ." I take a couple of deep breaths to keep myself from crying. "I'm sorry you lost Nora. I hope you can someday get to a place where you don't blame yourself."

That makes him choke up and smile.

"When something terrible happens, we want to blame somebody," I say, the words pouring out of me with clarity and a measure of peace. I didn't know that saying these words would be freeing. "I've been thinking a lot about the accident. I blamed you at first. Then my mom. I even blamed my dad for making her go out. The crazy thing is, I couldn't decide who I wanted to blame more. Sometimes there is nobody to blame, and you just have to try to make peace with that. Y'all's secrets and silence and lies made all of this worse. I've never been close to loving anyone. Orion was . . . I don't know if I can ever trust . . ." If I keep talking, I'll begin to cry, and I didn't come here to cry in front of Orion's dad.

I fold the paper and return it to my pocket. Mr. Roberson has wiped his face dry, but his eyes are still red. I force myself to hold his gaze.

"I don't really know what it looks like—it might take a long time for me to truly let everything go. I will miss Orion. He's the best boy . . . the best person I've ever known. Or . . . I thought I knew."

"You precious girl. I'm so sorry." His words are a congested mess of tears. His shoulders slump. He holds his chin up when a tear slips from his lashes. He's somewhere between agony and shame. "I'm so sorry."

"I . . . thank you. Thank you for that." I don't know what else to say that I haven't said. Jinx jumps out from behind him and rubs herself against my legs, making one long, slow circle around my feet.

"Jinx hates going outside," he says, wiping his nose and trying to regain some composure. "She must really miss you."

"Okay, well, I should probably go. Please say hello to Mrs. Roberson."

"Oh, she's staying with her folks in North Carolina for a while . . . until we figure things out. She didn't know . . . I'll tell her you came by. She'll be glad to know it, for Orion's sake."

I wave and walk toward my car.

"He didn't know."

I stop but don't turn back.

"He didn't know. I told Orion everything right before you got here. He wanted to tell you. He was going to tell you after dinner, but . . . well . . . My boy loves you. *That* I know. He's not the same. If you love him . . ."

I keep walking, faster this time.

He didn't know?

He didn't know.

It's the only thing my brain has space to process the whole drive home.

I pull into my empty driveway and park the Jeep. Not ready to be in the house just yet, nor having the emotional energy to be in the tree house, I roll the windows down and recline in the seat. A warm breeze whips through the car, and I turn my eyes to the clouds rolling slowly and steadily by. With each breath I take, a calm inches into me, as one thought runs through my mind on repeat: *He didn't know.*

The first thing I do when I'm finally inside is check the answering machine. No messages. I check my phone again and, just as I wished, there's a text from Orion.

> **Orion:** Jupiter, my phone died. I wanted to call you. My dad told me you came by. I came to see you too, but you weren't home. I guess you were here. I'm sorry about how upside down everything is now and about not telling you right away. There are things I need to say to you, but I need to say them to you in person, so you can see how much you mean to me. Come to open mic, where we had our date. Tomorrow night, 8:15. I'm not trying to recreate our first date or anything like that. I know it's gonna take more than that to fix this. I pray to God we can . . . I . . . can fix this. I might not get to call you before then. Please tell me you don't hate me. Please tell me you will be there. P.S. Jinx and Lotus miss you too.

Orion's handsome, smiling face is sandwiched in between his two cats in the photo attached. I laugh at the sight, and then cry a little, remembering how easy it was to be with him and knowing deep down that it'll probably never be that way again.

The impulse to reply and spill my heart out to him and tell

him how much I miss him is strong, but the pain is still too raw. Do I really want to open up to him again, just for something else to come between us down the road? This hurts too much. Maybe I should just cut my losses and go on with my life. I let myself love him, and look where it's left me.

> **Me:** Orion, I don't hate you. I hate the situation. I miss you, too, but everything is just so fucked up now. I just don't see how we can come back from this. I leave for school the day after tomorrow and have a lot of packing left to do. This summer has been the best summer and the worst summer of my life. Whatever happens, you should know that the best parts were with you. I can't promise you that I'll make it to open mic. I'll think about it.

I hit send and collapse onto my bed. Brick by brick, my head starts to rebuild the wall around my heart. The longer I lie here, the stronger the wall gets, and the safer and lonelier I start to feel. Yet my heart still longs for Orion, who is everything . . . wrapped in barbed wire.

THIRTY-FIVE

Orion

What was I thinking?

I had zero plans to do anything at open mic—ever—in my life. But I can't ignore what I saw in Ray's poems—how vulnerable she is and how much she sacrificed to even hang with me. I have to show her in a big way that I'm willing to make myself vulnerable to be with her, too.

She may never express her feelings to me the way she expresses herself in her art, but I have to show her that she can trust me. I need her to feel my love. I hope she gets to, before she leaves for school.

I pull into the Target parking lot and whip out my phone. I search *How to make a CD mixtape* and *DIY CD sleeves*.

Inside the store, I toss blank CDs, heavy card-stock paper, tape, and a pack of colorful Sharpies into my basket. On my way to check out, I swing by the men's aisle. I want to pull out all the stops tomorrow. I don't wear cologne, mainly because I swim every day, which means I shower constantly. I generally smell like soap and chlorine. But this big night calls for something extra . . . more deliberate.

I scan the scented body washes. I quickly browse through confusing scents like "bearglove" and "swagger," but ultimately go with a simple bottle that just says sandalwood. When I get home, I don't bother waiting for the gate to the carport to open. I park on the street and run through the front door, startling my dad, who almost jumps up from the couch.

"What the hell?"

"Sorry, Dad. I need to use your PC in your study for about an hour, maybe more."

"Okay, sure. What you got cooking?" He cranes for a better view of my Target bag.

"A plan to get Ray back," I say, winded but ecstatic.

He chuckles. "Well, all right, then."

I dash past him and up the stairs, jumping over Lotus on his step, and into my room. I put the body wash in my bathroom and find my copy of *Black Boy* by Richard Wright on my bookshelf. I toss it into the Target bag and head down to my dad's office.

Before I get started, I text Mo.

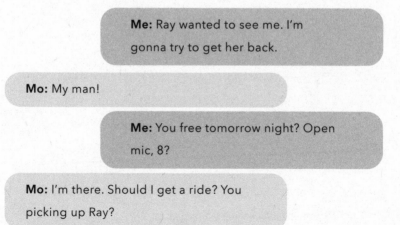

Me: Ray wanted to see me. I'm gonna try to get her back.

Mo: My man!

Me: You free tomorrow night? Open mic, 8?

Mo: I'm there. Should I get a ride? You picking up Ray?

Me: Not 100% sure she's coming. I'll pick you up.

Mo: I thought she wanted to see you.

Me: I'll fill you in later.

I power on the computer and wait for the screen to come alive. I don't know how any of this will turn out, but I'm going to pour as much of my heart and soul into it as I can muster. I just hope she shows up.

THIRTY-SIX

Ray

THE LAST DAY OF SUMMER

It's late afternoon and I'm staring at a room full of stuff that somehow has to be shoved into a suitcase before I leave for school tomorrow. I had the selfies Orion sent me printed at Walgreens. Our YMCA poolside photo smiles at me from my lap, next to one of Momma's scratch-made lemon pastries. A peace offering. I take another bite, staring at Orion's face. Maybe it was just meant to be a summer romance. Maybe it was meant to exist for a moment, leave its mark, and . . . disappear.

I finish eating and am feeling antsy. I'm home alone and pacing through the house aimlessly, looking for something to do. I don't feel like packing or watching TV. I don't feel like reading or creating, which reminds me that in my rush to go to Orion's house yesterday, I didn't pack up the tree house. I can do that now.

The pieces of my birthday poem from weeks ago are still arranged just how I left them—like a sad puzzle made up of the sad pieces of me. I wonder if Orion came up here looking for me, or if he just called up from the yard. If he did come in,

I wonder what he saw . . . really saw in these pages. Part of me hopes he did see.

A ray of sunshine peeks at me from the window, and I lean in to feel it on my face. The garden rustles, lavender dancing. I imagine my father's whisper on the wind.

I grab my pencil and fill in the last page of poetry in my summer journal.

Love ends, but . . .

I tap my pencil for several moments, but the words won't come.

<hr/>

It's almost closing time when I press my back against my father's headstone, and the moon is high in the still-bright sky. The dead honeysuckle vines have been cleared away, but the dried lavender is surprisingly still here. It's still fragrant and calms me instantly. I kick off my shoes and dig my toes into the earth, willing myself to feel him.

"I told you I'd come back and tell you about the dinner." I snort. "You'd never believe how that went . . . or maybe you would." I glance around me, and as far as I can tell, I'm the only living soul around. I tell him everything, sparing no details. When I get to the actual dinner, I get a little emotional, but mostly I relay the whole thing like a recap of one of Tyler Perry's soap operas. When I'm finished, I'm sad, but there are no tears, which is . . . oddly healing.

I graze the grass around me with my fingertips and lie back, looking up at the cloudless blue sky. "I wish you didn't die." A hollowness settles into my gut and I have to struggle to fill my lungs. I've thought countless variations of this inside, almost constantly, especially in the summers. I've expressed it in many forms through my poetry. Somehow, speaking the words gives them more power. "I wish I got to see you love Momma. I wish I got to feel you love me."

I let the truth of my words wash over me. For a few moments, I imagine what my life would have been like—who I would be—had my parents just stayed home that night.

"If I'd known you, the way Momma got to, I think I would have recognized how safe Orion is . . . I might have trusted him sooner. But it's no use thinking about what could have been. I think I'm ready to focus on what is."

The wind picks up and I look to the sky. I'm so tired of feeling alone.

"He invited me to open mic tonight, but I'm afraid . . . to love him, because that means risking losing him. And that's scary as hell."

I let the silence sit on the humid air, and Momma's words play on repeat in my head. I'm a product of her choosing love, despite the risk. She is proof of the power of true love even after her true love is gone.

My fingers itch for my journal, but I remember I didn't bring it. Now I know the end of my poem. "Thank you, Dad." I hop up, dusting off my pants. "I don't think I'll be back here before I head to school. But I'll look up more often and tell you about how I'm doing. Promise."

THIRTY-SEVEN

Ray

I picked one of my favorite party dresses, a neutral one with a sparkly tan crew-collar tee for the bodice and a gray layered tulle skirt that stops just above my knees. The silver-banded waist ties in the back. I'm standing in front of my mom in the hallway trying to decide which shoes to wear.

"Chucks or gladiators?" I alternate standing on one foot, so she can see the outfit with each shoe. There's still a strange, new, hesitant energy between us. Hopefully I can feel the ease of our friendship again one day.

"Gladiators. You wear those Chucks all the time. Plus the dark leather sandals almost match your skin tone and really showcase those legs. Here, you should wear this. Can I tie it on for you?"

Momma holds the flower crown she made for me, now fixed. We step into the bathroom so I can help position it before she ties it on. The last time this flower crown was between us, I wasn't sure I could ever be friends with her again. We still have some rebuilding to do, but I know that she's always got my back.

My cell phone rings, and it's Bri, FaceTiming. I tilt my chin up and look sidelong at the camera before I connect the video call.

"Okay, purple ombré braids with the matching flower crown! You giving woodland fairy princess. Let me see the outfit." I turn the camera around to show my reflection in the mirror. "I see you!"

Bri's enthusiasm makes me laugh hard and blush.

"Thanks, girl," I say, cheesing.

"I know you're about to go, but I just had to see you before you head out. I'm glad you decided to go."

"Yeah, me too."

"Call me *as soon as* you get home tonight, no matter what time. I want to hear every detail about how y'all end the summer. Promise?"

"Promise."

I check myself out in the mirror. She's right. The flower crown and the sparkles from my dress do give fairy vibes. I enhance the look by drawing a tiny silver star high on my cheekbone, just outside my eye, with a metallic liquid eyeliner. I smudge a deeper purple eyeshadow on the middle of my eyelids with my finger, and that's the only makeup I'm wearing tonight. A little lip balm and I'm good to go.

"All right, I'm going. I shouldn't be out too late," I say to Momma before I leave.

"If you are, I know you're in good hands. Have fun, baby."

She kisses my cheek and I'm out the door.

I'm running a few minutes behind, hard as I tried to hustle here. But any fears I had about missing whatever Orion wanted me to see vanish as soon as I'm inside the door.

Orion is taking the stage.

I go dizzy for a split second, blinking until I believe what I'm seeing.

With his guitar strapped across his back, he stands in front of the microphone, holding papers. His hands tremble.

The place is pretty crowded, so I snake my way in a little farther, keeping to the edge of the room. If he looks a hair to the right, though, he'll see me.

His voice is shaky in the mic, but it stills me all the same. Orion—sweet, *I never sing in public* Orion—is onstage.

"A special person once told me that no one knows the last day of childhood while it's happening. You never get a chance to say goodbye. It just fades away without you even noticing. One day you look up, and it's gone."

A wave of chatter in agreement erupts from the crowd.

"I know, right?" he says, chuckling. "She was always saying deep stuff like that." He looks down for a few seconds. "You rarely remember last times. Them first times, though?" A beautiful smile washes over his face, and he shakes his head as the laughter around us crescendoes. His voice is more even, and his foot is still bouncing, but less. "Until the day I die, I will remember every single first we shared."

There is a smattering of grunts of approval from the audience. A warm glow settles in my stomach.

"She writes these poems . . . finds them in the pages of

books. She explained to me that she liked to find beauty—poetry—in the pages of the story right when things start to fall apart. I gave it a try, but I like the part of the story where things start looking up. I found these poems on the pages of my favorite book, *Black Boy* by Richard Wright."

Heads in the audience nod.

"It's funny what you can do in a room full of people that you can't seem to do in front of one person." Laughter bursts from the audience and a few people shout out *Love Jones*—the film that line is from.

"On these pages, Wright figured out how to outsmart his illiterate grandmother, who'd outlawed reading in her house, to get her to support him reading. I'm a huge fan of optimism. This whole night is an exercise in optimism for me. Because what's the point of living if you can't have hope?"

Applause.

"Okay, so this girl, sh-she changed me. Knowing her . . . loving her made me a better version of myself. I have a poem to share and a song I'm gonna try to sing. So bear with me." He takes a deep breath and reads.

This heart in agony.
The air is not enough to satisfy Me.
She had already given Me, lucky Me, her proMise
    in her eyes.
I waited anxiously.
For the first tiMe in My life, I was claiMed by love
    I hungered for.

Tall.

Black.

A dime.

His gaze darts in my direction and his eyes land on mine. A hint of a smile turns up the sides of his mouth. The emotion in his eyes almost brings me to tears. He recites the last line of his poem.

I want you.

Hoots and yells, applause and whistles, fill every inch of the cafe and can probably be heard outside. A few people follow his gaze and realize I'm the girl. I flash hot, then cold again, and I can't stop blushing.

"O-okay . . . now for the song." He clears his throat. "I—I've never done this in front of anyone before." Orion strums his guitar and wipes sweat from his brow, and it takes everything in me not to shout, "You can do it!"

"This song goes out to the person who lit up my summer days and kept my summer nights aglow. To my girl from outer space. If you look up on a clear night, you might see her in the sky." He winks at me. Now everybody knows I'm her. I look over and see Cash and Mel smiling my way. Orion must have invited them. Then I spot Mo recording in my direction. *Ha, wow.*

Orion begins to play a sweeping intro on his classical guitar, and the notes melt on the air. I sway, watching his fingers glide over the strings, so swift and sure. He sings the first line.

Of course he's singing "Find Your Love" by Drake, his favorite singing rapper. He keeps the rhythm, tapping the body of his guitar.

His eyes are closed, and I remember how he told me that this comforts him—to feel invisible in the spotlight. I can't imagine how hard this must be for him: to be singing, so beautifully and so passionately, in front of this crowd. They don't know how shy he is about singing. He's doing this for me.

The poem. The thought of him combing through those pages, finding the words, makes me want to cry. He went out of his way—out of his comfort zone—just to reach me.

He's facing his greatest fear.

And he knows that for me to be with him, I will have to face mine, too.

Reflexively, I wrap my arms around myself and squeeze. I'm not cold or anything. My mind is racing with one million what-ifs, and I'm overcome with too many emotions to manage. I need to feel grounded—to get myself out of my head, to be present, right here, for every second of Orion's song.

There is so much tenderness on his face as he sings the chorus. My heart swells with every note, verse, and refrain. As the song comes to an end, his eyes find mine again.

"'I bet if I give all my love, then nothing's gonna tear us apart.'"

My ears are ringing, either from the applause in the room or from the blood rushing to my head. I will my hands to move and clap for Orion. Something wet drips on my chest, and I realize that I'm crying. I'm aware of faces turning my way and people patting me on the back, but it all feels like it's happening underwater. I need fresh air.

I don't know how I get there, but eventually, I'm outside, pacing, filling my lungs and trying to calm my nerves. There are things I need to say, and I want to be calm enough for him to hear me. After a few more deep breaths, I regain my composure. And thank goodness, because Orion comes strolling out the building with his guitar across his chest.

"Hey, I'm so glad you came." He rubs his palms on the outside of his jeans.

We both start talking at the same time.

"I—please let me go first," he says, and I nod. "Ray . . . Jupiter . . . I'm so sorry. That night, I wanted to tell you. I planned to tell you. My dad told me right before you got there, and I didn't know what to do. If I had known . . ." He shakes his head.

"Orion, listen, you don't have to . . . Your dad told me you didn't know until that night. I know you'd never hurt me. Not on purpose. When I left that night, I was so angry and confused. I thought we'd never . . ." Orion winces as if my words have stabbed him. My hands ache from wringing them, but that's the only thing giving me the strength to say what I'm about to say. "I thought I'd never see you again. I don't know if I could survive that. You made me . . . I need you. But I can't see any clear path forward for us. That scares me more than anything. How do we even begin to . . ."

Orion removes his guitar and rests it against the building. He steps forward, and I ease into his embrace, sliding my arms around him. I have to force myself to cut the hug short—it feels too good, and I'm still so confused about what we are . . . what we can be now.

"That seems like a good place to start," he says.

"You smell good."

"Thanks. You look pretty," he says, and gently pinches my chin. My insides turn into Jell-O.

"Thanks. I'm gonna go out on a limb and guess you sing a little bit?"

He smiles and covers his face.

"Nah, don't get shy now—we're not going back there. It's a new day."

We laugh, and he reaches out, lacing his fingers into mine.

"Is this okay?" he asks.

I nod. He tugs my arm, and we take slow, measured steps toward the end of the sidewalk away from the small crowd accumulating outside the cafe.

"Seriously, that was amazing," I say. "Drake would be jealous of the way you were hitting those notes."

He laughs, hard, and the muscle in his arm tenses. I go warm all over.

"I did it for you, so as terrified as I was, how *I* felt wasn't the most important thing."

I look at him, and his gaze is so full of love and longing. "And the poetry . . . Orion, it was perfect."

"I learned from the best," he says.

"Thank you, for everything," I say as he stops walking and pulls me to him. His arms are tight around me, and I swim in his eyes, working up the nerve to say what I need to say to him.

"Hey, I made this for you." He motions behind him, and

Mo emerges from the crowd. Without a word, Mo gives Orion something, salutes us both, and then goes back into the building. Orion flashes a broad grin and hands me what appears to be a CD wrapped in a paper jacket. "It's a mix, so we can always remember this summer. I have the playlist on my phone. I'll send it to you. But I know you like CDs, so . . ."

I run my thumb under the flap, and the CD jacket opens up to a four-pointed star, surprising me with a collage print of all our selfies. It's like Jupiter-and-Orion wrapping paper. A laugh escapes my chest.

"What?" I flip the jacket over and read a few of the songs on the track list, which he has handwritten with a fine-tip pen. I see a Sade song and blush, and "XO" by Beyoncé, and I feel so seen, so understood, and so loved right now. I climb up on the curb so we're eye to eye.

"Thank you. You did good," I say.

"All I ever want to do is do good by you."

"Where did you come from?" I repeat a question that he's asked me before.

"Outer space," he says, repeating my answer, which makes me giggle. Then sadness sweeps through me.

"How . . . Orion . . . I leave for school tomorrow."

"Then let's make the most of tonight."

"So we're gonna figure it out?"

He presses his forehead to mine. "Yes, we'll figure it out. I love you, Jupiter." At the sound of his voice, saying those words to me, it's like something in the universe that has been wrong all along is set right. But how can I trust it?

"Orion, I'm so scared."

"I know. But I'm right here with you. I'll be brave for both of us, until you're ready. You can trust my love, Jupiter. You can trust me." My head checks in with my heart for a space willing to let love back in.

"I love you." The words rush out of me, joining his truth with my own.

It turns out they're the easiest three words to say to Orion. So I say them again, and press a kiss against his lips.

"I loved you the minute I saw you, girl."

"I know."

Smiles are plastered on our faces as everything else fades away. We are all that exists in the universe. His arms are locked tight around me, and my hands cup his big, handsome face.

In his eyes, I see the moonlight and Jupiter—tragically unlucky, hopelessly unsure, and loved.

Love ends, but . . .
While it shines, you stand in the sun.

AUTHOR'S NOTE

I created the poems for this book before I ever had a story. I knew the main character would be a teen Black girl, but I had no idea who she was. I knew she would create poetry, so I wrote a poem (the one performed on Jupiter and Orion's date night) and I kept exploring. I considered haikus and rhymes before landing on found poetry. I sat down with three of my favorite old books from my school years—*The Great Gatsby, Their Eyes Were Watching God,* and *Black Boy.* I tabbed the moments in each book that marked the height of emotion for the main characters—where the language is the most expressive—and got to work finding poems.

The first piece that appears in this book is the first one I created. There, I found the story of a girl who had never known the love of her father. I created most of the other poems that same afternoon. Miraculously, they all told parts of the same story. My debut novel became an exploration of how children with physically absent or emotionally unavailable fathers regard, experience, and engage in love.

As readers, we enjoy the thrill of losing ourselves and finding ourselves within the pages of books where the main characters may be animals, monsters, aliens, magical beings, or humans from cultures other than our own. What a treat to read a story where the hero and the villain feel like home! No matter where you're from, dear reader, I hope that some part of *Finding Jupiter* felt like home. I hope that you're inspired to find poetry wherever there are words and that the writers among you have been inspired to write stories that feel like home to you.

QUOTATION SOURCES

p. vi: "I was complete . . .": F. Scott Fitzgerald, *The Great Gatsby*, 131.

p. 46: "Who are you": Fitzgerald, 134.

p. 70: "She insisted . . .": Fitzgerald, 136.

p. 80: "His memory made . . .": Zora Neale Hurston, *Their Eyes Were Watching God*, 184.

p. 128: "Where you touch . . .": Fitzgerald, 37.

p. 141: "I love her . . .": Jackson R. Bryer and Cathy W. Barks, eds., *Dear Scott, Dearest Zelda: The Love Letters of F. Scott and Zelda Fitzgerald*, 8.

p. 142: "Had I run him . . .": Hurston, 182.

p. 178: "Fooled around outside . . .": Hurston, 169.

p. 201: "So he waited . . .": Fitzgerald, 111.

p. 202: "In the dark . . .": Hurston, 99.

p. 218: "Convenience? Love?": Hurston, 101.

p. 254: "don't feel . . .": Hurston, 183.

p. 270: "The boy was . . .": Hurston, 177.

p. 303–304: "This heart in . . .": Richard Wright, *Black Boy*, 142–143.

BIBLIOGRAPHY

Bryer, Jackson R., and Cathy W. Barks, eds. *Dear Scott, Dearest Zelda: The Love Letters of F. Scott and Zelda Fitzgerald*. New York: St. Martin's Press, 2002.

Fitzgerald, F. Scott. *The Great Gatsby*. New York: Scribner Classics, 1986 (Original work published 1925).

Hurston, Zora Neale. *Their Eyes Were Watching God*. New York: Harper & Row, 1990 (Original work published 1937).

Wright, Richard. *Black Boy*. New York: HarperCollins, 1989 (Original work published 1945).

ACKNOWLEDGMENTS

Adriane and Terri, my blood sister and my chosen sister, thank you for big, deep love and the constant reminders that it was time for me to write a book—any book—and the subsequent, exacerbated queries as to when said book would be written. Yolanda King, my Austin person, you said, "I'm going to write a book." Then you did it repeatedly. You are my forever inspiration. J. Elle, you saw something in my quiet love story among hundreds of YA fantasy manuscripts during Pitch Wars 2019. To say thank you is an understatement. My dear friend, you changed my life.

Chelsea Eberly, my extraordinary agent. You are brilliant and I'm so happy to be on this destined journey with you. To my editor, Phoebe Yeh, I bow down to you. From our first conversation, we were like old friends. I knew that our partnership would be a breeze. You're so sharp, kind, and generous, and an amazing editor. Please acquire all my future books for Random House and just never leave me. Elizabeth Stranahan, you are so clutch and part of the best editing team I could ever wish for. To my visuals Dream Team, cover designer Ray Shappell and artists Delmaine Donson and Bex Glendining, *chef's kiss*. To Gráinne Clear and the entire team at Walker Books UK, thank you for an amazing world debut experience! Film agents Dana Spector and Berni Barta, thank you for making it fun for me to dream bigger.

Karen Valby, you magical earthling. You were the first friend to read my book and your response was like calcium to her bones. Thank you forever. Kay, Angela, and Kaila, thank you for listening to me dream this book up during the months and years our boys played on the playground! Tyrese and Mischia, our lunches gave me fuel and momentum. Karmon and Aziza, I'm so thankful our life paths have joined. Your love, friendship, and encouragement on this leg of my journey means the world. To the best neighbor, Lisa, you brought Jupiter and Fred into my life right when I needed signs. Fred Campos, thank you for kindly nodding at my questions about constellations and planets and listening to my theories about life and stars. Dr. Tracy Asamoah, your friendship and expertise as a child psychiatrist are precious things to me on this journey. My dear nanny, Ka'lia, you are my life jacket. Thank you.

Summer, my best friend, thank you for listening to every detail about this entire journey in real time, for being with me during life's big things and for always holding me up and holding me down. Life is a funny thing, girl. Momma, my favorite person and my biggest cheerleader. Thank you for your unconditional love and for instantly and enthusiastically supporting all my dreams. Billy, my husband, thank you for being my big teenaged love story and showing me that I deserve love. Zack, my son, you are the wind beneath my wings. Zāli, my daughter, you are the sun. Rodney, you respond to all my big announcements like they are a given. Your high expectations of me and the affirmations you've spoken to me our entire lives sustain me. My twin, I remind myself that we are made of the same stuff when I feel silly for dreaming big or dreaming at all. I keep going because you keep going. To my dad, aunts, uncles, cousins, and ancestors, thank you for shaping me into the person I am. Huge shout-out to my teen early reviewers—Azana, Riley, Ben, Zare, Zack, Avery, Gavin, Marlee, Reed, Nia, Matisyn, and Siena. To my Austin village of fantastic sister-moms (including you ladies who moved away), thank you for existing. Queen Squad, we out here!

Octavia Butler, I promise to always look to the stars. Toni Morrison, I promise to always make everybody Black.

Kel

ABOUT THE AUTHOR

KELIS ROWE is a Beyoncé fan who writes Black young adult summer love stories—well, two at least. She graduated from Central High School in Memphis, Tennessee, where she was an honors student. She decided to apply to college the summer after graduation because she found out she exceeded the height limit to be a flight attendant for Northwest Airlines, which had been her dream job. She met her husband at Christian Brothers University in Memphis, Tennessee, where she graduated with a bachelor's degree in psychology with a marketing minor. She worked in market research for seven years before becoming a homeschooler. The year after her son enrolled in traditional middle school, she finished her first novel, *Finding Jupiter*. The following year, she signed a book deal, had a baby, and started writing her second novel. She writes out of her suburban home near Austin, Texas, or a rented coworking space in the city if she feels like putting on outside clothes that day. Discover more about Kelis on her Instagram and on her website kelisrowe.com.